Pride Publishing books by Matthew J. Metzger

Single Books
Best Behaviour
Enough

Starting Over
The Divorce
The Other Man
The Wedding
The Third Date

ENOUGH

MATTHEW J. METZGER

Enough
ISBN # 978-1-83943-838-7

Interior text design by Claire Siemaszkiewicz
Pride Publishing

Published in 2019 by Pride Publishing, United Kingdom.

Pride Publishing is an imprint of Totally Entwined Group Limited.

ENOUGH

Chapter One

He could smell the fire.

He was blind. His eyes streamed. The curling wallpaper crackled and hissed. His skin was burning. The air in his lungs seared him from the inside out. And there was nowhere to go—no escape from the heat, no escape from the orange towers and acrid black smoke, no *air*.

"Ezra!"

The smoke wrapped itself around his teeth and tongue like a grotesque mockery of a kiss, and there was no reply but the roar of hot air and climbing fire. The house was burning. *The house was burning!*

"Ezra! *Ez!*"

A scream. A piercing scream, like nothing he'd ever heard, but before he could move, the wooden boards crumbled to ash and he was falling, tearing through the shreds of stairs into the inferno, and—

Jesse hit the carpet with a thump and jarred himself awake.

The flat was quiet. The streetlight touched the other side of the curtains with a faint orange light. There was no smoke, no fire, no sound. Nothing.

Jesse dragged himself back onto the bed. The sheets were impossibly tangled and his tank top stuck to him with sweat. His wrist ached in its brace where he'd bumped it, but the panic hadn't quite eased its grip on his heart or his lungs, and he fumbled for his phone, ignoring the pain.

Thank God for speed dial.

The clock on the side said two-fifty-eight, and the phone rang six times before the line coughed and crackled and a sleepy voice, tinged in the early hours with the fading edges of a Welsh accent, mumbled a vague sort of question.

"Ez?"

There was a rustle of sheets. "Jesse?"

"Oh, God," Jesse breathed. The air escaped in a rush, loud and hard. His lungs shook with the effort. "Shit. I just— I needed to check—"

"Jess? What's happened, sweetheart?"

The soft roll of his vowels, the accent entirely muted when he was properly awake, was as comforting as a hug, and Jesse coughed out, "Nightmare," before thinking twice. Ezra was okay. He was okay. It was all okay.

"Oh, sweetheart," Ezra murmured, low and crooning. "Do you want to tell me about it?"

"I need—can I come over? I know it's late and I know you have work in the morning, but—I just—I need—"

"No," Ezra interrupted, and Jesse's stomach twisted violently.

"*Please*, Ez, I—"

"Hey, hey, hey." Ezra cut him off. "Hey, stop, calm down, sweetheart. I *meant* you can't come here. You don't sound okay, not to me, and I don't want you to go out like this, so I'll come to you, all right?"

Jesse exhaled, the twist easing. "Okay."

"You okay if I hang up, or do you want me to put the phone on speaker?"

"Can—speaker," Jesse swallowed against the nausea. He was still shaking, he realised faintly. "I just—I couldn't find you, Ez. The house was burning and I couldn't find you, and I—I need to hear you. You don't have to talk to me, but I need to hear you."

"Okay." The phone crackled again and clunked, and suddenly Ezra's voice was loud and echoing. *Soothing.* The Welsh hint was fading, and Jesse could suddenly hear him dressing, but he was *there*. "Was it my house or the one last week?"

"Yours," Jesse said. "I was on the stairs, and they gave way, and I woke up. I couldn't find you."

"If my house was on fire, I would probably be in the kitchen having caused it," Ezra said, and yawned loudly. "Make yourself useful, sweetheart, and make up a brew for me? I've not slept long."

Jesse knew better than to apologise. He shrugged out of his sweat-soaked pyjamas and pulled on a pair of jogging bottoms before taking the phone through the narrow hall into the kitchen. The kitchen window overlooked the main road. A police car trailed idly by on the prowl. Phone to his ear, he listened to Ezra swear sleepily at his cupboard, and the soft sounds of those narrow feet padding downstairs.

"Sweetheart?"

"Mm?" Jesse listened to the front door and the heavy sound of the key.

"I'm going to hang up while I drive. You all right for ten minutes until I get there?"

"Yeah," Jesse croaked. His heart had come down out of the rafters, and he could breathe. The streetlights didn't look threatening anymore. He just felt…shaky. Sick and shaky and scared. "Yeah, Ez, I'll be fine."

"Okay. Love you."

The dial tone was immediate. Jesse dropped the phone to the counter and switched on the kettle, staring out of the window and waiting, arms folded against the chill. It wasn't the first nightmare, and it wouldn't be the last. He usually managed one a week without fail, and the injury hadn't helped matters. But they didn't usually involve Ezra in burning buildings. They didn't usually involve losing him.

And Jesse couldn't stomach the thought of losing him.

Which was a bit scary in itself. They'd only met eight months ago. At a gay bar, of all places—the one place where he went to meet sex partners, not *partner* partners. Jesse had thought the freckled blond with the dark eyes was pretty in the neon lights and had bought him a drink, talked him into a dance, bought him another. Kissed him at the back of the dance floor—and had promptly found himself alone, but with a phone number in his back pocket.

He'd wanted sex. That was all he'd been after. Sex with a pretty guy. But then they'd gone on a date and he'd met Ezra *properly*, and he was lost. Ezra wasn't just a handsome face and nice legs. Ezra was the world. He was *Jesse's* world, and it had only been eight months, but Jesse still knew that this was it, for him. Ezra was it. There would never be anyone else like him.

So he stood in a tense vigil at the window, waiting for the faithful little Peugeot 207 to creep around the corner. Waiting for Ezra to come, because there was emotional shock and there was sense, and the two weren't in line right now. He *knew* Ezra was okay. He knew it. He'd answered the phone. He'd been sleepy and understanding and sworn at his cupboard. He was fine.

But Jesse still needed to reach out and touch him, just to make sure. *Somehow.*

The little blue car was lonely on the three-in-the-morning road, and Jesse propped the door of his flat to creep down the communal stairs and open the main door. Ezra had gotten sort-of dressed, in jeans and an open check shirt, feet shoved into his trainers without socks, and his hair was wild and fluffy, in gleeful disarray, as he locked the car and wrapped himself around Jesse in a tight, warm hug.

Jesse clung back until something creaked, and pressed the side of his face against that wild hair.

"You're all right, sweetheart," Ezra murmured.

Jesse squeezed again until Ezra's grip on the nape of his neck tightened in warning, then he let go and dragged Ezra up the silent stairs by the hand. Concrete stairs. They wouldn't collapse in a fire until the whole building came down.

He didn't say a word until he'd pressed the requested tea into Ezra's hands, locked the door again and bundled them both back to the messy bed. Ezra was equally silent, taking a couple of mouthfuls before abandoning the tea, stripping to his underwear and crawling into the mess to mould himself into Jesse's arms.

"There you go," he murmured lowly, kissing Jesse's encroaching stubble and stroking a hand gently through his hair. "Feel better now?"

"Mm," Jesse pressed his nose into Ezra's neck, tangling their legs together. He could feel a strong pulse in Ezra's jugular. He could feel the rough skin of the bumpy scar on Ezra's shoulder under his fingertips. He could feel the fuzzy mess of Ezra's hair, usually styled and stiff in that messy-but-it's-on-purpose-so-it's-okay manner, now just loose and wild. He could feel *him*. "Thank you."

"Thank me again tomorrow afternoon when I'm grumpy and exhausted after two hours of the Year Nines."

"Okay," Jesse agreed, sliding his arms completely around Ezra's back until he enveloped him. They didn't often sleep cuddled together—or even together at all, between Ezra's eight-to-four and Jesse's shifts—but he needed this. He *needed* it.

"Mind if I go to sleep?"

"No," Jesse squirmed until Ezra got the hint and tucked his head under his chin. His hair tickled. Jesse kissed the top of his head and wished he had the easy grace with language that Ezra did. Wished he could express himself properly. Wished he could talk as easily as he hugged. But all that came out was, "I just needed to touch you."

Ezra said nothing to that, simply shifting until he was comfortable, one arm over Jesse's ribs and the other tucked over his own waist in a casual sort of drop. Ezra was *long*—long limbs, long neck, all willowy lines and bendy joints, and he settled like water into the bulkier, stiffer contours of Jesse's body.

But he fit, and he fit perfectly, and Jesse wrapped him up and held him, breathing in the smell of store-brand shampoo and cheap aftershave until the last traces of the nightmare-induced fear washed away.

It was still a long time before he slept.

* * * *

Bzt, bzt, bzt, bzt –

Jesse swatted at the noise, and a low laugh and blessed quiet were his reply. "Urgh," he said.

"Mm," Ezra agreed. "But some of us have jobs to go to."

"I have a job," Jesse grumbled, still refusing to open his eyes.

"They just don't want you," Ezra teased, and Jesse cracked open an eye to glower at him. He'd *escaped*. He was standing by the bed buttoning the spare shirt he kept in Jesse's wardrobe. *Bastard.*

"C'mere." Jesse made grabby hands. Ezra stepped back.

"No," he said. "It's already quarter past. It's just as well I brought the car."

Jesse blinked up at him and stretched luxuriously. He'd not gone to sleep until half-four, wrapped around Ezra like a blanket, and he knew for a fact Ezra hadn't slept deeply either.

"It was a bad night," Jesse said eventually. "You should call in sick."

"And let some poor ineffectual supply teacher get a test tube shoved somewhere painful by the more creative ones? I don't think so." Ezra buttoned his collar and bent over the bed to kiss Jesse's hair. "But it's the last day. And after that, you get me all day and every day until occupational health clear you to go back to work."

Jesse caught his shoulder and sat up, deepening the kiss until Ezra sat gingerly on the edge of the mattress. He smelled of Jesse's shower gel and his hair was damp in its mousse-induced style. Ezra had very light, almost wispy hair. He'd used to spray it into its perfectly-styled, deliberately messy cloud until Jesse had come along and vetoed the flammable spray. The mousse wouldn't burst into flames, and it had the added bonus of not feeling so disgusting.

"Get your hands off that," Ezra murmured, and Jesse ran his hands down his back instead. "Mm. Jesse, I need to go."

"In a bit," Jesse coaxed, kissing his neck. He knew better than to bite above the collar—Ezra had nearly strangled him the one and only time he'd done that—but he couldn't resist open-mouthed kisses down the length of lightly freckling skin. The hot spring was taking its toll. "In a bit!" he added when Ezra began to push at him, and he tried to hang on, but Ezra did *yoga*, the bendy little savage, and escaped without so much as a struggle.

"I said *no*," he reiterated sternly, before grinning, kissing the top of Jesse's head and pushing him back onto the mattress. "Get some sleep and come and catch me after work. It's their last day, so make sure you turn up with the biggest bottle of whisky you can afford."

"Yessir," Jesse grinned, mouth still tingling, then Ezra was gone, shutting the bedroom door behind him. Jesse listened in mute love to the off-key singing as Ezra put his shoes on and clattered with keys—then the front door closed and the flat was silent.

It was April. The sun was high already, and the sky a deep, clear blue. Jesse could hear the sea from his flat in the winter, but in the spring it was too sedate to be picked out over the rush-hour traffic and the wail of an ambulance siren flying down the main road to the hospital. He bathed luxuriously in the light washing across the bed until he heard the cough and rumble of Ezra's car disappear into the melee of suits and drones going to work, and—finally—Jesse swung himself out of bed and faced the day.

Jesse was twenty-five and had had the same flat since he was seventeen. It was a *box*, Ezra insisted, but then Ezra had a degree and a last name that replaced 'I' with 'Y' because that looked fancier. Jesse was just Jesse Kevin Dawkins, and a box was all he needed. The kitchen was too small to close the door properly, the bathroom was the sort where taking a crap and washing his feet in the shower and hands in the sink at the same time was wholly possible, and the bedroom had a double bed with absolutely no floor space whatsoever. He'd had to take the door off the cupboard to fit the bed.

But it was *his* flat. Jesse had spent most of his childhood being bounced from place to place with his mother, and to have somewhere that was *his* was a big deal. Ezra could call it a box all he liked, but the only way Jesse was moving was if the flat burned down, or Ezra wanted them to live together.

Then they'd make a new home. The two of them.

It was a bit early for it, Jesse reflected as he jammed bread into the toaster and rummaged through the fridge for the grapefruit juice, but maybe once their anniversary arrived he could ask Ezra to live with him. Even if it meant bringing the stupid cats, and a whole bathroom counter of Ezra's hair products. All fifteen billion of them.

His phone buzzed on the counter where he'd abandoned it last night, and he smiled when he slid it open and Ezra's name popped up, cheerfully bright in the shimmering morning.

Ezra <3: Oh my God, one of the little shits has slashed the tyres on the head's car! Do I laugh or look mad like the rest of them?

Jesse laughed.

Me: Look mad. You look stunning when you laugh and that physics teacher has a thing for you. Don't encourage her!

Ezra <3: Sap ;) Love you too x

His heart hiccupped, and Jesse clutched the phone like a brainless newly-wed until the toaster popped.

* * * *

The Thomas Oxley School was a dreary sort of school named after a dreary sort of man. It was a squat redbrick construction, brooding at the side of a hectic main road, scowling under a mismatched slate roof and losing at least four students a year to the traffic outside, and another ten or eleven to youth offending institutes, mental health wards, suicides and very mobile broken families. Last year, the school had made national news when one student had murdered another on school grounds. It was the kind of place that had briefly had a metal detector to stop the kids bringing in knives.

Sometimes, Jesse thought Ezra's job was more dangerous than his.

He waited outside the chain-link fence to the car park at three-forty-five. Most of the little reprobates had dissipated, but Ezra's car sat obliviously in the sun and baked itself happily. The headmaster's car was made obvious by the AA van and the bloke changing every one of the ruined tyres. Jesse would feel sorry, but by Ezra's account the head was a dick and deserved everything the kids gave him.

When Ezra finally did emerge, he looked exhausted. Jesse met him halfway, took the stack of wobbling books from him and received a weary smile.

"Bad day?"

"Don't even," Ezra warned, unlocking the car and popping the boot to dump his stuff. "I want to sleep for the entire break."

"I can drive if you want," Jesse offered.

"Would you?"

"Sure."

Ezra tossed him the keys. Jesse spent ten minutes readjusting the mirrors, because Ezra insisted on sitting bolt-upright in the car instead of lounging like any self-respecting, *comfortable* driver would. By the time he put the car in gear and reversed out of the tight space, Ezra was already half-asleep.

They lived the wrong way around. Jesse lived not ten minutes' walk from the school, while conversely, Ezra's house was a fifteen-minute drive in *good* traffic, never mind the half-four build-up, and yet it sat not five hundred metres from the fire station where Jesse spent most of his working day. Really, they ought to swap—except that Jesse's landlord would never allow cats, and, frankly, Jesse preferred the nest of his flat to Ezra's airy, open house.

"C'mon, gorgeous, out you get," Jesse coaxed once he'd pulled up in the driveway. Thankfully, the cats were nowhere to be seen. He wasn't as practised at avoiding small animals as Ezra, and the tortoiseshell especially had a habit of just running under the car, even if it was moving.

Ezra lasted roughly five minutes. He dropped his backpack at the door, his tie over the living room doorknob, rejected his shoes by the coffee table and collapsed onto the sofa with a mumble that might have been a request for coffee. Jesse ignored him. By the time he'd locked the door and tidied up the abandoned clothes, Ezra had twisted half onto his side and fallen asleep.

Even twisted up in a rumpled shirt and boring trousers, he was gorgeous. Jesse touched his hair lightly, then left him to scout out the kitchen and the potential for food. He was a better cook than Ezra—which wasn't hard—and had been stocking up his kitchen for the last three months. It had a proper wok and everything now, whereas a proper frying pan was pushing the spatial boundaries of Jesse's kitchen.

The cat-flap rattled, and a chirping *mraow* sounded from somewhere around his ankles before Kitsa, Ezra's ADHD-afflicted tortoiseshell kitten, leapt nimbly up onto the tiny kitchen table and meowed plaintively for attention.

"Hello, darling," Jesse crooned, holding out a hand. She rubbed her whole back under it, purring. Kitsa was a small cat, and his hands were large—he could have picked her up in one without much difficulty. "Hungry?"

She meowed again and rubbed her face on his knuckles. He liked Kitsa. Kitsa was friendly and purred and chased laser pointers and thought butterflies were legitimate food. Apparently, she'd been an unwanted Christmas present for the neighbour's grandson, and Ezra had taken her. The elderly lady next door couldn't have managed Flopsy, his big lazy cat, never mind Kitsa. Privately, Jesse couldn't imagine anyone not wanting Kitsa. Even *he* liked Kitsa, and he wasn't a fan of cats.

He set down fresh food for them both before getting to work on dinner. Predictably, the moment the can opener popped the top off, Ezra's other cat materialised, but the horribly-named Flopsy had no time for Jesse. She barely had time for Ezra. She was a seventeen-year-old Ragdoll, and thoroughly ignored the entire universe in favour of making nests in clean laundry and destroying flowers. Jesse ignored her, she ignored him and Kitsa bounced around his ankles like a hyperactive toddler once she'd decided that tuna wasn't going to be as good as whatever he was making.

"Cats don't get cheese," he told her, tossing a block of Cheddar onto the counter. Spanish omelette, he decided, and Kitsa voiced her disagreement from around his left foot. "Or potato, or egg or any of it," he said. Flopsy slouched out after decimating the tuna. If cats could belch, she would have.

He lost himself in the radio on the end of the bench, the sunlight streaming through the back door, the cat winding herself around his legs and hopefully putting her paws up on his shins every now and then, and the soothing rhythm of cooking. It was a mindless sort of activity for Jesse, even if he was paranoid about switching off the oven at the wall when he was done, or triple-checking the fire alarm and monoxide monitors before he even *thought* about firing up the hob. He'd seen too many gutted houses and ruined lives from his day job to be any other way.

He was warned of an imminent boyfriend when Kitsa meowed and abandoned him. A moment later, Ezra shuffled in—foggy-eyed and yawning, hair sticking straight up on one side where the mousse and the sofa had conspired against him. He looked stunning, and Jesse's heart twitched.

"Hey."

Jesse didn't answer, just reeled him in by the waist and kissed him deeply, locking an arm around his hips so that even when Ezra huffed and pushed his face away, he was kept close.

"Too hungry for sex!"

Jesse laughed. "I just wanted a kiss, not a shag. Anyway, it's almost ready."

Ezra tucked his head into the crook of Jesse's neck and shoulder. "I want to work," he said, "at a school where the students don't try to set fire to each other with Bunsen burners."

Jesse curled his fingers around the narrow jut of hipbone and rubbed his thumb into the gap where Ezra's shirt had worked free of his trousers. His skin was hot to the touch from sleep and spring. Ezra's scalp pushed at the underside of his jaw—the height difference wasn't usually great enough to allow it, given that Jesse was five-eleven and Ezra five-nine, but post-nap Ezra slouched. A lot. And Jesse kind of liked it.

"I want to work," Ezra continued blithely, "somewhere where twenty-five doesn't make me *old*. Somewhere where the kids use their pencils to draw ionic bonds, not on each other, and not badly spelled various racist, sexist and homophobic remarks."

"Bad day?" Jesse repeated.

"Jesse, I *seriously* had to tell a kid why the phrase 'buttfucking faggot' couldn't possibly apply to Katie Micklewood."

"Okay, that's…yeah."

"He couldn't even *spell* 'fucking.' Or 'faggot' for that matter. It took me a good minute to realise it was supposed to be an insult."

"Even I'm not that thick."

"You call yourself thick again, I'll show you some of the mock GCSE papers from last January," Ezra grumbled. "I teach a few hundred children in a week. Maybe *ten* of them have *any* brains whatsoever, and of the ten, maybe six of those brains have intellect suited to science."

"You're an awful teacher. You're meant to encourage them."

"I do, I just bitch behind their backs," Ezra yawned and squeezed both arms around Jesse's waist. "Omelette?"

"Spanish."

"Mm."

"You awake enough to come out tonight? It's Danny's leaving do. Crawl starts at The Bell and heads towards town from there."

"Oh no. I'm not showing up at my mother's tomorrow hungover, and neither are you."

Jesse winced. He kind of wanted to. He was meeting Ezra's family tomorrow for the very first time—Ezra's very distant, very judgemental, very *Catholic* family. He was scared shitless.

"I know that face," Ezra murmured. "Don't be so scared."

"I can't help it. And you can't tell me they're going to like me."

He'd managed to keep putting it off. Christmas was too soon, and they were too new. He'd been working on Ezra's birthday so couldn't make it all the way out to Norfolk with him. The drugs had made him too loopy right after the accident at work.

But eventually he'd run out of excuses, and Ezra had started to get that pinched look on his face. Like he wasn't believing them anymore. Like he was wondering if Jesse wasn't serious about them.

So when his grandmother's birthday had rolled around, and Ezra had mentioned that he visited every year, and it would be nice if Jesse could come too—

Jesse had agreed.

And he'd been shitting himself ever since.

"You're going to have to meet them at some point," Ezra said. "And it'll be fine. Grace won't like you, but Mum will come around once she really sees you, and Nana's a loopy old bat anyway, so nobody listens to her."

Jesse wasn't listening either. It wasn't that he wanted Ezra's family to *like* him—there was no chance of that anyway. He was a dropout who'd had about ten shelf-stacking jobs before joining the fire service, had no education worth shit, and was a *man*. They weren't going to like him. But he didn't want Ezra to be…put off. To change his mind once his mother was all disapproving and shit. Because it was his *mum*, and she called him every Sunday evening to talk, and even if Ezra was about as Catholic as Jesse was Hindu, he still loved her.

Ever since he'd proposed visiting them and introducing Jesse, way back in February, Jesse had been…

Scared.

"Come out?" he tried again. "I'm going. And we don't have to drink a lot, but you have to admit it's been ages since we went out properly. I want to see you in your tight jeans and your tipsy face."

"You could see that here," Ezra grumbled, but finally unpeeled himself and rummaged for plates. "Fine. Okay. But not *long*. I'm tired, and we'll have to start out early, and—"

"Relax." Jesse ran a long hand down Ezra's spine, feeling the languid ripple of him. "It'll be fine."

It had to be, right?

Chapter Two

"I fucking hate London."

"Hanging?"

"*Yes.*"

God, was Jesse ever hanging. His head was pounding, his eyes were screwed up even behind the sunglasses, and who had decided it had to be unreasonably hot this Easter? It was never hot at Easter. They usually got right through until August before the temperature even approached warm, but oh no, the one day he'd been hungover in months, and it had to be a scorcher.

"Do you believe in God?"

"Not anymore," Ezra said.

"Did you believe he was an arsehole even when you did believe in him?"

"Not *usually*," Ezra said, changing gears as he finally, finally left the M25 for less horrifically congested roads. "But read the Old Testament sometime. He's pretty much canonically an arsehole."

Jesse groaned. "I want to *die*."

"That's what you get for getting slaughtered even though you said, *three times*, you'd stop at two pints."

Jesse winced. Ezra huffed, then seemed to soften.

"We'll go to the hotel first and I'll medicate your hangover away before going to Mum's. How about that?"

"Marry me."

Ezra snorted. If he were in less pain, Jesse would have been enjoying the view. Ezra's little Peugeot was old and knackered. He was saving up for a new car rather than waste money attempting to fix the old one, so the air conditioning had bust a long time ago. Judging by the lack of electric windows, a couple of *centuries* ago. Which meant they had the windows wound down, the grimy North London air was toying lightly with Ezra's hair, there was a burst of freckles beginning to pop into life along his forearms *and* he was wearing a sleeveless shirt.

Well, maybe Jesse *was* enjoying the view. But he'd be enjoying it more if not for the hangover.

"I couldn't help it," he whined. "Mac's doctor said he'd fully recover from his burns—it's worth celebrating!"

"I get it, you hose-monkeys are all party animals."

"Can we just stay at the hotel and say we got there unacceptably late and meet your family tomorrow instead?"

"No."

Jesse scowled and closed his eyes. *Worth a shot.* He didn't want to meet Ezra's family—he was *terrified* of meeting Ezra's family. Meeting them *hungover*—well, that wasn't going to be a great first impression, was it?

"They're not going to eat you alive, Jess," Ezra said softly, and Jesse sighed.

"I just—I want them to think I'm good enough for you."

"Good luck with that," Ezra said briskly. "Anything short of Jesus himself is not going to be good enough for Nana. Or Grace," he added, and grimaced. "Urgh. I hope she cancelled."

"Not helping."

Ezra shrugged. "Telling the truth, babe," he said easily. "But they're not going to have a good old-fashioned gay-bashing. They'll be all stiffly polite, and you'll love Nana anyway because she's absolutely insane, and Mum'll come around in her own time. They won't like you—trust me, you'll be keeping me gay or some other such crap—but once they've actually *met* you, they'll work out that you're a nice guy and not Satan in tight jeans."

Jesse bit his lip. "So if I were someone else, *any* other guy—?"

"No *boy*friend would ever be enough," Ezra said, and took advantage of a straight stretch in the road to briefly reach over and squeeze Jesse's hand. "You're enough for me. That's all that counts."

Except it wasn't. Jesse knew better. People cared about what their families thought of their other halves. If Ezra's family hated him, Ezra would eventually listen. Then he'd break up with him, and Jesse knew it was insane to think it only eight months in, but he *needed* Ezra.

"Hey."

He glanced over the top of his shades at Ezra's summons. There was a smile playing at the edges of that stupidly kissable mouth.

"Love you."

Jesse bit his lip, then leaned over and kissed Ezra's cheek.

He couldn't fuck this up.

* * * *

Technically speaking, Ezra was Welsh. He'd lost most of his accent to some mix of Norfolk, London and the south coast, but Jesse had noticed early on that if he was drunk or tired, that lilting Welsh began to creep back in.

So he'd asked. And the tricky bastard had promptly said he was born just north of Abertawe, and laughed himself sick when it had taken Jesse two months to realise he was referring to Swansea.

He'd been raised near Cardiff for most of his childhood, as far as Jesse knew. He didn't speak Welsh, and he never claimed to actually *be* Welsh, but Jesse liked the faint lilt to his voice, and he had mental images of Ezra on some wild mountainside in watery Welsh sun. They would have to take a holiday to Wales over the summer.

'Mum's Welsh,' Ezra had said, the one and only time they'd discussed it. *'Swansea. Dad was from Bristol.'*

He'd refused to say anything else once Jesse had teased him with a poor West Country accent, and so Jesse found himself outside a small converted farmhouse just outside of Norwich with very little idea about the people who lived there.

They'd arrived in the late afternoon. Ezra had booked a room in a small bar-restaurant-hotel hybrid thing in the centre of Norwich rather than stay with his family, and he had indulged Jesse's pounding headache by going there first and letting him take a kip in the darkened room. By the time he'd been woken—with a welcome kiss and a glass of orange juice Ezra had pilfered from the bar downstairs—he'd felt a little more able to manage this.

That was, until Ezra's Peugeot crunched over the gravel driveway of the converted farmhouse, and Jesse caught sight of a crucifix nailed to the gatepost.

"Seriously?" he asked, pointing at it.

"Seriously," Ezra said, and laughed, waving out of the open window. "Nana!"

The front door was open in deference to the sun and the heat, and a green garden chair had been placed by the step. A tiny, wizened old woman, who must have been eighty if she was a day, squinted at them before a toothless smile creased her already very creased face and she began to slowly and painfully haul herself up, leaning on a walking stick that must have been as heavy as she was.

"You're late!" she scolded as Ezra hauled on the handbrake and bounced out of the car to hug her. He was almost a foot taller than she was, and her fiercely white perm seemed to glow against his dark top. "And you've grown. Come here. Let Nana see you."

He had to stoop to let her cup his face. Jesse took the keys out of the car and locked it up, shifting nervously on his feet. Ezra had said Nana was crazy, but he obviously loved her to bits. What if Nana didn't like him?

"Too thin," Nana said, and slapped his cheek. "Your wife is not feeding you! Divorce her. Immediately. Mildred at church has a very nice granddaughter, she's your age—"

"I don't have a wife, Nana," Ezra said gently.

"Well, get one," she snapped, and smacked his shoulder as he straightened up. "No wonder you're too skinny. Ceri! *Ceri,* come here! Who are you?" she added, squinting at Jesse. She had ferociously blue eyes, like chips of ice, and they gleamed viciously in her collapsed face.

"Nana, this is Jesse. My boyfriend," Ezra said, and drew Jesse closer by the hand.

"Boyfriend?" Nana snapped, then sucked in a breath. "I would have thought your father would have beaten that nonsense out of you by now."

Jesse flinched. Ezra didn't so much as twitch.

"Where is he? Useless, worthless layabout, drifter like his father. Zach! Zach, get out here and sort this nonsense out!"

"Mum, what *are* you talk—Ezra!"

A woman on the cusp of being elderly appeared in the open doorway, drying her hands on a tea towel. While Nana looked nothing like her grandson—probably thanks to her age—this woman was very obviously Mrs Pryce. She had the same beautiful dark eyes, the same length to her face, the same long limbs and delicate hands. Her hair was greying from a light brown, and cut fashionably short, and when she came down the steps to hug her son, she moved with the beginnings of age-related stiffness.

"I was beginning to worry," she crooned, hugging her son close, and Ezra looked lanky between his diminutive Nana and his equally tiny mother. "And this is…?"

"Jesse Dawkins," Jesse introduced himself, holding out a hand. She shook it, although a little warily. "I'm Ezra's partner."

He saw the flickering gaze as she took him in, and knew what she was thinking. The visible tattoo of the fire service crest on his bicep. His biceps in general. His big hands. His height, and his—density, Ezra called it, because Jesse wasn't particularly wide or bulked up, but he was rock-solid with muscle, and it showed. The shaggy fair hair that Ezra had banned him from shaving off. The braced wrist.

He saw the way she shrank back a little too. She didn't like him already.

"Oh," she said. "Yes. Of course. Well. Come in, both of you." She turned away from them hastily. "Come on, Mum, it's nearly dinnertime. I've made Swedish meatballs."

"Pah!" Nana scoffed.

Ezra hung back, pulling Jesse back to the car and unlocking the boot under the pretence of getting something. "You all right?" he murmured, and Jesse grimaced.

"She doesn't like me," he said, and he wasn't sure which one he was referring to.

"It doesn't matter if they like you or not," Ezra soothed.

He swallowed, trying to believe him. He fished for something else, staring up at the door as the women argued on the step.

"So—is—is Nana your mother's mother, or—?"

"Dad's," Ezra said. "Nana Lindquist."

Wait, what?

"Lindquist? How does that work?"

"She's Swedish," Ezra replied. "She came over with her fiancé in the fifties, then he ran off with a barmaid in Bristol. Dad was her only son, and she claimed he was the bastard of the bloke in the bedsit below hers. James Pryce."

"Oh. So your Dad was—"

"Zach Pryce," Ezra confirmed. "Technically speaking, we should be Lindquist, but she put Pryce on his birth certificate, so here we are. But she's been living with my parents ever since they got married, hence Mum just calls her Mum."

"Jesus Christ, your family is confusing," Jesse muttered.

"Get used to it," Ezra said, and used the open boot as a privacy screen to cup his face and kiss him. "Be grateful Grace isn't here. She's a right bitch."

"Ezra!" one of the women called.

"Come on," Ezra said, taking Jesse's hand again and slamming the boot. "Don't look so serious! They're not going to lynch you."

That wasn't what Jesse was afraid of.

The house was of the small and cosy variety. The kitchen was lit by the slowly setting sun, baking the brown and cream tiles in a golden hue. A border collie was stretched out in front of the cooker, as old as Nana judging by the greying fur and the complete lack of interest in newcomers, although one brown eye regarded them warily for half a second. A fat tabby cat was curled up on the windowsill and showed a little more interest when Jesse hesitantly scratched its ears, nudging its face into his fingers and purring lightly.

"See, *this* cat likes me," he told Ezra snidely, who maintained that his own cat, Flopsy, didn't hate him.

"Jingle likes everyone," Ezra sniped back, and pulled out a chair at the enormous kitchen table. Nana, already seated, had rustled up some knitting from somewhere. "What's that, Nana?"

"A sweater for Grace."

Jesse privately thought Grace must be eight feet tall and two inches wide, but kept his thoughts to himself, directing his nerves into petting the appreciative cat.

"Do you like animals, then, James?"

"Jesse," Ezra corrected his mother sharply.

"I guess," Jesse said, and swallowed. "I like playing with Ezra's cats when I visit. Don't have any of my own, though, my job's too unpredictable for pets."

"What do you do?"

"He works for the fire service," Ezra said.

"Oh!" Mrs Pryce looked startled. "A firefighter? Well. I thought...well, I supposed that Ezra had met his...partner...at the school."

Jesse shrugged. "Nope." He didn't think telling Mrs Pryce that they'd met in a gay bar would help his cause.

"Sit!" she said, plonking a tray of sloshing teacups onto the wood. "I'm afraid we don't know anything about you. None of my children are all that communicative."

Ezra rolled his eyes and took a cup. Jesse warily took another, wondering if she'd put holy water in it or something, to see if he was possessed by Satan. Did people still pull that kind of shit?

"So," Mrs Pryce wrapped her hands around her mug. "Where are you from?"

"Originally?" Jesse swallowed his nerves. They couldn't find fault with him here. "Portsmouth. I've been living in Brighton for years, though."

"With your family?"

"Um, no, just me. My..." he hastily fudged the truth. "My parents both passed away a few years ago."

He had expected some noise of sympathy but didn't get it. She hummed, but her face and tone didn't change.

"How old are you, then?"

"Twenty-five. Twenty-six in November."

She hummed again. Ezra had definitely gotten the habit from her.

"Are you a Christian?"

"Um."

Ezra snorted. "*No*, Mum. He's atheist. Like me," he added pointedly, and the corners of her eyes tightened.

"Were you *ever* Christian?" she demanded.

"Um, no," Jesse said. He couldn't have lied about his religion if he'd tried—he'd been in a church once in his entire life, and that was for his mother's funeral. He just didn't know enough to lie passably. "No, I—my parents raised me atheist."

She rolled her tongue over the front of her teeth. "I see."

"Can we not have this argument again?" Ezra snapped. "What do you care if Jesse goes to church? I don't go either."

"It's better than that Jewish boy," Nana piped up.

Judging by the looks Ezra and Mrs Pryce gave her, Jesse wasn't the only one struggling to find the meaning in that. Jewish boy?

"Okay then," Ezra said slowly.

"You don't want to be hooking up with no hellbound hebes," she said sternly, wagging a crooked finger at him.

"Mum!" Mrs Pryce exclaimed, and went pink. "You can't say those sorts of things!"

Nana puffed up, and an argument briefly stormed around the table. In the midst of it, Ezra squeezed

Jesse's hand and smiled at him. "You're doing fine," he murmured, and Jesse grimaced.

"Grace is coming the day after tomorrow," Mrs Pryce said, once Nana had huffed and gone back to her knitting with fierce jabs of the needles. "Ezra. She's your *sister*."

"She's a jumped-up, born-again nutjob," Ezra muttered darkly.

"Ezra!"

"She is!" Ezra protested.

"Don't talk about your sister like that. I bet Jesse doesn't talk about *his* sisters like that."

"I haven't got any," Jesse interrupted on reflex, and mentally winced when he realised he'd spoken out of turn. Damn it. "I'm, um, an only child."

She cupped her hands around her near-empty cup of tea. "Any particular reason for that?" she asked primly.

"I don't know," Jesse said honestly. He'd been eight by the time his parents had split up. Plenty of time for more children, they just...hadn't had them.

"And what did your parents do?"

Sweet fuck-all, but he knew better than to say it. "Er—"

"Mum, you're being nosy."

"I need to know the kind of...*people* that my children are seeing," she said carefully.

"You're picking out reasons to tell all your church friends that I've been swayed to the dark side by some only-child atheist firefighter from the wrong coast," Ezra said flatly, and Jesse would have laughed if he wasn't so anxious about this whole disastrous meeting.

"Ezra—"

"Mum." Ezra let go of Jesse's hand to lean across the table towards her. "I know what I'm doing, all right? I know you don't like it, but it's not going to change.

Whether it's Liam or Jesse or someone else, it's always going to be a *man*, and right now, it's *this* man. So how about you try getting to know him instead of picking holes?"

Mrs Pryce's face tightened in an irritable expression that Jesse knew all too well. The pinched mouth, the deepening lines in the forehead and around the eyes—he *knew* that face. If she'd been standing, he would have been willing to bet money she'd have folded her arms over her chest just like Ezra did.

"If only your father were still here," she said quietly.

Ezra's face closed down. When he spoke again, his voice was tight. "It's nothing to do with Dad."

"Boys need fathers. Without them—how old were you when your father passed away?" she asked Jesse.

"Mrs Pryce, being gay isn't—"

"Homosexual," she interrupted instantly. "Gay means happy. The word is homosexual."

Jesse had never actually heard anyone say homosexual before. It jarred. It felt almost like a swear word. For a moment, Jesse had no idea what to do—then he realised that Ezra was grinding his teeth, and Jesse's nerves at pleasing this hostile woman were overridden by his instincts. He wrapped his fingers around Ezra's lightly and squeezed.

"It's nothing to do with Dad not being here. You don't go gay, Mum, and I won't spontaneously recover or whatever you think is going to happen and spontaneously go straight either. I'm gay. I've *always* been gay."

Jesse wanted to hug him, but was unsure of how it would be received. He tightened his grip instead, and felt a faint answering pressure.

"Audrey Hepburn was a lesbian," Nana interjected, then her knitting needles thumped the table when she dropped her hands. "Ceri, for goodness' sake, it's five o'clock!" It was quarter past six. "When's *dinner*?"

* * * *

They escaped at eight.

Dinner had been tense, hostile and awkward. Mrs Pryce had asked probing questions the whole way through—if Jesse had had girlfriends, if Jesse liked sports, if Jesse was interested in fashion, even if Jesse had HIV. Anything else, anything that might not relate to her definition of gay as a picnic basket, had been studiously ignored.

Ezra had made their thinly veiled excuses at eight and gotten them out of there, heading back to the hotel in silence. It was buzzing with activity when they got back, but they bypassed it all. Ezra hauled Jesse up the stairs to their room by the hand, unabashed by the milling people. It looked to be a wedding reception or something similar, and the jaunty atmosphere was at odds with the dark cloud over Ezra's expression.

In their room, though, it lightened. He shut the door on the noise and immediately pushed Jesse down onto the edge of the bed, climbing onto his lap and settling his head on Jesse's shoulder with a heavy sigh. Jesse stroked a hand down that long back and kissed his wavy hair, which was beginning to finally escape from its mousse-induced tidiness.

"You okay?" he murmured.

"Mm," Ezra wound his arms around Jesse's shoulders and kissed his neck. "She just exhausts me.

She's always like that. It's been like that since I came out."

"Who's Liam?"

He hadn't meant to ask. Jesse had *meant* to console and say it was fine and he hadn't really expected them to like him anyway, and he would have meant it because Ezra was sitting in his lap and hugging him, and it hadn't made him question the wisdom of being with Jesse—yet—but it slipped out.

"Liam? My first boyfriend," Ezra murmured, and grumbled incoherently into Jesse's T-shirt.

Jesse pushed it aside. He'd known Ezra had had a boyfriend before him. He'd not *said*, but he hadn't been as nervous as Jesse about getting together. He had been all cool and practised and confident. Jesse, who'd only had one-night stands and casual sex before Ezra, had been a nervous wreck.

Was still a nervous wreck, truth be told.

"Did they not like Liam?"

"Nope."

"Was he Jewish?"

"Nope. No idea where Nana got that from. Anyway, Mum and Grace hated him—they won't like anyone who isn't a girl, and preferably a Catholic one—but Nana liked him fine," Ezra said. He slid to the side, leaving his legs draped over Jesse's lap. "Urgh. I should do my routine."

Jesse considered it. Ezra's routine was a long and gruelling yoga session, the point of which—for him—was flexibility, strength and stress-relief. Or—for Jesse—live porn. Nothing got him turned on faster than walking in on Ezra being bendy in his clingy yoga blacks.

But Ezra's tone suggested it wasn't what Jesse was going to get tonight.

"Or?" he prompted.

"Kind of just want a drink," Ezra admitted.

"I could get with that."

Ezra eyed him. "You sure? Your wrist not bothering you?"

"Nah. Brace'll probably come off when we get back." Jesse wiggled his fingers at Ezra and grinned. "Anyway, an excuse to see you tipsy? Yes please."

"I still haven't worked out if you get handsy when you're drunk, or if it's because *I'm* drunk."

"Definitely you." Jesse squeezed his knee before pushing his legs off to the floor. "Come on, beautiful. Couple of drinks, then you can show me where you used to hang out here?"

"There's very few places," Ezra warned. When he stood, Jesse rose from the bed to hug him from behind, tucking his chin into the top of Ezra's shoulder and squeezing him tightly. "What was that for, hm?"

Jesse shrugged, swaying them lightly before kissing the side of Ezra's head and letting him go. "Felt like it," he said, and smacked his arse to get him moving. "Let's go. I have the feeling I'm going to want to get drunk every night if I'm going to cope with this."

Ezra laughed, opening the door. "Oh, it'll be worse when Grace arrives."

"Your sister?"

"Unfortunately."

"Older? Younger? Twin?"

Ezra rolled his eyes. "Younger. She's twenty with the attitude of a sour, eighty-year-old nun. I've got students with more sense of proportionality and priorities than she does."

"*Ouch*, Ez."

"It's true," he said dismissively as they reached the bottom of the stairs and the hubbub of the party. It was a christening party, Jesse vaguely realised, not a wedding. And lots of people had babies. "Let's go down the road. Jackie's is noisy but it's good-music noisy, not baby noisy."

The darkness had well and truly swept in. The street was quiet in the early night, the streetlights all glowing an ill-looking orange, and the faintest fumes in the air from the petrol station over the road. A drunk couple staggered past, giggling to each other, and Jesse felt the urge to get into a similar state—but a contented urge, somehow. Mrs Pryce hadn't liked him very much, but Ezra was so *hostile* to that dislike…maybe it would be okay.

Jackie's was a loud cross between a bar and a club, with a sticky dance floor populated by both straight and gay couples, and a tiny LGBTQ+ flag above the bar with a sign declaring it to be a safe space. Jesse had no idea what that was meant to mean, but he grasped that it was okay to be gay in here, and slid an arm around Ezra's waist at the bar.

"You're clingy," Ezra said lightly, but tucked his head briefly against Jesse's neck in a kind of half-hug pose. "You okay?"

"Yeah," Jesse said, and slapped Ezra's hand down. "I'll get this round. I want you to get tipsy, and you'll never do that if you stick to your bloody lager."

"Mr Dawkins, are you trying to get me drunk?"

"Yes," Jesse said, handing over a twenty to the bored bartender. In the pause as the guy wrestled with the till, Jesse twisted to kiss Ezra soundly, transmitting his exact intentions with his tongue and his hand possessively low on Ezra's hip.

"Mm." Ezra hummed as he pulled back, and his eyes were just a little darker. "Maybe I'll get a *little* bit drunk."

"You do that," Jesse said, and pressed the glass into his hand.

Jackie's livened up a little as the bar slowly filled and the money kept changing hands. Jesse kept Ezra on the vodka, relishing the chance to be *able* to get him drunk. Jesse couldn't usually drink—he couldn't chance not being called out—and Ezra didn't like to drink alone. So it was nice to let go a little, to drink a bit more than the two-pint maximum, to feel the first fuzzy edges of poor coordination and disjointed thinking take over his brain. The music was kind of shitty—late-nineties stuff he hadn't heard in years—and the bartender was stingy with the doubles, but it was fairly cheap and it was nasty enough to work, and when that wide, beautiful smile bloomed across Ezra's face when a tiny little lesbian and her girlfriend dragged him to dance with them, insisting they knew him as insistently as he said that they didn't, Jesse felt *happy*. Despite Mrs Pryce, despite Audrey Hepburn being a lesbian, despite the crucifix on the gatepost, he felt happy.

He drained his glass and went to the gents', relieving himself clumsily in a definitely nasty bathroom with the telltale streaks of sticky white powder on the counter that said that at least one part of sex, drugs and rock and roll was going down in here on the average evening. Rinsing his hands off, he wondered if another round was called for, or another bar. Obviously, they'd keep going a bit longer. He could still *think*, for one. And thinking was counterproductive for later, when he'd get Ezra's long legs wrapped around his waist and try to suck all the alcohol back out through his mouth. Or his neck. Or other places.

Then he left the bathroom and saw *him.*

Ezra had escaped the tiny lesbians and was leaning very precariously against the bar, a fresh drink in hand, and smiling—beaming—at a man who was just offensively good-looking. He looked like one of those underwear models or something. Tall, too-tight T-shirt, spiky dark hair in a style that could have been achieved with an electric razor but which he'd probably paid fifty quid for at a salon aimed at women. A waxed chest, judging by the naked V of skin visible below his neck. And smiling a chiselled, perfect, cologne-ad smile at *Ezra*. People could model cologne and underwear, right? Because this guy definitely did.

Jesse hesitated at the bathroom door and a shaky warmth bubbled up in his stomach as the underwear model reached into his back pocket and passed Ezra a thin bit of card. His number, maybe? Why the hell was some underwear-cologne model giving Ezra his number?

Why the hell was Ezra putting it in his pocket?

Ezra turned from the bar, eyes scanning the room and that placid, drink-smudged smile widened when he locked eyes with Jesse. He leaned back against the sticky wood, weight on his elbows, and beckoned with one long finger. It was as though an invisible rope reeled Jesse in. As the underwear model glanced Jesse's way and melted back onto the dance floor, Jesse's anger went with him. Mollified, he planted his hands either side of Ezra's waist, bracing himself against the bar, and crowded Ezra against it to kiss him and taste the drunken want on his tongue.

"You ran away," Ezra accused, tugging on Jesse's hair lightly.

"You started talking to other guys," Jesse murmured, and yet with Ezra's hand playing with his ear and the wide, blissfully peaceful expression he wore when he was drunk, it somehow didn't matter.

"Only because you ran away," Ezra teased, and bumped his nose clumsily against Jesse's.

"Can we go?" Jesse whispered, dropping a hand to slide it around Ezra's hip and down to the top of his leg, rubbing lightly against the denim of his jeans. "Back to the hotel? I have designs."

"On what?"

"On you and the bed and being bendy."

Ezra grinned, and downed the rest of his glass in one expert motion, his back and neck flexing like liquid in suspension.

"I knew you got me drunk," he accused, and Jesse laughed, putting a hand into Ezra's back pocket to hook him in and guide him out. The night air was cold after the heat of the bar, and the underwear model had vanished like an ugly, sexy mirage.

"You shouldn't talk to underwear models," he blurted out, and Ezra laughed too loudly in the street.

"I only talk to *your* underwear," he retorted, then all the sense of it was slipping away, and Jesse simply forgot in favour of other things.

For the moment.

Chapter Three

For the second morning in a row, Jesse woke up feeling vaguely like he'd died.

Or was very ill, at least. Dead people were out of their misery, but the steel drum solo going off between his ears was proof he hadn't actually shuffled off the mortal coil during the night.

Pity.

Waking up in the hotel room was weird. The light was all wrong, the ceiling the wrong colour, he couldn't hear any sirens either from the main road—his flat—or the fire station—Ezra's house—and Ezra himself was right there. Jesse didn't often get to spend the night at Ezra's, and Ezra didn't like his flat, so waking up to an unusual warmth in the bed was good enough compensation for the headache and the nausea.

He reached out. Ezra grumbled but let Jesse wind himself around him in a hug, pulling that long back into his chest. Ezra clung to his pillow, dragging it with him, and buried his face in it until only his hair, wild with the mousse he hadn't washed out the night before, was left sticking up out of the mess.

"Don't I get a hug?" Jesse mumbled, and kissed the back of his neck.

"Go die."

Jesse grinned and squeezed. Ezra's grumble turned into a growl. "Suffering?"

"Jesse Kevin Dawkins, if you so much as—"

"But, Eeeeez—"

"Shut *up*."

Jesse kissed his neck again, then his shoulder, then rose up on his elbow to lean over and push the pillow down far enough to find a cheek. Ezra swatted at him, but Jesse caught the hand and kissed that, too.

"Breakfast?" he coaxed. "A big greasy fry-up and enough coffee to give you the shakes?"

"Try enough coffee to kick-start a minor South American economy," Ezra mumbled, but finally gave in to Jesse's persuasion and unburied himself, twisting over enough to kiss his cheek and scowl at the window. "Oh, Jesus, and it's *sunny*. Whoop-de-fucking-do."

"I'll buy," Jesse offered, nosing at the surprisingly spiky hair.

Ezra grumbled and pushed him off, staggering out of the bed with a complete lack of his usual grace. He was entirely naked, and Jesse *knew* he needed breakfast and a decent hangover cure when his dick didn't so much as twitch at the sight.

It was a slow start. Ezra attempted to drown himself in the shower, and Jesse didn't blame him. The sun refused to abate, and it took two rounds of teeth-brushing, a heavy-duty pair of sunglasses and a lot of promises of extra bacon to get Ezra to even *think* about going outside. In the end, Jesse threatened to carry him.

"I have carried heavier people than you through burning buildings, so stop your whining and *move,*" he commanded.

Ezra's reply was to give him a look that could have started those fires that burned down the buildings.

His mood did improve—marginally—once they got outside. The humidity had eased, and there was a quiet café not far from the hotel that smelled of Ezra's much-needed coffee and advertised a full English breakfast for not too much money. The man was prickly enough in the mornings without caffeine—without caffeine *and* hungover was a lethal combination that Jesse was wary of dealing with too often. So he forked out for the coffee, and stayed very quiet until the edge of danger had passed.

"Are we going back to your mother's today?" he dared, once the first obscenely large mug of coffee had been downed and replaced with a tall, cold glass of juice.

"Not until this evening," Ezra mumbled, rubbing at his eyes behind the sunglasses. "Grace is arriving this morning and she likes her time with Nana and Mum without me hanging about."

Jesse winced.

"Don't give me that face. It's a wonderful agreement," Ezra muttered. "The less I have to see of the spiteful little cow, the better."

Jesse mentally decided that another coffee was definitely in order, and signalled the waitress.

"She can't be that bad," he tried.

Ezra put the glass of juice down abruptly. "One of my *favourite* students in 9A," he said coldly, "is a simply *lovely* little girl by the name of Miranda. If she's not throwing anything that's not bolted down at the other students, she's trying to set fire to Melissa Dunlop's hair with a Bunsen burner. On my first *day* teaching at that school, she told me she was going to get her daddy to complain about the faggot teaching chemistry. She was *eleven years old.* Only last month, she hit another girl so hard her braces had to be removed by a doctor at the hospital, and the best part? She's never dealt with, because the other kids are too scared to tell tales on her. Know what I call her? Grace. She's *just like Grace.*"

"Uh—"

"Grace is my *younger* sister, Jess. She's four years younger than me. Know what she does? Nothing. She's sitting pretty on a bribe that'll keep her from needing to work for the next two years because she got a secretarial job, had an affair with the boss, videoed it, then got him to pay her off to keep quiet so his wife and kids wouldn't find out. And when the money runs out, she'll do it all over again."

"How can you be sure that—"

"Because she told me."

"Jesus," Jesse muttered.

"She's a sick, twisted, bitchy little girl who spent most of my teenage years calling me everything she could think of for being gay and threatening to out me to the rest of the family. Frankly," he snapped, "I wish *she'd* been in the front seat of that car."

Jesse blinked. "What?"

"Nothing."

"Ez—"

Ezra pulled his hand away when Jesse reached across the table. "I don't want to talk about it, Jesse."

"Hey," Jesse bit his lip. "Hey, I'm sorry. I didn't mean to upset you."

Ezra sighed heavily, massaging his temple with one hand.

"No," he interrupted. "I'm sorry, I shouldn't have gone off on one. I just *hate* her and Mum insisted she come for Nana's birthday too, the minute I said we were coming, and I'm pissed off about it."

Jesse opened his mouth, wanting to ask about what Ezra had meant by a car, and thought better of it. Instead he finally caught his hand and squeezed it lightly.

"I'm still sorry," he said. "I mean, I know you were always a bit meh about your parents being all religious and stuff, but I didn't figure that your childhood sucked at all."

Ezra shrugged. "I was the middle child. I got bullied by both of them."

"Both of them?"

"I had a brother. Josh."

"Had?" Jesse asked delicately.

Ezra shook his head.

"Another time," he said eventually, and slid his hand out from under Jesse's. "Not—not right now."

Jesse bit his lip. Ezra could be moody when he was hungover, but it tended to be little things. The sun, noisy kids, crappy eggs. He wasn't entirely sure what to do with this emotional ranting, and warily kept his thoughts to himself as Ezra viciously stabbed at his breakfast. Maybe they shouldn't go and see Grace, if she upset Ezra so much? But it wasn't like she could bully him *now*, right? They were both adults, and Jesse would be there. It wasn't like—

"Ezra!"

The call of Ezra's name halted Jesse's hesitancy in its tracks. Ezra twisted, scowling, then the scowl just *melted* off his face, and Jesse's tipsy irritation from the night before surged right back up as a man crossed the café to their table, grinning widely.

Mr Tall, Dark and Handsome. The underwear model. The underwear-cologne model with the waxed chest. Coffee in hand, and *God*, that smile was like the rest of him. Disgustingly perfect.

What the hell? Was Norfolk just crawling with weird, good-looking stalker types?

"Liam!"

Jesse's brain screeched to a halt.

Liam.

Liam, the first boyfriend.

Liam, the ex.

Liam, the university graduate that Ezra had dated before.

What the hell?

Ezra didn't scowl, didn't recoil, didn't ask exactly who Drop-Dead Gorgeous was or what he thought he was doing here. Instead, he stood-the-fuck-up and *hugged* him, beaming from ear to ear.

Jesse's world flexed like he'd shoved a fish-eye lens into each eye.

"Jesse, this is Liam," Ezra said, and tugged the newcomer into the spare chair by the sleeve. Like they were still familiar or something. Perfect Liam extended a hand. Jesse shook it like a dead rat and dropped it as soon as was polite. What business did Ezra have with stunning ex-boyfriends and taking their phone numbers? "Liam, this is Jesse, my boyfriend."

Any warm feeling Jesse usually took from hearing Ezra introduce him that way was distinctly absent, and a cold wash flooded through his system when Liam raised a perfect eyebrow—seriously, did he pluck them or something because nobody had eyebrows *that* fine—and said, "Really?"

"Yes," Jesse said shortly, and took Ezra's hand over the table.

"Well," Liam said, and laughed. That sort of short, affected laugh posh people did. "You don't really have a type, do you, Ezzy?" Then he turned back to Jesse and said, "I was his first, you know."

Jesse's stomach clenched.

"In university," Ezra explained, and rolled his eyes. "I got *so* much stick for that, dating a *law* student. God, the way the other chemists went on, you'd think I was selling state secrets to the enemy."

"Selling them to a lawyer is just as bad," Liam smirked, and even his smirk was sexy. Jesse clenched his toes inside his boots. A lawyer. A well-educated, well-spoken *lawyer*. He was probably rich, too.

"So, uh, how long were you together?" he asked.

Liam raised his eyebrows. "Ezzy hasn't told you everything?"

"Never heard your name in my life," Jesse said shortly. He wanted to add 'and stop fucking calling him *Ezzy*,' but didn't. Ezra would probably smack him for being rude to his ex. Who he was apparently still friends with. And could make him smile and laugh. And whose number he took in bars.

"I'm surprised," Liam said, smiling over the lip of his coffee cup. "I taught him everything he knows."

Ezra pulled a face. "Oh, come *on*."

"You were so virginal it was painful!"

"You're right, it *was* bloody painful," Ezra muttered darkly, and Jesse squeezed his hand, not liking the course of the conversation. "Liam was the first guy I was ever with," he clarified. "And I was terrified. I was barely atheist. It took me a lot longer to shake off the feeling I was doing something wrong."

"Very wrong," Liam said, and winked.

"Well, he doesn't think I'm doing anything wrong," Jesse said sharply, and Ezra raised his eyebrows in silent admonishment. Jesse ignored him. He didn't like this stupidly good-looking guy just waltzing in here and making cracks about their sex life together, even if that sex life was well out of date. And was going to stay that way.

"So what do you do, Jesse?" Liam asked smoothly. "Another teacher? A waste—no offence, if you are—but a waste of a profession for Ezra. He was a brilliant chemist. He should be working for one of the American pharmaceutical companies."

"I like Brighton," Ezra said mildly.

"I don't teach," Jesse said tightly. He knew the type. He was going to have to show his hand, reveal his lack of an education, and Liam would be polite about it, would say what a great job he was doing, and how fulfilling it had to be, but there'd be that look in his eye. The one that asked why the brilliant chemist was dating a dumb fireman without so much as an A-Level to his name.

"Jesse works for the fire service," Ezra said.

"Oh, I see," Liam said, and there it was. The condescending smile. "That's—wow. That must be a really fulfilling sort of job."

Bang on the money. Jesse congratulated himself bitterly for the prediction, and smiled tightly.

"I've had to get used to waking up to someone who wasn't there when I went to sleep," Ezra teased, rubbing a thumb over Jesse's knuckles. Jesse tried to smile, but failed, the unease niggling at him.

"Do you live together?"

"No," Ezra said, and laughed. "We've only been together eight months. I brought him to meet my family."

"How's it going?"

How indeed. Jesse almost—*almost*—wanted to be back in that Christ-ified living room with the Virgin Mary's reproachful stare from over the mantelpiece. At least she was quiet. At least he didn't have a whole childhood of Mass and the Bible telling him he was a sick pervert. And Nana Lindquist was kind of funny, anyway, but this *Liam* creature was just—just—

"Oh shit," Liam said suddenly, and something was chiming. He dug a phone out of his pocket—designer jeans, Jesse noted irritably—and unlocked it. "Argh, Christ. The office is calling. *Again.*" He rolled his eyes, and Ezra laughed. "I gotta run. Hey, you in town for the next week or so?"

"Probably another ten days," Ezra said, and pulled a face. "Assuming Grace doesn't try and drown me in holy water or something before then."

Uncertainty flickered across Liam's face, and Jesse seized on it with far too much glee.

"His sister," he said flatly. "He didn't tell you about Grace?" he added snidely, and maybe he was a horrible person to go with the general lack of living up to this model-standard ex, but he couldn't help the flush of vindictive pleasure at Liam's genuine surprise in that moment.

"Call me," Liam said, turning away from Jesse altogether. "We should get together. Have a drink, catch up. Talk."

"We'll see," Ezra said cryptically.

"Nice meeting you, Jesse," Liam said. He didn't mean it.

"You too," Jesse replied. He didn't mean it either, and he watched with no small amount of relief as those designer jeans swept out of the café, very expensive phone already held to his ear.

"Can I have my hand back?" Ezra interrupted the musing.

Jesse tightened his grip. "In a minute."

"Mm," Ezra hummed. "I do believe you're jealous."

Jesse winced.

"Oh, come on, Jesse, you practically went green when he introduced himself."

"I just—he was so *familiar* with you—"

"He's held my cock in his hand," Ezra said, the unusual vulgarity startling Jesse for a brief moment. Ezra had his unreadable face on. The blank one. Jesse sometimes called it his teaching face, when he was hiding whether someone had said something monumentally stupid. But right now, it could be his gearing-up-for-a-row face.

"I'm sorry," Jesse jumped the gun. "I'm sorry, I just—I don't like—the idea of you being with someone else."

A half-truth.

"Mm."

Oh shit, he was sceptical.

"Look at it from my point of view," he coaxed, wrapping both hands around Ezra's and stroking the back of it lightly. "I just found out your ex is, like, the most attractive man east of Birmingham, and a *lawyer*, so he's well-off and clever and—"

"Boring as fuck."

Jesse blinked.

"He's boring, Jess," Ezra said, winding his fingers around Jesse's thumb and squeezing gently. "He's a *lawyer*. He's one step up from an accountant."

Jesse snorted, the wave of humour taking him by surprise. Ezra wasn't mad at him. And he wasn't crushing on Liam again.

"Look at it from *my* perspective," Ezra challenged. "I have a stupidly good-looking boyfriend—I'm serious, you manage to look good covered in ash, and that's not an easy one to pull off—who whines when I try leaving the bed too early on the weekends, tried to drown me in the Channel because, and I quote, 'it seemed like a good idea when I did it, Ez!' and keeps a laser pointer in my kitchen for the sole purpose of driving my kitten insane. *And* breaks into my house to do so."

Jesse flushed hotly.

"You have nothing to be jealous of," Ezra said gently. "A lawyer whose idea of a fun day is screwing a client for another five hundred pounds just doesn't come *close* to measuring up to you."

The blood receded from Jesse's face, and fast.

"Is your hangover feeling a bit better?" he asked.

"Um. Well, I guess so, short of a couple of aspirin—"

Jesse was already standing, pulling Ezra after him by the hand, barely pausing long enough to let him grab his bag. "Let's go back to the hotel," he said as the door clinked shut behind him, and Ezra huffed, his face flushed slightly under its freckly outcrop.

"Oh my God, you're a walking sex machine," he said, but made no move to remove his hand from Jesse's.

Liam might have taught him, but Jesse had every intention of going over the lesson. *Repeatedly.* And right fucking now.

* * * *

"I'm disgusting."

The declaration was betrayed by the heave of Ezra's ribs under Jesse's arm, and the very slow shift of his eyes from lust-blown black back to beautiful brown. The sheets were tangled hopelessly around their legs, and the mess drying between them was sticky from the heat, the exertion and the possessiveness Jesse hadn't quite managed to keep in check. Although judging by the scratches on Jesse's shoulders, Ezra hadn't been complaining.

"Mm," he hummed, and kissed the bruise on that long neck. Ezra was going to murder him when his brain kicked in enough to realise what Jesse had done.

"I need to shower."

"Mm."

Jesse still felt boneless. There was something heady about Ezra he'd never gotten from any of his casual fucks or one-night stands. Something that just wrenched the bad out and left only this blissful sort of haze, like lounging in heaven. Maybe this was what doing heroin felt like. Maybe Ezra was a drug.

"Jesse," Ezra whined, wriggling. Jesse tightened his arms, drawing him further in. "*Jesse*. I need a shower. Seriously, I feel rank."

Jesse grumbled. He didn't want to let go. Ezra was warm and bruised and ruffled. His hair was sticking up in every direction, and Jesse was tracing his fingers rhythmically over an exposed hip, because he could feel Ezra's pulse there, and the way it was dropping down into the same laziness that Jesse felt. Why couldn't Ezra just *lounge*?

"I'll cuddle with you after my shower," Ezra bargained, peeling away Jesse's arm and kissing him. He tasted of salt and sex. "Okay?"

"Fine," Jesse grumbled. "But be quick about it."

Ezra grinned. Jesse pulled him down for another kiss by the rumpled hair, and finally let him go, watching that perfect body disappear into the en suite. When the shower started up, he rolled over and groped by the side of the bed for his underwear.

And found Ezra's jeans, a bit of paper sticking out of the back pocket.

Jesse paused, blinking the orgasmic haze away, and slid the paper out. It was card, he discovered, and he turned it over to see the black lettering of a business address, along with a scrawl of handwritten blue.

William Quesne, divorce and separations solicitor. And just underneath the 'call now for a free quote' spiel, scribbled in a looping cursive, *my new number – call me, gorgeous xxx.*

Gorgeous?

Jesse carefully ripped the card into four and prised himself out of the mess of bed to cross the room and throw it away, rearranging a couple of chocolate bar wrappers to hide the pieces. New number, his arse. Ezra didn't *need* the prick's new number. Who did Liam think he was, giving his number and flirting with his ex? His ex *who had a new boyfriend.*

Jesse felt a bit sick. Why had Ezra taken it? Hell, why had he kept it?

In the crumpled pile of clothes, something beeped. Jesse resisted the temptation to find it. He knew the tones of Ezra's phone, and knew he'd be in a world of trouble for spying on his texts, so he returned to the bed, curling up on Ezra's side and breathing in the smell of him from the pillow, heavier than usual thanks to *why* they'd been back in bed by lunchtime.

"Ez?" he called.

Ezra always left the bathroom door open, and Jesse usually didn't like to invade. It wasn't an invite. Ezra got twitchy if the door was closed on small rooms with only one exit, and absolutely refused to lock it. But right now, the glimpse of gleaming tiles and the sound of the shower were too tempting.

"*Ez?*" he called again.

"What?"

"Can I come in?"

"If you want, I guess."

The hotel bathroom wasn't sophisticated. It was a toilet, a sink and a bath with a shower installed over it much later, judging by the poor tiling job. It was cramped, despite the management's attempts to make it look bigger by installing lots of mirrors, and it took about ten seconds for Jesse to abandon the sheets, cross the cold tiles, pull back the curtain and step into the bath.

Ezra squinted at him suspiciously, the water plastering his hair to his head for once and turning it a deep honey-gold colour. Jesse sat on the ledge where the bath met the wall, and beckoned for Ezra to sit in his lap—one of Jesse's favourite positions to cuddle him in, because it meant he could squeeze the life out of Ezra and he wouldn't feel trapped or suffocated, but one that Ezra tended to find bemusing at best.

"What's gotten into you?" Ezra asked, but obligingly perched on Jesse's thigh, nosing at his cheek. He was hot from the steaming water and Jesse wound his arms around that tight waist.

"Just wanted a hug."

"Mm." Ezra toyed with Jesse's hair. Jesse's was heavier than Ezra's, tending to fall around his face and look permanently damp because of the thickness of it and the way it refused to drift or float around. Ezra began to slick it back with wet hands, exposing Jesse's forehead and kissing it absently. "You've been very clingy ever since we left Brighton, you know."

"I saw Liam at Jackie's," Jesse blurted out.

Ezra's hand stilled in his hair. "And?"

"I saw him flirt with you and give you his card and just— I don't know. I didn't like it."

Ezra snorted and smiled against Jesse's temple. "Mm, I know. You hate other people flirting with me. You go into caveman mode."

"I—what?"

"Me Tarzan, you Jane. All that guff," Ezra clarified, and kissed Jesse's damp skin again. "It's kind of sweet. Kind of hot, too, sometimes. You do realise the reason you refuse to come to any of the socials with *my* colleagues is because you think the head of physics has a thing for me?"

"She *does*," Jesse grumbled. "She practically took her top off for you at that retirement do you made me go to in February."

"Never mind that I'm gay and wouldn't notice?" Ezra prodded gently. "Jess, you're the jealous type. Admit it. It doesn't matter that Liam's my ex, it—"

"It does. It makes it *worse*."

"Why?"

"You fancied him once!"

Ezra shook his head and laughed quietly, returning to his self-appointed task of styling Jesse's hair with nothing but hot water.

"You're terrible," he accused. "Yes, Liam flirted with me. Yes, I was pleased to see him, because he might be boring but he's a very nice guy and we didn't have an ugly break-up with things being thrown, you know."

"You kept his card."

Silence. Jesse winced and dared to glance up at Ezra's face. The eyebrow was up.

"It was in your jeans."

"*Was*?"

"I threw it away."

"Mm."

"He called you gorgeous!" Jesse defended himself. "And he put kisses on it."

"One of your analysts calls me gorgeous."

"What, Iggy? Iggy calls everybody gorgeous."

"My point exactly," Ezra muttered, and huffed, tugging a little too hard on Jesse's hair. "You're awful, you are," he grumbled absently. "Stop fussing. I'm not about to go running off to shag Liam again. In fact, after that performance, I won't be running off to shag anything at all for at least two days."

"Sore?"

"Just a bit."

Jesse tried to look contrite, but actually just felt a bit smug. If he was sore, he'd be reminded all the time of what they'd just done. And he knew from experience that if Ezra kept thinking about sex, he'd *want* sex more, too. Which was, really, most of Jesse's intention.

"Stop fussing," Ezra repeated, dropping a teasing kiss to the corner of Jesse's mouth. "I love you, remember? Seeing Liam again doesn't change that, even if he's discovered how to lighten up since we split."

Jesse caught his mouth properly and kissed him back, tugging on that swollen bottom lip with his teeth. Sliding his hands up Ezra's back, hot and slick with water, he felt the first prickles of arousal in his groin, and Ezra laughed, pushing back.

"Oh no you don't," he said. "I said at least two days, and I meant it."

He got up and reached for the shampoo, batting Jesse's hands away from toying with his hips. His cock was right there in front of Jesse's face, soft and alluring, but the attempt to get to that was denied, too.

"Lay off. We have to go to Nana's birthday dinner this evening, and you get to meet Grace."

And just like that, Jesse wasn't turned on anymore.

"Oh, shit."

"Oh, shit indeed," Ezra agreed, and kissed him one last time.

Chapter Four

Grace answered the door, and the silence was telling.

They arrived at six for dinner. The moment that Ezra parked the car, light spilled out from the opening front door—and Jesse got his first look at Grace Pryce.

Ezra was open about his friends and closed about his family. He didn't have any of them on Facebook, or any pictures. As far as photos were concerned, Ezra had popped spontaneously into existence at the age of nineteen, drunk, at some barely-remembered house party at university. Jesse had never seen even an old picture of his sister, yet—

Yet.

Grace was very much Ezra's sister in appearance. She had the same tall, long-limbed, lithe figure. She had the same fair hair that shimmered like caught sunlight in the dusky evening. She had the same long face and slightly too-large nose that lent an imperfection to her face and made it pretty rather than stunning. She had the same firm cheekbones, and a long elegant neck. Her eyes were the same large, captive shape and placement, but a ferocious blue instead of hypnotic brown, and her skin was a smoother, creamier shade of white than Ezra's freckle-prone tones—but they were still so obviously siblings.

Physically. The pursed shape of her mouth, the wrinkle in her nose and the raised eyebrows formed an expression that Jesse had seen on Ezra's face, but never in looking at somebody he actually liked.

"Ezra," she said coldly, and flicked that blue gaze to Jesse. "Is this the fuck?"

"He's my partner, and you don't refer to him like that," Ezra returned, equally coldly.

"Partner," she drawled, and the wrinkle in her nose deepened and radiated out into her lip and cheeks. "Playing at commitment, are we?"

"I'm playing at nothing," Ezra snarled.

"Really," she said flatly. "We all know gays can't *commit*, Ezra. It was *commitment* that had you running from that law student. What does he do now? Divorce law for faggots who tried it?"

Ezra's fist curled. Jesse took his wrist and stepped forward to flank him. "I don't appreciate the use of that word," he said, half-diplomatically and half-coldly. Such blatant hostility wasn't something he was a stranger to, but nor was it something that he expected from Ezra's family. Not *that* blatant. He was suddenly grateful for Ezra's warning.

"That's not my problem," she said flippantly. Her eyes flicked to Jesse's fingers around Ezra's wrist. The sneer deepened one final time, then she turned on her socked heel and marched back into the house, leaving the door wide open.

"Fucking *bitch*," Ezra hissed under his breath, and Jesse worked his fist open to hold his hand and lace their fingers together.

"We can go whenever you want," he offered hopefully.

Ezra shook his head, but his face was tight and upset. Jesse stopped him at the stairs and pulled him in by the hand for a brief kiss.

"I'm okay," Ezra murmured against his mouth, and Jesse nosed his cheek.

"You're not," he corrected gently, and squeezed his hands. "Did you live here?"

Ezra blinked. "Um. Yeah. Moved in about eight months before the—Dad died."

"Then say your hellos and show me your old room?" Jesse coaxed. It would prise open some of the secret that was Ezra, and it would hopefully shake off the bitch for a while. He couldn't imagine, if that was their version of hello, that it was going to get better.

Ezra nodded, and led him into the kitchen by the hand. He looked calm again, but his grip said otherwise, and Jesse made no move to let go. He was hating the Pryce family more and more as this visit went on. He would *have* to talk Ezra out of staying so long.

Grace had disappeared. Nana was sat at the table, knitting the eight-foot sweater again, and looked up as they came in with a cheery smile and an, "Ezra, darling, there's biscuits in the tin!" There was no visible tin.

"Hi, Nana," Ezra said, letting go of Jesse's hand to hug her. "Happy birthday! How you doing?"

"Don't be silly, dear. It's not my birthday. And we're waiting for Zach," she said cheerfully, knitting away.

"He's late again, daft child. Where's Josh? Is Josh with him?"

"Yes, Nana," Ezra said after a momentary pause.

Mrs Pryce, watching from the sink, bit her lip. Jesse frowned at the reference he didn't understand, and wondered if Josh had died at the same time as Ezra's father. He didn't know the details of Mr Pryce's death, only that Ezra had been a teenager. Ezra had simply said, "Accident," and changed the subject. Had Josh been in the accident, too?

"Where's Grace, then? She has a ballet lesson at five. She'll be late."

It was nearly quarter past six.

"Grace doesn't do ballet anymore, Mum," Mrs Pryce interjected, beckoning Ezra for her own hug. She stroked back his hair, but said nothing to him directly.

"I'm going to show Jesse around," Ezra said. The tension in the kitchen rose, but for once Jesse felt as though he wasn't quite the source of it. When Ezra took his hand again to drag him back into the hall, the weight in the air was almost suffocating.

"What was that?" he asked as they climbed the stairs on a worn carpet runner that was a murky brown and had probably started its life as red.

Ezra shrugged. "Nana often asks where people are," he said lowly. "Even people who aren't coming back. It's just—painful. She doesn't know she does it."

Jesse bit his lip. "Did Josh...die in the accident?"

Ezra took a shaky breath.

"Yes," he said shortly and pushed open the first door on the landing. Another flight of stairs wound up inside. "Welcome to my room," he said and climbed them gingerly. They were ancient and creaking, dust exploding from the flex of the old wood as Ezra and

Jesse climbed, and they opened into an attic room that had been frozen in time, so abandoned that even the dust hadn't formed, the air stale with age and immobility.

It was a large room. A window let the setting sun pour gold and red beams of liquid light into the otherwise dim space, the ceiling was little more than the wooden eaves of the roof itself and the air was chilly in a way that spoke of how exposed the walls were to the outside world. The furniture was dark wood and wrought iron, a double bed dominating the west wall, bathed in a waterfall of colour from the sunset outside, and the duvet was still rumpled from its last use, years ago.

For all the space, it smacked of a cosy haven. Photo albums were stacked under the desk and an armchair in one corner was littered with old clothes—a football scarf, a pair of trainers lying abandoned between the front legs, a woollen beanie over the back with holes diligently eaten into it by the moths that now littered the desk, dead and gone. There were pale squares on the wall where posters and pictures had hung, and when Jesse glanced back down the stairs, the rusty padlock was still affixed to the inside of the door.

"You nested up here," he said, and Ezra laughed.

"Mm, a little," he admitted, bouncing down on the bed and toeing his shoes off to fold his feet up under himself in the lotus position. "I could lock everyone else out."

It seemed a sad and lonely existence, and Jesse's heart twinged. "You didn't like your brother either?" he tried.

"No," Ezra said simply.

Jesse stared at him. "Ez—"

"I was a lonely kid, okay?" Ezra offered, staring around the room with an oddly empty melancholy expression. "We moved around a lot. Dad always had big ideas, was always changing jobs, always on the move. I mean—Jesus, I'd moved eight times by the time I was thirteen. We only stopped after he died. Mum refused to leave the grave behind us."

"Where've you lived, then?" Jesse asked, opting for safer waters.

Ezra laughed. "Oh, God. Swansea, Rhys, two places in Bristol, Northampton—but not for long, we left really quickly—then Milton Keynes. Ealing for a little while, but the job fell through. Then we came here, and—" He shrugged. "Then Dad had the accident."

Jesse perched on the edge of the bed, leaning gingerly against the pillow. "Do you have pictures?" he asked gently.

Ezra bounced off the bed to the desk, returning with two binders that had faded from exposure to the light along the spines, but were still a brilliant forest green on the sides that had been hidden. He crawled up the bed with them to settle on the pillows beside Jesse, opening one across their laps and revealing a picture of a very young Mrs Pryce, long brown hair fluffy around her face, in a hospital bed, a pink bundle clutched to her chest.

"Grace," Ezra said, but Jesse wasn't looking at the baby.

A man sat behind the bed, a young boy on each knee. The man didn't look much like Ezra, aside from the flyaway fair hair and the brilliant wide smile that Jesse knew so well. He had a huge hand wrapped around the middle of each boy, who were both around the age of five, and dressed in identical jeans, red trainers and blue T-shirts with cartoon fish on them.

Ezra, as a—Jesse worked it out—four-year-old was just like any other blond four-year-old boy in the universe. He was beaming toothily at the camera, tousled fair hair in the disarray that it would maintain for the rest of his life, and looked frankly identical, if a bit smaller, to his brother.

"Josh?" Jesse guessed, pointing at the older boy.

"Mm."

He turned the pages slowly. It was a generic family album, pictures mainly of the children growing up, the odd foray into birthday parties and Christmases with ugly jumpers, and often of a new house. As Ezra grew older, Jesse noticed that the unabashed grinning lessened. By the time he was eleven, the spontaneous pictures of a laughing family had been replaced by the kind of formal pictures that hung in people's hallways, and he always stood at his father's side, as far from his siblings as possible.

Jesse's heart *ached,* and he slid an arm around Ezra's back.

Apart from the formal pictures, Ezra was often absent altogether. There were many pictures of Josh and Grace together, but very few of Ezra at all. The odd time a more natural photo occurred, he tended to be with his father.

"I just wasn't like them," Ezra said, when Jesse tentatively asked. "Josh and Grace were—they were like twins. Josh adored her. They were like the same person, and I…wasn't. I was quieter. I wanted to read, and find bugs in the garden, and I kept begging Dad to take me to the science museum in London for my birthday." He shrugged. "We didn't get on."

Jesse rested his cheek on the top of Ezra's head and kept turning the pages.

He jolted when he found the last picture, taken outside a chapel on some sunny day. It was unmistakable what the day had been. It showed nothing but Mrs Pryce, Ezra and Grace on either side of her, standing by a dark blue car and dressed in formal black.

Mourning black.

"The funeral?" he whispered.

Ezra just nodded and pushed the other album into Jesse's hands. He didn't dare linger.

Time jumped between the two albums. On the one hand, Jesse was disappointed. He'd seen no pictures of Ezra growing up before, and the gap between fourteen and nineteen missed most of it, including the point of learning to shave and whatever had broken Ezra's nose as a teenager. He claimed a rugby match, but Jesse couldn't see Ezra playing rugby.

But on the other hand, the first picture—a group of young men outside the University of London Students' Union—showed a *happier* Ezra. His smile was genuine. He looked relaxed. He looked at home, even if he was in public, and he looked so much more like the man that Jesse had seen across a dance floor in a gay bar eight months ago.

"See, this is you," Jesse said, tapping the picture, and Ezra laughed.

"Mm. Me with a booze problem. I swear I don't remember most of my first year."

Jesse grinned—and kept grinning through the drunken photos of people Ezra couldn't name and weekends away to Amsterdam or Edinburgh or Barcelona. One picture of Ezra and another boy with pink glitter and lipstick on their faces that Ezra passed off as, "Ibiza and too many shots," and Jesse's day was made with the discovery of evidence of Ezra at Brighton Pride in his second year, wearing a leather jacket and looking surprisingly hot.

"Kind of badass," Jesse admitted, turned the page, and scowled.

Liam beamed up at him. It was a formal-ish shot in a pub, the prick in a suit and looking like an even hotter underwear model at twenty-odd. Ezra was arm-in-arm with him, also in a suit, and Ezra grimaced against Jesse's shoulder.

"Christmas ball, second year," he said. "We'd been together about three weeks."

"He looks like a boring tosser," Jesse decided.

"He was," Ezra said, and laughed. "Mind you, I was just as bad back then. Took nine months before I had sex with him. Too scared I was going to get smited at any minute or something."

Jesse ran his hand down Ezra's side to pinch his hip. "Three weeks," he said smugly.

"Two and a half," Ezra countered, and stretched up to kiss his cheek. "You might not like him, but Liam *did* get my ingrained Catholicism to fuck off and stop thinking I was sick every time I wanted to do so much as kiss."

Jesse grunted and kept turning pages. Liam was *everywhere* now, and he skipped a lot of pictures to avoid that perfectly styled hair and practised smile. And the arm he always had around Ezra's waist. It was irrational—the pictures were *years* old—but he wanted to smack him and tell him to get his hands off.

"Two years?" he said.

"About that," Ezra agreed. "We split up when we graduated."

"What, the same day?"

"Mine," Ezra said. "And yes. Right after the ceremony."

"And you dumped him?" Jesse couldn't help asking.

"Get me drunk one day and I'll tell you the whole sorry story," Ezra said, and paused. "Actually, in hindsight, it's kind of amusing, but it can't have felt nice for Liam."

"That's fine by me," Jesse said, pushing the albums away and turning to press Ezra down into the mattress. "Did he do something really stupid that I should avoid doing?"

"Yes, but I doubt you'd be that thick," Ezra murmured, tilting his head back when Jesse began to kiss his neck.

"Did you ever bring him home?"

"Mm, no," Ezra hummed, pushing his hands up under Jesse's shirt and tracing the muscles in his back. "My family met him at my graduation. Same day I dumped him. It was a bit awkward."

Jesse rubbed a hand over the front of Ezra's jeans and toyed with the button. "So you never brought him home to christen your old room?"

Ezra laughed breathlessly. "I've never so much as had sex in this room," he said, and drew his right foot up towards his hip, opening up invitingly under Jesse's weight. "And I'm not having sex now, but I wouldn't say no to a bit of…manhandling."

"Oh, I can—"

"Ezra! Dinner!"

The shout from the landing was like a bucket of iced water over the head. Jesse jolted up, and Ezra laughed and caught him again for a quick kiss before sitting up.

"Maybe after dinner," he said, tracing his fingers over the shell of Jesse's left ear. "I could lock the door and everything."

* * * *

"So, Jesse"—Grace speared a piece of pasta on her fork as though it were Jesse's balls and held it up in front of her face to examine it critically—"how long do you intend on being with Ezra?"

"Er—"

Ezra's face twisted.

"What do you mean?" Jesse hedged.

"Exactly what I said."

"What you said doesn't make sense."

"Of course it does," she said flippantly. "Gay relationships are about sex."

"Grace!" Mrs Pryce exclaimed.

"It's not just—" Jesse began, exchanging a startled glance with Ezra. Or, rather, he offered surprise, and Ezra met it with a weary shrug.

"Of course it is." Grace waved his objection aside, ignoring her mother. "Men can't commit. It's a fact. Two men trying to commit to one another? It doesn't happen. So how long do you suppose you'll put up with Ezra?"

"I don't *put up* with Ezra, I—" Jesse tried.

"Even if you're deluded, he's not. Liam offered *commitment*, and Ezra ran a mile. It's the way he's built."

Ezra flushed an angry red. Jesse was half-curious and half-derisive. Because what the hell did Grace know—what did she mean by Liam offering Ezra commitment?

"I'm in it for the long haul," Jesse said, as diplomatically as possible, and squeezed Ezra's thigh under the table. From the way her eyes flickered downwards, Grace caught the flex of his biceps and guessed his action anyway. The disgusted look intensified marginally.

"However long *that* is in your book," Grace muttered, almost to herself. She stabbed another piece of pasta. "I suppose it's from moving around so much in childhood, having no stable male influence after Dad was killed, then turning out gay thanks to that lack of influence. I suppose it was inevitable, *really*."

"Grace, I swear to your stupid fucking God—"

"Ezra!" Mrs Pryce yelped. Nana crossed herself, eyed her knitting needles, and crossed them too, apparently for good measure. Wouldn't do to have blasphemy-tainted knitting needles, after all.

"Do you keep in touch with your ex?" Grace demanded of Ezra.

Ezra narrowed his eyes. "Not really."

"Shame. You could invite him over and ask him to—"

He made a sharp motion, she shrieked and Jesse surmised he'd kicked her. Mrs Pryce snapped both their names with an exasperated, futile sort of air, like she'd been hearing the same old crap for the last twenty-odd years. Probably not how she phrased it, though.

"Look"—Grace threw up her hands, turning to their mother—"I just don't understand why he's *here*."

"Because it's Nana's birthday—"

"It's not my birthday," Nana chirped.

"Yes, it is, Mum. And Ezra hasn't visited since—"

"*He's* in the room," Ezra snapped, but they both ignored him.

"He shouldn't *be* here, Mum!" Grace interrupted hotly. "He's sick, and until—"

"Grace Mary Pryce, don't you talk about others like that!"

"It's true!"

Ezra stood up abruptly, his chair screaming on the tiles, and stormed out. Jesse threw down his fork and followed, Mrs Pryce saying, "Oh, *Grace,*" tiredly over his shoulder, and he felt a vicious wave of anger towards the woman. Who just *let* their daughter say that kind of thing to their son?

"Ez!" he called and caught up to him at the front steps. It was dark outside by this point, but some motion-sensitive floodlight boomed into life as Ezra's shoes crunched onto the gravel, and highlighted the sheen in his eyes. "Oh, Ez, don't."

Ezra's jaw worked furiously, then he gave in to Jesse's hands and let himself be hugged, clutching at the back of Jesse's shirt briefly.

"Let's go?" Jesse pleaded, stroking Ezra's hair lightly. He could feel him shaking. "Let's just go. I know it's your nan's birthday, but she doesn't know. She won't miss us. We can get dinner at the hotel and just…put the TV on, lounge around, be us. Don't let Grace ruin tonight."

Ezra took a shaky breath. "That," he croaked, "has been every fucking dinner since Dad died."

Jesse winced and kissed the side of his head. "I'm sorry," he whispered.

Ezra shook his head and clung a little harder for a moment.

"Ezra, put him down!"

They broke apart when Nana called, shuffling out into the night waving a crooked hand at them.

"We have to go, Nana," Ezra said, wiping away the tears with the heel of his hand. "I'm sorry, I know it's your birthday, but—"

"Come here," she ordered imperiously.

He went. Jesse hovered at the bottom of the steps as she hugged her grandson. She really was ridiculously small.

"You're just like me," she said, and patted his cheek. "Stubborn to the end. You won't let a thing sway you, not even God."

Ezra offered her a half-smile and a shrug, neither of which was convincing.

"Spiteful little cat," Nana said suddenly. "She needs a good smacking. Zach never smacked any of you enough, no wonder you all turned out funny. Ceri! Ceri, for goodness' sake, where's the belt! I'm still young enough to belt these hooligans into shape!"

She turned away, and Ezra stepped down into Jesse's open arms with a half-laugh, hugging him tightly once more before letting go and nodding.

"Okay," he said, the rasp fading from his voice. "Let's go and be us or whatever it is you said."

Jesse squeezed his hand, and finally got a smile that looked genuine.

"I really hate your sister," he offered as they got in the car, Ezra apparently aggravated enough to not bother saying goodbye to his mother.

"Join the club," Ezra said, and glanced at Jesse with a half-smile in the light of the dashboard. "I love you, you know."

Jesse smiled, propping his elbow on the door and his chin on his hand, watching Ezra out of the corner of his eye. The upset seemed to have passed or been locked down and Jesse turned over the information in his head before gently saying, "You know, I'm a little bit—glad."

"Glad?"

"That you don't get on with them," he said. "Because if you did, maybe you would have stayed here. Or come back after uni. Instead of coming to Brighton."

Ezra huffed and shook his head, but he was smiling, so Jesse pushed his point.

"I mean, why Brighton?"

"The school offered me a job and I wasn't picky."

"If you were picky, you wouldn't have given me your number."

"Oh, I don't know," Ezra said, shifting gears. Whatever he said, Jesse *swore* he handled the gearstick like a porn star with a dildo. "Maybe in ten years you'll look like the back end of a bus, but that night, you were doing everything right."

Jesse flushed and subsided. Ten years. Ezra didn't think the possibility of them being together in ten years was stupid. But then, Grace had said that Liam had offered commitment, and Ezra—

Maybe Jesse had been doing everything right in the club, and maybe he'd been lucky since—but how long until he was doing everything wrong?

Chapter Five

"You have a plan," Jesse said, when Ezra came back from paying for the petrol with a cheap bunch of carnations.

"Mm," Ezra said, putting the flowers on the back seat. "I forget, sometimes."

"Forget what?"

"How much you don't know," Ezra said, and shrugged. "I'm just—I guess I'm used to everybody knowing things. This trip's made me realise how much you *don't* know."

Jesse felt lost and said so.

"Sorry," Ezra said, and gave him a rueful smile. "I mean...with Liam, you know, I was working through a lot of crap. I didn't like myself, I didn't like being gay, I didn't know what I was going to do. And, you know, it was natural for Liam to get to know everything in helping me through it. But with you—I don't have those issues, so I've never, you know, had a meltdown all over you—"

Jesse couldn't quite imagine Ezra having a proper meltdown at all. He'd seen him irritable and he'd seen him scared and he'd seen him upset, but never more than Ezra could reasonably manage on his own anyway. A meltdown? Not likely.

"I forget how much that means you don't know."

"I'm still lost."

"We're going to see Dad," Ezra finally clarified. "I'm going to tell you what happened."

Jesse winced. "Ez, I—if you don't *want* to tell me, I—"

"I'm happy to *tell* you," Ezra said. "I'm just—" He shrugged. "I think it'll be easier to explain this way."

It was only a short drive before Ezra pulled his Peugeot through the open iron gates of a cemetery. It was a small one but had the look of the chapel being attached for the purposes of funerals, rather than the graveyard having been born of the presence of a church. The shaved-down grass, the shiny black headstones and the long gaps of unturned land said that burials here continued. The charred remnants of the chapel said that funeral services now happened elsewhere.

"It burned down about four years ago," Ezra said, catching Jesse looking. He pulled the car up about a third of the way inside and hauled on the handbrake a little too harshly. "Come on."

"You okay?" Jesse asked lowly.

"Mm," Ezra said. "It's—difficult. I don't visit as much as I should."

Jesse took his hand once they were out of the car. The flowers were mockingly gaudy in the sombre silence, and Ezra squeezed his fingers with a tight smile.

The grave was amongst a cluster of new, flower-heavy resting places. It was taller than most, with a space between the names. *Zachariah James Pryce, beloved son, husband and father,* had been forty-four. A space waited for his wife's name to be added later. His son, *Joshua Christopher Pryce,* had been only sixteen.

"'Resting in the arms of Jesus,'" Jesse recited, and frowned. "Um."

"Yeah, I know," Ezra shrugged, kneeling at the graveside to pull out the dead flowers from the vase. "Hi, Dad," he said softly, but gave his brother no greeting and said nothing more. Jesse had heard of people chatting to graves, but Ezra seemed unwilling to say anything else. He knelt beside him and waited for the flowers to be arranged to his satisfaction before putting an arm around him.

"Tell me," he said.

Ezra took a deep breath.

"It was a car crash," he said finally. "Head-on collision with a van. Dad and Josh were in the front, and me and Grace were in the back."

"Oh, Christ," Jesse whispered. "Oh, *Ez.*"

"That scar on my shoulder? My seatbelt," Ezra said quietly.

Jesse had—wondered. He had always wondered about that scar. A thick run of ruined skin, pink in the winter and unfreckled in the summer, that crossed Ezra's collarbone like a skid mark of damage. Ezra had never—as far as Jesse knew—been the kind of person to go in for rough sports or dangerous hobbies. He did yoga and running. He hated motorbikes. He made Jesse clean his upstairs windows because he refused to go up the ladder himself, and what was the point of a fireman boyfriend if one couldn't make him go up ladders occasionally? So Jesse had wondered, but never asked—and now wished maybe he'd asked earlier.

"I broke my collarbone. Grace fractured some ribs. Dad—Dad died instantly, he just died, and Josh—Josh died in hospital later, but he was unconscious, so, you know, he never felt it. But it took—it took them three hours to get me and Grace out, and we were just *trapped*, and—we knew. We knew Dad was dead and I was fourteen and she was ten and—"

Jesse squeezed Ezra's shoulders tight under his arm and kissed the top of his head, his heart clenching tightly in his chest. Fourteen years old, trapped in a car with a dead parent for three hours—God, no *wonder* Ezra was claustrophobic.

"Babe, I'm so sorry, I'm—"

"It's okay," Ezra squeezed his knee. "It was nearly eleven years ago. I miss them, but—life goes on. And it was quick. They never knew. Even Josh—he never woke up again. He didn't feel it."

Jesse pulled him close until Ezra dropped his head onto his shoulder. When he did, Jesse kissed his hair again. "Tell me about them."

"Josh was a prick," Ezra said unexpectedly, and Jesse felt his cheek crease in a smile against his T-shirt. "No, really, he was. He used to beat me up and call me names. He bullied me. We never got along, and if he was alive now, he'd probably have given my name and address to the BNP for being gay."

"Oh. Er—"

"I don't miss Josh," Ezra said. "I really don't. I mean, yeah, I was shocked and it was really weird not having to hide under the bed every time he came home from football practice and Mum and Dad were out, but—it was Dad I cried for. They had a joint funeral, and it was Dad I was crying about."

Jesse rested his cheek against Ezra's hair and half-smiled. "I get it. I don't think I'd cry at my old man's funeral. So what was your dad like?"

Ezra hesitated. "I'm—honestly?"

"Yeah."

"I'm—kind of glad he's dead. Now, I mean. Because—look, it was easy for you. You said so yourself. You figured out you were gay and that was kind of that. Right?"

"Yeah."

"Well, I was a sixteen-year-old Catholic schoolboy when I worked it out. Josh and Grace had been bullying me for it for years, but I was sixteen when *I* worked it out. And I was terrified and I hated myself and I thought it was sick and wrong and I was going to go to hell. And that was so tightly ingrained that even after I stopped believing in God, it still— I didn't feel good, really. Not about myself. Liam taught me a lot about not being disgusted with myself. You might not like him, but you owe him a lot, because without him, I would never have been comfortable enough to go to a gay bar, or give a hot guy my number, or go out with said hot guy, or bring the hot guy home to meet my mother."

Jesse didn't trust himself to say anything and squeezed Ezra tightly instead. "So—"

"Dad would have disowned me," Ezra said flatly. "And I loved my father, Jess. I thought the world of him. If he'd disowned me for being gay, it would have absolutely destroyed the both of us. He'd have blamed himself for the way I turned out, and I would— I—"

Jesse kissed the top of his head and murmured, "It's okay."

"I'm kind of glad. Now. I can keep the dad that just played football with me and encouraged me to hit my brother back when he was bullying me and took me out to feed the ducks when I was little and jealous of the new baby. I can keep that father and never have to know what he would have become or said to me if he knew."

Jesse didn't know what to say. On the one hand, he knew what Ezra meant. He'd never have told his father either, even if he'd suddenly reappeared and given Jesse the chance. But was he *that* convinced his father would have reacted badly that he was glad the man had died? How could he be *that* certain?

"Mum never got over it," Ezra said, bending his knees and tucking his feet up into the crooks of his knees in the lotus position, though he never shrugged off Jesse's arm. "She changed after Dad died. She used to proper bollock me and Grace for yelling at each other, she used to keep it all under control, much as she could, but after—she just gave up. We raised ourselves a little bit. Grace went wild, I disappeared into my room and it's like—it's like Dad and Josh haunt the spaces between us, you know? Nothing was enough for Mum after Dad died."

The remnants of the Pryce family began to click into place in Jesse's head, and he felt bitterly sad. Ezra had had all the ingredients for an amazing childhood. Both parents, at least one grandparent, siblings to play with, everything—and yet it had all been completely wrong, too.

"This is why you don't like small spaces," Jesse said finally. It was the only thing he *could* say.

"Mm," Ezra hummed, and laughed. "Silly, isn't it?"

Jesse snorted. Ezra had told him about being claustrophobic—though not the reason—early on, mostly because Jesse had jumped to the wrong conclusion and panicked. Jesse wasn't much taller than Ezra, but he was pure muscle, and Ezra had always jokingly referred to him as a concrete block. He was heavy and outweighed Ezra by probably a good six stone. And the first few times they'd had sex or been messing around and he'd trapped Ezra with his weight, Ezra had just seized up and panicked—

Well, claustrophobia hadn't been what Jesse had thought about first.

"No," he said firmly. "I would be too."

Ezra huffed.

"Come on, Ez. If it's not silly that I have to call you in the middle of the night because I've had a nightmare about some of the things I've seen at work, then how is it silly you don't like feeling confined after you spent *three hours*—?"

"All right, Jess, I get it," Ezra said a little tightly, and Jesse bit his lip, rubbing his hand softly up and down Ezra's arm.

"I'm impressed you ever got back in a car," he admitted.

Ezra shrugged. "Still don't like the backseat. Or when other people drive, really."

"You lucked out with me, then," Jesse said. He could drive but couldn't comfortably afford to run a car on his salary and, given that he could walk to work, had never seen the need to bother buying one anyway. He drove Ezra's Peugeot occasionally, but he wasn't technically insured to do so.

"In more ways than one," Ezra said, squeezing his thigh and frowning at the grave. "He'd be spinning down there if he could see us."

"Well, he can't," Jesse said bluntly, and sighed. "Ez? Let's go home."

"Mm?"

"You're miserable here," Jesse said flatly. "You're tense and upset all the time, and I hate it. You shouldn't be that way, you should be all sarcastic and taking the piss out of me and gorgeous and shit."

"How romantic."

"Like that." Jesse prodded him in the ribs, and Ezra squirmed in his arm with a scowl. "You've been, you've visited, we brought Nana a gift and said happy birthday, we've been introduced, now let's go home."

Ezra sighed and ground the heel of his hand into his face. "I—"

"Come on," Jesse coaxed. "We still have a week and a half before you go back to work, and my appointment with the physio isn't until the sixteenth. We can just go home, laze around your house, go out. Let me prove Flopsy hates me."

"Paranoid."

"It's a cat. Of course I'm paranoid. They're evil."

Ezra huffed a little laugh and pressed his head onto Jesse's shoulder again, still staring at the grave.

"All right," he said finally. "I mean—I keep somehow expecting it'll be better each time I visit, but it never is, so—okay. Let's go home."

* * * *

They pulled up in front of Ezra's little house at half-eight in the evening. Dusk was only just hinting in the sky, and the cat flap rattled before Ezra had even opened the car door. The minute he did, Kitsa leapt up into his lap and immediately started purring.

"It's nice when somebody misses you," Ezra crooned, scratching her under the chin and picking her up as he got out. She dug her little claws into his shoulder and eyed Jesse speculatively as he rescued their bags from the boot.

"Don't even think about it," Jesse warned her, and she decided against the leap, butting her head against Ezra's ear instead and meowing plaintively. "I swear your cats are more like your kids. Your loud, needy kids."

Ezra laughed, and Jesse watched his face light up with it. He had made all the protestations and argued about losing their money on a hotel room they weren't using, but Jesse had seen the way the pinch around his eyes had disappeared. By the time they'd left Norfolk, he had been relaxed. By the time they'd reached the outskirts of Brighton, he'd been *himself* again. And Jesse was startled to realise how much he'd missed him in those scant few days.

Flopsy was less than impressed to see them. While Ezra fussed over the cats and put down fresh food, Jesse dumped their bags in the hall and locked and bolted the front door, having no intention of going home tonight. He toed off his boots, set the post on the side table and padded back through to the kitchen to wrap his arms around Ezra's waist from behind and mould himself against that slender back for a hug.

"Mm, hello." Ezra scratched his scalp like *he* was a cat, too. "I recognise this."

"This what?"

"This clingy, leech-like behaviour."

Jesse peeled away the edge of Ezra's T-shirt and left a deep bruise with his mouth at the base of his neck, soothing it with his tongue and kissing it lightly when Ezra grumbled in a vaguely incoherent manner and pulled his hair.

"I take it you're staying the night?"

"Can't trust you to cook."

"Even I can stick a lasagne in the oven."

"Yeah, that gross frozen stuff. I'll make chicken salad?" Jesse offered, shamelessly using the favourite to butter Ezra up. A little buttering never hurt.

Ezra hummed. "You're trying to soften me up."

"Yeah," Jesse said, worming his hands under the hem of Ezra's T-shirt. His stomach was very warm, and Jesse curled his fingers pleasantly. Ezra squirmed. "Is it working?"

"I don't know. You haven't offered me a kiss or anything. I don't feel very softened up."

Jesse turned him around by the belt loops on his jeans and pressed him up against the fridge to kiss him, coaxing his mouth open and brushing his hands back up under the T-shirt when Ezra dug his hands into his hair.

"Mm." Ezra smiled against his mouth. "*And* chicken salad?"

"With extra dressing."

"Deal," Ezra said, nosing at Jesse's cheek.

It took another few minutes to peel himself away from Ezra's mouth, and Jesse felt suddenly struck by how at home he felt in this kitchen that wasn't his. It wasn't just knowing where everything was, or being allowed to make something here without Ezra's help—not that Ezra's cooking skills constituted *help*, really—it was the sensation of it being natural to cook in Ezra's kitchen. It was the feeling that, while it was nice that Ezra remained, sitting up on one of the counters, cross-legged like a child, he didn't *need* to be there. It was the way it felt right to have Kitsa meowing at his feet as he diced the chicken, and the sound of the clock on the wall being harmonious instead of out of place.

They talked about inconsequential things—work, the fussing cats, Jesse's appointment with occupational health next week, all the little things going on in their lives that didn't involve Ezra's awful sister and his not-quite-as-awful-but-still-pretty-bad childhood. In the warmth and easy atmosphere of his little kitchen, Jesse could look at the fair-haired man sitting up on the counter with his upturned feet in the lotus position that looked simultaneously easy and painful, and not see the solemn, unhappy child in the pictures.

"What are you staring at?" Ezra asked as he stole a tomato from the salad bowl and bit into it contentedly.

"You," Jesse said honestly.

"Why? Have I got something on my face?"

"Freckles."

"Ha bloody ha."

Jesse shrugged. "You look nice."

"Gee, thanks."

"Fine, you look pretty. Happy?"

"Don't make me sing it," Ezra threatened, and Jesse laughed, leaning up to kiss him and steal back the salad bowl. "Aw, no, give it back!"

"It's not chicken salad without chicken, idiot," Jesse told him, taking the pan off the heat.

Once he'd combined the two, however, Ezra just took the bowl back, and Jesse opted to stand at the counter and share the cobbled-together meal out of it. He never felt particularly hungry after travelling anyway and snatching bits of chicken from Ezra's fingers with his teeth gained him several of those beautiful smiles and exasperated eye-rolls that said that Ezra was feeling better after the disaster of a visit.

"You're impossible," Ezra murmured, leaning forward to kiss him, and Jesse curled his fingers into the denim of Ezra's jeans.

"You love me anyway, though, right?" he asked.

"Mm, usually," Ezra smiled, taking the last salad leaf and brushing it over Jesse's lips before eating it himself.

"Harsh, Pryce."

"Man up."

Jesse put the bowl aside and kissed him properly, wrapping a hand around the nape of his neck to pull him into it. After a moment, Ezra draped his arms around Jesse's shoulders and melted into the touch, pushing past Jesse's mouth like he was trying to memorise him. Jesse slid his hands from Ezra's neck to his shoulders, down the curved run of his spine, and to the spread V of his legs, still crossed between them on the granite countertop.

"I want you," he murmured lowly.

Ezra made a questioning noise.

"I want to take you upstairs and pour you back out of these jeans and lick that bit where your hip juts out at the front, the bit that makes you sigh."

Ezra ran both hands through Jesse's hair, gathering the dark blond strands into clumps and tugging on them in a way that sent tingles buzzing through his scalp.

"No teasing," Ezra murmured. "Just you tonight. No games, no teasing. Just you."

Jesse tapped his knees. Ezra unfolded and dropped his feet, but before he could slide off the counter, Jesse pushed his hands under those taut thighs and lifted, picking Ezra up almost effortlessly, and grinning when Ezra wrapped those long legs around his waist and clung, stealing every bit of air from his lungs with a hungry kiss.

Jesse managed to carry him all the way upstairs, one arm under his legs and the braced wrist against his back. Ezra didn't weigh much—Jesse had definitely carried heavier under more dire circumstances—but the way he clung let Jesse feel his arousal stirring, and it was difficult to think about walking in a straight line when Ezra's tongue was wrapped around his.

The bed was wide and inviting. The darkness of Ezra's eyes when Jesse dropped him onto the sheets was nothing but sinful, and the way he rolled his hips up to let Jesse pull off his jeans was worthy of a high-class whore. Jesse palmed the erection freed by the jeans and was seized by the hair in another hungry kiss, forcing him to remove his own jeans by feel alone, and step clumsily out of them onto the bed.

"Take your shirt off," he breathed into Ezra's mouth, nearly ripping the buttons on his own in an attempt to remove it quickly, the rush of colder air from the bedroom when he succeeded doing nothing to cool his blood. "*Ez,*" he persisted, when Ezra's hands and mouth moved lower on his collarbone and chest. "Shit, Ez, take your fucking shirt off."

"Busy," Ezra whispered, and grazed a rough thumb over a nipple. Jesse swore at the bolt of lightning that shot over his ribs, up his spine and straight into the base of his skull before ricocheting back down towards his dick and taking most of his blood with it.

"Ez, take the shirt off, or I will."

"So do it," Ezra murmured, sucking him back into a kiss, shifting his hips until they lined up, and bracketed Jesse's waist with those long, bendy legs.

Jesse took both sides of the T-shirt collar in his hands and tore.

Ezra jumped and laughed breathlessly, the rip of fabric loud in the otherwise quiet room, and the remnants of the shirt came away in Jesse's hand. He threw them aside, dropping back into the kiss that Ezra insisted on and running a hand down the freshly-bared ribs to the jut of hip that was, frankly, the sexist sweet spot on Ezra's entire body, naked or otherwise.

"I'll kill you in the morning," Ezra whispered.

"I'm sure you will." Jesse grinned, kissing a path down the heaving ribs until he found that jut, the point of bone that only revealed itself when he pushed Ezra's leg flat *just* so, and that when he rubbed his tongue broadly over it—

"*Oh* my God," Ezra said, and his hips jerked in Jesse's hands. "Oh fuck. *Fuck.*"

His hand was tight in Jesse's hair, and Jesse laughed, biting at the jut before licking it again, running his tongue into the low, concave dip of Ezra's abdomen, hauntingly close to the top of his still—barely—present boxers.

"*Jess,*" Ezra whined, head straining back on the pillow. "Don't *tease.*"

"Okay, okay," Jesse said, kissing the jut apologetically, and reached for the top drawer.

It didn't take long. A long day, a stressful week, and the blown lust in Ezra's eyes were too much for Jesse to handle all at once. He loved this stage. It was new enough that he had tired of nothing, found nothing of Ezra naked and so turned on it hurt that he had grown bored with, and yet old enough that he knew exactly where the sweet spots were. He knew when to twist his fingers and kiss that hip-bone at the same time. He knew just when to start and when to stop. He knew the breathy sighs of contentment from the first edges of pain if he went too fast, and how to wring out all the best noises. All the right noises.

Ezra hooked a foot over his back once he was fully inside, whispering some incoherent endearment against his mouth. Jesse loved this. The closeness, chest to chest and tangled in the sheets, only permitted when Ezra was mindless with lust. The dampness of his skin, the flush in his lips and the way their mouths clung as though their lips were hugging instead of kissing. The strange kind of disarray that Ezra's hair only adopted when they had sex, and the way that, right near the end, Ezra would tangle both hands back in Jesse's hair and pull him close to gasp into his mouth, not quite kissing and not quite talking.

I love you, Jesse thought, as loudly as he could, at the precise moment that Ezra fell apart, jerking under him in a short seizure of bliss. The moment that his eyes went blank, his brain momentarily paused, was the moment that Jesse followed, and the white-out pleasure was somehow strangely intense that night, tearing him out from his toes to his scalp, and burying the remains deep in the heaving ribs that protected Ezra's heart.

Deep *in* Ezra's heart.

"I love you," Ezra whispered breathlessly as they came down together, too hot and tangled up and still completely intertwined. "God, Jess. I love you."

Jesse kissed him, barely a brush against his swollen mouth, and nosed wordlessly against his damp neck.

Then Ezra kissed his ear, whispered, “Mm, I know,” and Jesse knew that even if he didn’t say it out loud, Ezra heard him anyway.

Chapter Six

"So," Ezra said when Jesse answered his mobile. "I hear my hero is back at work?"

Jesse blinked. "How did you—?"

He'd been cleared not ten minutes ago by occupational health.

"Iggy," Ezra said immediately.

"Bloody Iggy."

"Now you know why I let her flirt with me," Ezra said triumphantly.

"Yeah, yeah. Snitch."

"So when's your next shift?"

"I'm on light duties from the day after tomorrow," Jesse said. "No shifts yet. I haven't passed the grip test, so I'm stuck on paperwork duties and installing alarms and crap. Should be back to the proper job in a week or two. Celebratory drinks?"

"Mm, I could be persuaded," Ezra said, but Jesse strained his hearing, and could just about pick out the hustle of background noise that didn't belong in Ezra's house.

"Where are you?"

"Primark," Ezra said. "*Someone,* who shall remain nameless, ruined my last stretchy T-shirt by *ripping* it."

"So you're buying more?"

"Mm."

"Good, I like those," Jesse said approvingly, and Ezra laughed. "So, meet you in the Wetherspoons for lunch in fifteen? My treat."

"I never say no to a free lunch," Ezra said. "See you in a bit. Love you, baby."

"You too," Jesse managed, and grinned when he hung up. He wasn't comfortable with words like Ezra. He didn't like voicing his feelings very much, not when it mattered, and Ezra *mattered.* That little 'you too' was a step in the right direction.

He had a bounce in his step as he walked the half-mile into the town centre. Jesse loved his job. He had been cursing himself every day since the accident for getting injured in the first place, even if it had at least been around some of Ezra's own holiday time. Even light duties were better than nothing.

Ezra had beaten him to the pub, but not by much, and Jesse grinned to see that Ezra had bought the first round, two pints of Stella gleaming in the watery noon sun.

"Hey, gorgeous," he said, catching him by the shoulders from behind and absorbing the startled flinch, bending over to kiss him briefly despite the public setting.

"Get off, you animal," Ezra said, shoving his shoulder, but he was smiling as Jesse let him go and took his seat, and the clank of their glasses in cheers was loud. "Congratulations," Ezra said. "Now you'll stop moping around like someone killed your puppy."

"I do not," Jesse said.

"You do," Ezra corrected, checking his phone when it beeped. "Day after tomorrow, huh? Nine to five?" he added, replying to whatever text had distracted him.

"Yep," Jesse replied. "Mostly paperwork. And probably some liaison shit. The boss was saying how the police want to do this community safety drive and want us on board."

"Exciting," Ezra said, his tone saying it was anything but. "Well, I'm thinking that once your nine to five is over, I live within spitting distance. And I need someone to distract me from lesson plans."

"I think I could manage." Jesse grinned, then paused and chewed on the edge of his lip. "I've, um—I've been saving my holiday leave, and I talked to the boss today, and he said if I get in early enough, he'll prioritise my leave request this year."

"Lucky you," Ezra said.

"No, listen. I was thinking maybe we could go on holiday. A proper one, away. It was—your family aside—leave it," he added, batting the phone away when it beeped again and Ezra opened the text. "Your family aside, it was nice getting away somewhere new with you. We could, I don't know, go for a city break somewhere, or hiking somewhere."

Ezra was smiling, turning his phone over and over in his hand absently.

"That sounds nice," he said, the smile widening when Jesse's face flushed hot. "It would have to be August. I spend most of July working on my lesson plans for the next year so I can actually take August off, but—no, going away sounds nice," he finished, firing off a quick text before putting the phone aside again. "Depends where."

"We can look on the web when I get back from work on Wednesday," Jesse said, and grinned. "Somewhere hot, though."

"I'll burn."

"You'll *freckle*."

Ezra threw a menu at him. "I'll *burn*," he insisted. "Anything more intense than Brighton in the summer, and I go scarlet. Pick your lunch."

His phone beeped. Jesse rolled his eyes and scanned the menu as Ezra dealt with whoever wanted him. "Think I'll go with a chicken burger," he said eventually, and the moment he did, Ezra was standing. "Hey, no, I said I'd—"

"And it's *your* good news, so *I'll* get it," Ezra insisted, then smiled. "You can pay me back after work on Wednesday."

Jesse raised his eyebrows. Ezra smirked and sauntered away with the menu, leaving Jesse to stare out of the window at the world passing by. The sun was trying to break through the clouds and mostly failing, and there was a hint of rain against the windows. A typical day on the south coast, then. Jesse loved days like this.

Ezra's phone beeped, and Jesse jumped. He started at the lit display for a moment, before glancing towards the bar. Ezra was leaning over it talking to the barman. So Jesse took the chance and slid the phone across towards himself, opening the *one new text message* notification.

"Fuck," he muttered.

From: Liam Q
Time: 13.32
Message: I saw the bruises.

Well, that made a whole lot of sense. He backed out of the text and went to the previous one, also from the underwear model.

Liam Q: I just didn't get a good vibe off him, that's all I'm saying.

Which made about as much sense. Jesse frowned at the phone, but Ezra's reply of *you're being an idiot* between the two messages didn't help. Why were they texting anyway? He'd thrown away the card with the number and the kisses on it. Had Liam gotten in touch some other way, then? Jesse honestly couldn't remember if he was one of Ezra's friends on Facebook. Neither of them used it very much.

The phone beeped again. God, this arsehole was persistent—and completely bloody cryptic and kind of patronising too, when Jesse opened *that* message to find—

Liam Q: If you ever need to talk, Ezzy, I'm here x.

"*Thank* you," Ezra said tartly, snatching the phone out of Jesse's hand as he returned. "What are you nosing about in there for?"

"It wouldn't stop buzzing," Jesse said.

"Mm."

"It's Liam."

"I know that." Ezra gave him a funny look, glancing at the latest message and rolling his eyes.

"Why do you have his number?"

"He sent it me on Facebook." Ezra shrugged. "In theory, we're catching up, but funny, you two have something in common. He's been your favourite topic since you met him, and you've been his since, oh, about the same time."

Jesse winced. He knew *that* tone of voice. "Sorry?" he tried. "I just—he *keeps* texting you."

"Because you're both idiots," Ezra said, turning off the phone and pocketing it. "What does it matter if I'm talking to my ex-boyfriend anyway?"

Jesse squirmed. There was no way to answer that without getting yelled at, or—or waking Ezra up to the facts. That Liam was *better* than him.

"Jesse," Ezra said firmly. "Stop it. Liam is not a bloody threat to you—or to us. He's my ex, he's my ex for a reason that hasn't changed, so *drop it*. I'm getting sick of the pair of you—you're both carrying on like absolute idiots since you met."

Jesse scowled at the phone where it now resided. "So he meant me."

"What?"

"He said he didn't get a good vibe or something. He meant me."

Ezra rolled his eyes. "We're not going there, Jesse. And seriously, *stop* snooping through my phone. You're being overbearing."

"He doesn't like me."

"Well, isn't that good, because you apparently don't like him either."

Then the first part of the exchange clicked in Jesse's head, and he felt a cold wash of dread flooding his system. "He—what bruises?"

"Oh, my God," Ezra groaned.

"He said he saw bruises."

"Jesse, I swear to God, if I catch you going through my texts again—"

"Ezra, *what* bruises!"

Ezra huffed. "Oh, for God's sake. You left fingerprints on my wrist, and Liam's got eyes like a bloody hawk."

Jesse felt suddenly cold. "I—"

"Jesse. *Jess.*" And suddenly Ezra's hand was over his, ignoring the setting. "Jess, sweetheart, stop it. I know that face. Stop it."

"I left—Ez, why didn't you *tell* me!"

He'd left bruises. He'd gripped hard enough to leave a mark, and sure, Jesse liked leaving love-bites occasionally, and sometimes he'd bruised Ezra's hips if they were a bit rough, but he'd never—had he? If he'd done it once, how many times had—

"I didn't notice."

His brain stalled, stuck and rebooted. "What?"

"I didn't even notice until he pointed them out," Ezra shrugged. "In the bar. Then he gave me his number. I didn't even think about it until he started carrying on like a bloody idiot."

"Ez, I—" Jesse croaked. "If I—"

"You didn't hurt me, Jess, come on. You know me, I'd have raised hell if it had hurt. Now stop it. A couple of bruises aren't going to kill me."

"I shouldn't leave them in the first place!"

Ezra rolled his eyes. "You're being overdramatic."

"Ez, that's—that's—" Jesse couldn't even bring himself to say it. He felt *sick*.

"How about this? When you deliberately leave a bruise, or a mark, or whatever, then we can start having rows about it and what you're up to," Ezra said calmly, squeezing Jesse's fingers.

Jesse swallowed and took a deep breath, pushing away the sudden onslaught of panic. He wasn't like that. He *wasn't*. He'd never hurt Ezra on purpose, and he'd—he'd have to be more careful, and—

"One chicken burger and one gammon and chips?"

Ezra offered the waitress a sunny smile and withdrew his hand. "The gammon's mine," he said. "Thanks." The moment she retreated, those dark eyes homed back in on Jesse's face, and he frowned lightly. "You all right?"

"Yeah," Jesse lied, and mustered up a smile. "Yeah, I'm, I'm okay."

"Mm," Ezra said, spearing a chip with his fork. "I think you and I need a bit of a talk about this."

"I'm *fine*, Ez."

"You completely overreacted. You've *been* overreacting ever since I suggested visiting my family, and I'm done pretending you're just nervous and you'll get over it, because you're not. So we'll talk about it—like rational adults, instead of you snooping around in my phone—and get this all out in the open. Okay?"

Jesse took a shallow, shaky breath, feeling the edge again. This was it, then. This was going to be when Ezra realised he could do better, that he *had* done better, then—

"Okay," he lied again, and watched those narrow wrists as Ezra reached for the salt shaker.

He couldn't see a single mark.

* * * *

"All right," Ezra said, the moment that Jesse had shut the flat door behind them. "Sit down and let's hash this out."

Lunch had been pleasant, if a little tense, and they had walked back to Jesse's flat together with Ezra's arm tucked into the crook of Jesse's elbow, for once ignoring the risks of bumping into homophobic idiots or, worse, one of his students. But Jesse knew he wasn't getting away with it the moment Ezra spoke, and he sighed heavily.

"Ez, can we just—"

"You can tell me what's going on," he said sharply. "I feel like I'm the only one working without a script here. Now I know why Liam's kicking up a fuss—it's a stupid reason, but it's a reason. You? No idea. So, talk."

Jesse dropped heavily onto his sofa. "What do you want me to say?"

"How about why you overreacted when I told you about the bruise?" Ezra tried, perching on the edge of the coffee table and leaning his forearms across his knees.

Jesse bit his lip. "I—nobody—nobody *normal* wants to think that maybe—"

"Jesse, you went white as a sheet and your hands started shaking," Ezra interrupted. "Something else is going on here. Come on."

Jesse said nothing, wringing his hands anxiously between his knees. He couldn't be like that, could he? There was—he *wasn't*.

"Jess? Talk to me," Ezra murmured.

"I'm not like him," Jesse blurted out, staring at the carpet. "I'm *not*, Ez."

"Like who?" Ezra prompted gently.

Jesse took a deep breath. This—this maybe he could do. Maybe if he told Ezra about *this* part, then he might not have to spell out for him how much better Liam was than Jesse. Because *this* part wasn't true. It *wasn't*.

"Like my dad," he said.

Ezra frowned. "You never told me anything about your father," he said slowly.

"I told you he left."

"But that was all."

Jesse took a shaky breath. "He left when I was eight," he said finally. "And good riddance to the fucking manipulative, abusive prick."

Ezra's breath caught, and Jesse couldn't look at him. "Oh, Jess," he murmured, then those beautiful, dexterous hands were winding into his and squeezing them gently. "He abused you?"

"Not *me*," Jesse whispered. "Not really. He never hit me. He yelled a lot, and he ignored me all the time, but he never touched me."

At all, in fact. Jesse couldn't remember his father ever hugging him, or carrying him around as a little kid, or wrestling with him, or even playing football with him.

Ezra squeezed his hands. "What was he like?" he said gently.

Jesse squashed the surge of anger that rose just *thinking* about his bastard of a father.

"He was a cunt," he said shortly. "A two-timing fucking cunt. I don't remember him ever being a *dad*, you know, and he was a fucking lousy husband, too."

"But he didn't hit you?" Ezra echoed, rubbing a thumb over Jesse's knuckles.

"No," Jesse said. "Ignored me, mostly. Mum. He'd hit her. They'd have shouting matches almost every day, calling each other all sorts, then he'd hit her and storm out and she'd just sit in the kitchen and cry. She'd have a black eye every week. He used to call her a slag, too, even though he was the one sleeping around. He'd go out to the pub every night and she'd just sit in the kitchen and wait for him. She cried a lot, even before he left."

"She loved him?" Ezra whispered gently.

Had she? Jesse couldn't understand it if she had. She'd depended on him, he knew that much. She'd been a weak-willed, painfully shy sort of woman who'd leaned on him too much. She hadn't worked—too meek to get a job—and she'd not had any friends, though Jesse couldn't tell if it was because the bastard had driven them away, or she'd never had any in the first place. When he was there, she hovered around him like an anxious, eager-to-please lackey. When he wasn't, she sat in the kitchen all day, sipping endless cups of tea, and cried for hours. Had she needed him? Yes. Had it been *love*?

Jesse couldn't think it was. He loved Ezra, he knew he did. But did he sit around and cry when Ezra was at work, or on the odd occasion when the other teachers or the guys from the running club persuaded him to go out with them? Of course he didn't. And Jesse liked to think that if Ezra started badmouthing him all the time, or hit him, or any of it—not that he would, but *if*—then he'd leave. Even if it hurt. So had Mum loved the son of a bitch?

"I don't know," Jesse said honestly. "I mean—I don't understand how she could have."

Ezra tilted his head. His face was wrought in gentle empathy, and Jesse drew on it for strength and courage.

"I love you," he said, and Ezra smiled softly. "I *do*, but I wouldn't stay if our relationship was like that, you know? I don't—you know, if you're not here, I get on with things. I don't sit and cry into my tea if you're at work or out with your mates or anything. And, you know, I know I get possessive sometimes, but it's not—"

"It's not the same," Ezra said gently, and Jesse could have kissed him for confirming it.

"It's not, is it?" he pushed anyway. "Because—he'd—he was horrible to her, Ez. If we went out—we'd not do it much, but if we did—he'd yell at her in public, call her useless and a slag and accuse her of flirting with other people, and I—"

"Jess," Ezra interrupted gently. "Listen to me very carefully. Yes, you don't like other guys flirting with me. Yes, you are overreacting about Liam. Yes, you get possessive, and don't think I haven't noticed the way you get very touchy-feely when we're in a gay bar and you're warding off the competition. But *it's not the same*. Okay? Listen. This is the key part." He ducked his head a little farther to hold Jesse's eyes. "I have *never*, not *once*, felt threatened by you. Okay? Not ever."

Jesse swallowed against the lump in his throat and pulled on Ezra's hands. "C'mere," he choked, and Ezra made a low crooning noise, following the tug until he was wedged between Jesse's hip and the arm of the sofa, his legs slung over Jesse's thighs and his arms tight around his shoulders.

"I love you," Ezra murmured, "but I'm not stupid. I don't do guys who think they can run my life for me. That's actually why I dumped Liam. No, don't, he wasn't threatening or abusive or any of that, but he made a lot of plans for when we graduated that assumed I would be following the choices he made for me. And I said no."

Jesse pressed his face into Ezra's neck. "I'm just scared of turning into my dad," he confessed bitterly, and Ezra kissed his hair gently.

"I have proof you're not like him," Ezra murmured.

"What's that?"

"Remember when we started sleeping together?" Ezra asked, and smiled. "Generally, babe, not the specific, gasket-blowing glory of it."

"Yeah," Jesse said, shifting his hold to eye Ezra's calm face suspiciously.

"You remember how I was so twitchy about you being on top of me if I wasn't exhausted enough or horny enough to not notice how heavy you are?"

"Yeah."

"Jess, you asked if I'd ever been raped," Ezra said flatly.

Jesse flinched. "I didn't!"

"Okay, yes, you put it a lot more delicately than that, but that was the gist of it," Ezra said dismissively. "But do you get my point, Jess? You wanted to know if *I* had been abused. It didn't cross your mind that I might have been afraid of *you*, personally. You thought I was afraid because *someone else* had done something, and you were *accidentally* triggering the fear."

Jesse opened his mouth, said, "I—" and closed it again.

"If it wasn't for Liam being a prat, it wouldn't have crossed your mind to think you were being threatening or abusive or any of the rest of it. *Yes*, you are possessive. You are a bit jealous. You don't like Helen Glover at school *purely because* she's sweet on me. You are prone to a little manhandling sometimes, but you know what? Sometimes I like a good bit of manhandling. And the key part is, Jess, if I tell you cut it out and leave me alone, you *do*. You might be domineering sometimes, but you're never *forceful*, and you have never been so much as a little bit nasty to me if someone else shows an interest. You are *not like your father*."

Jesse's lip wobbled dangerously, and he buried his face back into Ezra's neck, fighting back the burning sensation behind his eyes. Ezra murmured an endearment and scratched his scalp soothingly, waiting out the little fit.

"I look in the mirror, and I see him," Jesse croaked. He was the spitting image of his father. The same tall, powerful, athletic build, the same thick, dark-blond hair, the same long, strong-featured face. He even had his father's way of smiling, from one side to the other and back again, the same slight downward turn to the edges of his mouth that made the smiles look wry and exasperated even when they weren't. The same *fists*. "I see him, Ez, and I'm terrified of turning into him."

"I'm not," Ezra said gently. "You're behaving like an idiot over Liam, and I really do not appreciate the spying on my text messages thing, but if you will just get it through your head that Liam is no more threatening to your place in my life than a random drunk at the local bar, then you will calm down and this whole sorry mess will be forgotten about."

Except for the fact that if it wasn't Liam who was better for Ezra, somebody else would be, someday, but Jesse was wise enough to keep that stray thought to himself.

"You told Mum that your parents were dead," Ezra said gently. "I know your mum died a few years ago, but—?"

"I don't know about my dad," Jesse admitted. "He left."

"You lost touch?"

Jesse snorted. "He was cheating on her, I knew about that from when I was about six. I'm pretty sure I have a half-brother out there somewhere—I remember my mother yelling about 'that bastard boy of yours' once or twice—but they married before I was born. Then when I was eight, he said he'd had enough of her. He picked me up from school with some blonde tart, asked if I wanted to go to Dover with them. I said I wanted to go home. So he dropped me off home and that was the last we ever saw of him. I assume—I don't know, he said Dover—I assume he left the country. Went to France with the skanky bitch or something. I don't know. He never came to the funeral, and Mum left everything to me in her will, so—I don't know. He's gone."

Ezra bit his lip. "Do—do you—?"

"I spent," Jesse continued ruthlessly, "the next nine years going from house to house in Portsmouth with my mum. She just cried all the time, she couldn't keep a job for more than a month. She spent thousands of pounds of dole money trying to call him or send him letters. His sister took out a restraining order on her. She broke it twice. They threatened to take me into care more than once, and she'd straighten up for long enough to get the social workers to back off, then it would start all over again. Then after I moved out, not long after I moved into my flat—" He shrugged, the pain of the memory of that phone call flaring up in the back of his mind. "She—she drove down to Beachy Head and threw herself off."

Ezra inhaled sharply. "Oh, *Jess*."

Jesse shook his head but allowed Ezra to squeeze him tightly in another hug. He clung back, staring at the coffee table without really seeing it. "I changed my name," he said hoarsely. "Dawkins was Mum's maiden name, so I changed it. And my middle name. It was *his* name, so I changed it. Kevin was my first boss, took a shot on me even though I had no references and no experience and was new to Brighton. I didn't want anything to do with my father anymore, so I dropped his name."

"What were you?" Ezra asked curiously.

Jesse shook his head fiercely.

"All right, sweetheart, ssh."

"He ruined her, Ez. That bastard destroyed her, he as good as *murdered* her, and he's my *father*. So you know—you know what it does to me when Liam makes those insinuations?"

"Stop it," Ezra said sharply, and leaned back, taking Jesse's face in his hands. "Liam is a jealous idiot who knows my stance on that sort of thing. He *knows* if he could persuade me that you're some abusive scumbag, I'd be gone in a heartbeat. But given that you've never so much as punched the *wall* in my presence, he's got his work cut out for him."

Jesse managed a strangled sort of laugh. "I just—I *look* like my father, Ez. I look like him."

"And I look like my mother," Ezra said simply. "Doesn't mean I've been attending Mass behind your back."

"It's different."

"It's not," Ezra said simply. "Your father was a cunt. 'Scuse my French, but he was. You, on the other hand, are a generous, supportive, *dedicated* man who would never even think about hitting me in an argument. I *know* that."

Jesse cracked a watery smile. Ezra rested his chin on Jesse's shoulder until his nose was less than an inch from Jesse's cheek, and out of the corner of his eye, Jesse could see the answering smile.

"I love you," Ezra murmured, and Jesse slid an arm around his back and kissed his cheekbone, not quite trusting himself to kiss him properly and not get carried away with trying to show much he loved Ezra too, even if his bastard of a father had crippled his ability to actually *tell* anyone that he loved them in so natural a manner. "Hey. Let's forget about Liam and your father and silly mirrors, hey? We could watch daytime TV and get Chinese later and maybe have sex without a cat watching, for once?"

"Your cats are those voyager things."

"Voyeurs, babe."

"Those," Jesse agreed, and Ezra laughed, stroking his face with the back of one hand. "I—"

He wanted to say it. Needed to. But his tongue seized up and his brain sputtered, and Ezra cocked his head and kissed his lower lip gently.

"Love you too, sweetheart," he said, and it was enough.

It just—it *had* to be enough.

Chapter Seven

Light duties meant largely staying in the station. Maintenance, admin, that sort of thing. Paperwork was the scourge of the fire service just like every other public service these days, and Jesse's boss, Alan, was a pro at making sure the most physically useless people of the week did it.

Jesse didn't actually mind paperwork. Okay, it was boring, and he wasn't exactly the most educated guy, but it was all designed so that even a monkey could fill it out. Plus, he'd personally met some of the drones it went off to, and they weren't exactly geniuses either. It helped that they had a new transferee in the station too, and Jesse's first morning back was spent filling him in on the various community safety outreach things the higher-ups had them doing every month.

But the afternoon was for paperwork, and Jesse liked paperwork.

It wasn't the paperwork *itself* he liked. It was the fact that he was left alone to do it when a car hit a van on the main road and the police called for the fire service to come and separate what was left of the two vehicles. And that left Jesse on his own in the station, at the desk by the big upstairs office window, overlooking the park and the houses beyond.

One of which was Ezra's.

He wasn't close enough to really spy. He watched out at two for Ezra's habitual run around the park during his holidays but could only guess at which jogger he was around the right time. It was the principle of the thing rather than the actual ability to do it. Right over there was Ezra's house. After work, Jesse could wander over in less than five minutes. And he knew, because he'd texted and asked that morning, that Ezra would be home. He would be cross, because he was spending the day marking the Year Nine tests they'd done before the Easter holiday and apparently his Year Nines were complete morons and all going to fail every chemistry exam they ever took. And Jesse could get a bunch of flowers from the garage opposite the station, turn up with the offering and prise Ezra away from his work. And he'd succeed, because Ezra wanted to be prised.

In short, Jesse was back at work, and in a very good mood.

He felt…lighter, since telling Ezra about his father. Since telling Ezra about that nagging little fear that had always been there, and that Liam had neatly tapped into and brought bubbling up. He felt more stable, because it wasn't just going to be a matter of time before Ezra found out. He *knew* now, and if he knew, then he could watch out too, and maybe with both of them being careful, it wouldn't happen.

There was just no *way* Jesse was going to turn into his father.

It was a cloudy sort of day, and Jesse half watched the park and half watched his work for most of the afternoon. It was odd to think how close Ezra had been all that time. He had been teaching in Brighton for two and a half years, so for nearly two years, Jesse had worked not half a mile from him and never known. Never had any idea that he existed, not a clue that the perfect guy—even if he did have freezing feet in bed—was literally just around the corner.

I am so lucky, he texted Ezra before leaning the mobile up against the computer speaker and carrying on replying to the emails that had built up in his absence. Someone wanted him to come and help test some applicants for the recent recruitment drive. He'd have to ask Alan if he could be spared, but it might be fun. Scaring newbies was always fun.

??? was Ezra's reply.

Me: I found you <3

Sap, was Ezra's less-than-romantic response. He had to be a third of the way through his marking, at least. Maybe even half. *Shut up and get back to pressing buttons and pretending you're useful.*

Me: You're horrible to me.

Ezra <3: Get the fuck used to it, sweetheart ;)

Jesse grinned. Maybe he'd make it an extra big bunch of flowers this time. Ezra seemed to be in the mood for games. *Well, now I have your attention…*

Ezra <3: Get back to work. You're not paid to flirt!

Me: How much would you pay me???

Ezra <3: WORK!

Jesse snickered and left the phone alone, returning to the emails and forwarding the training request to Alan. It was either him or Mac, and given that Mac wasn't even close to being cleared for duty after his injuries…

His phone buzzed again.

From: Ezra <3
Time: 15.43
Message: …but don't linger after shift too long ;) xxx

* * * *

Ezra opened the door, and Jesse thrust the flowers at him. They were a gaudy purple, an almost violent colour, and would have looked like oversized daisies if not for the virulent hue. He didn't know what they were called, but they'd been the brightest, boldest bunch in the garage forecourt, so it had to be them.

"Oh," Ezra said, and grinned, taking them in both hands and sticking his nose in them appreciatively. "Is this just the flowers, or a full stripogram?"

"Depends on the size of the tip," Jesse said, leaning his hip against the door frame.

"You know exactly how big the tip is—and the rest of it," Ezra returned, and Jesse laughed, leaning in to kiss him hello.

"Mm, and it's not half bad either," he murmured, and Ezra swatted at him.

"Charming," he said. "Come in, I suppose."

"Equally charming," Jesse said, closing the door behind him and pausing to tickle Kitsa when she came to investigate his boots as he toed them off. "Mind if I change?" he asked, tugging on the shirt collar. "I hate this shit."

"Sure." Ezra waved him off, already halfway to the kitchen.

Usually, Jesse changed at work, but he'd not engaged his brain before going in this morning and realised that his uniform would be clean when he was done, and his actual firefighting kit wouldn't move from his locker all day. Which meant he'd spent all day in the blacks, and he hated the itchy material. But he kept a change of clothes at Ezra's for, well, maybe not *this* purpose, but for change-of-clothes purposes generally, and he jogged upstairs to raid the wardrobe in Ezra's room and change into the pair of jeans and loose T-shirt he kept there.

By the time he padded back downstairs and bounced into the kitchen, Ezra was arranging the purple monsters in a vase that was supermarket-brand plastic masquerading as fairly convincing crystal. His stereo was on, playing some nameless indie music, and Kitsa was sitting on top of a box of files by the table, the only evidence of what he'd spent his day doing.

"How was marking?"

"I'm a failure as a teacher," Ezra said, tilting his head to let Jesse kiss his neck and hug him from behind. "They're all criminally stupid. One superstar thought the chemical symbol for oxygen was 'air'."

"As in, the word air?"

"Yes."

"Well"—Jesse fidgeted, chin on Ezra's shoulder—"I only know it because of work."

"What's C?"

"What?"

"The letter C—what's that the chemical symbol for?"

"Um—" Jesse wracked his brains. "Um, calcium?"

"Carbon," Ezra said flatly. "But at least you guessed an element. The same genius wrote 'cat.'"

"What *is* the chemical symbol for a cat?"

"The equation would be about three hundred feet long," Ezra said and pointed at Kitsa, watching them avidly from the box. "And the equation for that one would have to include the element 'evil', which hasn't been found yet."

Jesse laughed, and squeezed Ezra tighter once he'd filled the vase with water and put it back on the counter.

"Night in with the telly?" he proposed. "I offer my cooking skills and my hands for a shoulder massage later."

"What about the rest of you?" Ezra asked, tipping his head back onto Jesse's shoulder to look up at him in a half upside-down, half sideways sort of move.

"Always there if you want it," Jesse grinned, and Ezra huffed, half smiling, and patted his cheek.

"You're a strange one," he muttered, and twisted in Jesse's hands to slide his arms around his chest and hug him. "I suppose you can stay for a little while, then, if you're going to make yourself useful."

Jesse beamed and kissed his cheek before letting go. "What d'you want, then?"

Much as Jesse was the more sociable one of the two, more prone to going out and getting plastered on his rest days with his mates from work or down the gym, he liked these evenings too. Puttering around Ezra's kitchen with the telly on in the living room, and Ezra flitting about doing his chores like it was totally irrelevant that Jesse was there. It was comfortable, a sort of comfortable they were only just beginning to fall into, and Jesse enjoyed it. He liked the implications of it—that he belonged here, that Ezra expected him to be here. The little house was beginning to feel less like his boyfriend's house near work and more like their home.

It felt like a home because it wasn't just Ezra here, it was Jesse, too. His presence was here, from the picture of them at the beach at Christmas—and freezing their nuts off, but it had been a great day out anyway, especially warming up afterwards in the living room—that Ezra kept on his bedside table, to the spare clothes in the wardrobe, right down to the mat by the kitchen door where Ezra put his boots and a tin of black boot polish. Ezra didn't *wear* black boots. Even his work shoes were more of the spit-and-buff-quality leather than properly polished. And yet he had a tin of boot polish for Jesse's uniform boots.

"When's our anniversary?"

"What?" Ezra asked from the washing machine, where he was stuffing a load of dirty clothes to wash while they had dinner.

"When's our anniversary? The day we met, or our first date, or what?"

Ezra blinked up at him. "Does it matter?"

"Well—" Jesse hedged. "Yeah? We should have one. It's coming up soon."

"In, like, three months," Ezra said, and cocked his head. "Honestly, I can't even remember the date of our first date."

"What about the night we met?"

"Eighteenth of October," Ezra said, eyes rolling towards the ceiling as he thought about it. "It was Lizzie's hen do, that's why I was there."

"Lizzie?"

"Used to work at our place. Silly woman, but it was easier to go than try and give her excuses," Ezra said, and grinned up at him. "Worked out all right, didn't it?"

Jesse abandoned the pan to briefly crouch down on the tiles and kiss him lightly.

"You're very affectionate this evening," Ezra murmured, running a hand through Jesse's hair. "Anyway, the first date must have been around the twenty-fifth. It was about a week later, and it was a Saturday."

"Twenty-fifth of October," Jesse recited, and beamed. "I'm going to plan something, then."

"Oh, God," Ezra groaned, and pushed him away. Jesse returned to the simmering chilli, grinning. He was going to plan something and knock Ezra off his feet. Just because he couldn't say all the romantic guff didn't mean he didn't know how to *be* romantic if he wanted, and their first anniversary had to be special.

"Did you and Liam celebrate anniversaries?" he asked before he could help himself, and Ezra gave him a look. "I'm just curious!"

"No," Ezra said flatly. "We always forgot. And it was hard to tell when we got together, because we were friends first and I kept running away screaming from the raging homosexuality of it all."

Jesse laughed.

"Trust me, I'm still not up for some of the gay staples."

"Like?"

"Rimming."

"Well, okay, it is a bit—"

"And to be honest, it took me almost full two years to get used to the idea of fingering," Ezra added, hefting the empty laundry basket into his arms and marching off into the hall with it. "You better never decide you want to switch positions, because you'll be bloody disappointed!" he yelled over his shoulder, and Jesse snorted.

"As if," he said. "Too much fun from my point of view already."

He caught Ezra by the waist as he came back in and reeled him in for a half-hug. Ezra moulded himself contentedly against Jesse's shoulder, kissing his ear and smiling lightly there before settling his head down and sighing heavily.

"Tired?"

"Headache."

"I—"

"You know, I love you second-best like this," Ezra murmured.

Jesse stilled. "What?"

"You like this. This is my second favourite...way you are. I can't explain it. I just—I love you the most, the absolute most, when we're messing about and being stupid and it's just fun, and you like this, this is the second favourite. Get it?"

"I think so," Jesse said slowly. "But—me like what?"

Ezra shrugged, head still on Jesse's shoulder. "Relaxed. Happy. *You*, I suppose. No jealous fits about Liam, no tension, just you and me and my cats."

"I could do without the cats."

"You are also a liar," Ezra said loftily. "How long before that's done?"

"Twenty minutes. Twenty-five if you're going to be a freak about having your rice overcooked."

"It's better soft!"

"*Riiight,*" Jesse drawled.

"Fuck you, I'm going for a shower," Ezra said, before kissing his cheek and escaping. Kitsa, lingering hopefully by her food dish in case any of the chilli might be coming her way, meowed plaintively.

"Yeah," Jesse agreed. "He's a bastard, isn't he?"

* * * *

They ended up on the sofa, entirely as Jesse had intended—him in the middle, facing the TV, and Ezra with his back to the armrest, bare toes jammed under Jesse's thigh and knees close enough to let Jesse wrap his arm around them and hug Ezra's legs in lieu of the rest of him. Jesse loved evenings like this, quiet and peaceful, all the walls down, with the potential for anything. Maybe he'd go home later. Maybe he wouldn't. Ezra had returned from the shower in sweatpants and nothing else, so maybe Jesse would peel them off later, and maybe he wouldn't. They were all there, every option, and he stroked a thumb over the hard edge of Ezra's kneecap and considered them all.

"You're quiet," Ezra said when the ad break flicked on, and Jesse shrugged.

"Feeling lucky," he said, squeezing Ezra's knee. It was the healing wrist, and his grip was almost back up to par already. He'd spent all day with that stupid stress ball the physiotherapist had given him. Tomorrow he'd start on the bolt cutters.

"Why's that, then?" Ezra asked, finishing off his chilli and putting the bowl on the floor. Kitsa instantly came running to shove her face in it.

Jesse shrugged. "I like my job, I have my health, and I have you. I'm doing pretty good at the minute."

Ezra snorted. "Right, yes. *You're* lucky."

"What's that supposed to mean?"

"Consider my position," Ezra said, and wiggled his toes. "I have a boyfriend who cooks, lifts heavy things, kills spiders in a very heroic fashion when required and is happy to cuddle after sex. And when I want him to go away, he goes home. What exactly do *I* bring to the table here?"

Jesse blinked. He was meant to joke back, but the humour died, and he leaned forward to put his bowl on the floor before freeing Ezra's feet and dragging him bodily towards the centre of the sofa.

"Jess, what—"

"C'mere," Jesse said, and pressed Ezra flat into the cushions, spreading himself out over him like a living blanket. Ezra laughed, scratching Jesse's scalp and wriggling until they settled more comfortably, Ezra's right leg dropping off the sofa, and his left pressed up against the back to let Jesse's lower body fit between them comfortably.

"Sap," Ezra murmured, and Jesse burrowed his head down until he could kiss his neck. "Mm. Kind of a nice sap, though."

"This okay?" Jesse asked, nosing at the warm skin just under Ezra's ear. He didn't often get to do this. Ezra hated tight spaces.

"For now," Ezra hummed, eyes closing. He stretched his neck back, a little like a cat wanting attention, and Jesse obliged, kissing his throat lightly before shifting his weight onto his elbow and moving up to find his mouth.

"You bring loads to the table," he said simply, and Ezra smiled, sliding his hands around Jesse's waist. Under the shirt, but not yet exploring. "You promised me a story," Jesse added, taking advantage of the calm.

"When?"

"In Norwich. You said one day you'd tell me how you dumped Liam."

Ezra laughed. "Well played, Dorks. Well played."

"So?" Jesse coaxed, settling against the back of the sofa and stretching out luxuriously over Ezra's left side, stroking patterns into his bare ribs with one hand.

"Mm. You want to hear the story?"

"Well, you did say it was on your graduation day and it was kind of funny."

"You want to hear Liam's suffering."

"Yes," Jesse said decidedly. Kind of bad for Liam meant kind of good for him. And maybe if he knew what Liam had done to fuck up, he wouldn't make the same mistake.

"Okay."

Ezra eyed the ceiling speculatively. Jesse stroked his arm and waited.

"July the seventeenth. Liam had graduated the day before, and on the seventeenth, it was my turn. And I'm in my suit, and my stupid robe and the mortar board, and the ceremony is over, but—they separate you, you know? All the graduates sit together and all the parents sit elsewhere, so—well, Mum and Nana came. Nana wasn't quite so batty back then."

Jesse smiled.

"I was waiting outside for them and Liam found me first," Ezra said. "He'd come to have lunch with my family and me, actually. He'd introduced himself that morning when they arrived and it had been a bit awkward so I was trying to find some nice way of telling him to sod off."

"Yeah, right," Jesse said.

"I was actually a nicer person back then." Ezra rolled his eyes.

"I *belieeeeve*," Jesse mocked.

"Do you want this story or not?"

"Sorry, sorry. Go on."

"Well—some context? I'd been thinking about breaking up for a while, actually. Once our exams were over, Liam had been making all these plans, you see. How he was going to get a job with the law firm that had him on internship, and that meant he'd be living in London, so it only made sense for me to get a job with one of the research groups that were in North London at the time, and we could commute in from Cambridgeshire easily enough, blah-blah-blah."

"You weren't impressed?"

"No. I wanted to be a teacher. Liam knew that, but he didn't really listen, you know? And I had my own plans, and if Liam didn't want those plans, then tough shit. I did."

"Harsh."

"But true," Ezra shrugged. "I prioritised my career plans over Liam. Kind of rams the final nail in the coffin, you know?"

Jesse hummed and rubbed a hand over Ezra's shoulder. "So what happened?"

"Well, he came and found me, and it was all the usual 'you look amazing' shit—and trust me, Dorks, you *don't* look good in a graduation gown. You look like a total prat, actually, and I was no exception, but it's the done thing. Then he said, you know, why don't we meet your family in the union bar and get a quick drink before we have to play nice at lunch? And I figured sure, so down we went. And it was about a five-minute walk to the bar through a little square—one of those fenced, green squares that London has, you know, stick four trees and a bench in it and call it a park?"

"Uh-huh..."

"So he stops me at the obligatory bench and is all, 'Sit down with me a sec,' and launches into this massive speech he's obviously written about how amazing it's been with me and how uni was always going to be awesome but I made it special, but we're adults now and we have to find our own way in the world—and I had this crazy moment of, 'Oh my God, he's dumping me!'"

"But you said—"

"Oh yeah, he didn't. He actually got out a ring box and went down on one knee," Ezra said, and shut up.

Wait.

What?

Jesse's brain hiccupped. For a long second, there were no thoughts whatsoever in his head. It was like shock-induced meditation.

Then he unstuck his tongue from the roof of his mouth and offered a paltry, "Holy shit."

"Mm."

"Wait, wait—he *proposed* to you? As in—as in, you know, marriage, a white picket fence, babies?"

"Well...marriage at least. I'm sure the babies bit would have come later."

"He *proposed*?" Jesse repeated incredulously, pushing himself up until he was straddling Ezra's thighs. Ezra grinned up at him.

"Yes!"

"He *asked you to marry him?*"

"Yes!" Ezra said, and laughed suddenly. "He actually thought I would marry him!"

"Talk about being on different pages—"

"Mm."

"So—what did you say? I mean—"

"I said no, what do you think?"

"No, but I mean—"

"No, really, I just blurted it out. Like—seriously, like if he'd asked me to join in a gang-rape with him or something. I was horrified. And when I recovered from the shock, I said no again, and I was like, 'How in the hell do you think we're supposed to get married when we're going in completely different directions?'"

"And?"

"And I dumped him. I just—I dumped him, then and there. I said we were never going to last after uni because neither of us was going to give up our dreams for the other, and we were over. And he's *still on one knee,* Jess! He hasn't moved!"

"*Jeeeeesus,*" Jesse breathed.

"So I—I just got up and walked away," Ezra finished. "I didn't know what to do, so I just—I walked off. And he never followed me."

"*Wow,*" Jesse said, and tried to wrap his head around it all.

"Actually—" Ezra blew out his breath in a low whistle. "That night in Norwich was the first time I've seen Liam since."

"Really?"

"Mm. I was startled. He just came up and started chatting like we'd parted on good terms instead of me…well, running away from his marriage proposal."

Jesse bit his lip. "Grace said he offered commitment and you ran."

"Yeah, but I ran because he offered commitment to someone I didn't want to be committed to," Ezra retorted. "I'm not against the idea of getting married someday. I kind of want to, in an abstract kind of way. But I'm not marrying someone I'm not totally convinced I want to spend the rest of my life with, sappy as it sounds, and Liam was *never* that guy, not to me."

Jesse squeezed his hip. "Good," he said. "Otherwise you'd not be here, not be with me—"

Ezra laughed and bent himself up to kiss him lightly. "It would have been a huge mistake," he agreed. "I feel kind of bad about the fact he went and bought a ring, but, Jesus. It came out of nowhere, too. I had no idea he'd been thinking like that."

"Well, I'll make sure to wait ten years, then drop loads of hints if I ever want to marry you," Jesse said, and Ezra stuck out his tongue.

"What do you mean *if*?" he demanded tartly and pushed. "Get off me."

"Why, where're you going?" Jesse demanded, even as he obeyed.

Ezra disappeared into the kitchen briefly, before returning with ice-cold beer. He tossed one to Jesse, followed by the bottle opener. "You'd marry me in a heartbeat, just to get to play with my hair for the rest of our lives."

"Not *just* the hair—"

Ezra grinned, and straddled Jesse's thighs to kiss him thoroughly. By the time he let go, Jesse had to gather his wits to remember what they'd been talking about.

"What else?" Ezra whispered in his ear.

"Oh, your arse, definitely," Jesse said, and Ezra bit his earlobe. "Um, your legs. Your bendiness in general really. I'd divorce you again if you quit yoga," he added, and Ezra pushed his hands up under Jesse's T-shirt. "Your, um, your mouth because—fuck, again, do that again—because *yes*, that. And your hands, same reason. And *oh fuck*—"

The rest of the reasons were lost to those hands and that mouth, and when Jesse finally pulled himself back together, cuddled shirtless and boneless on the sofa with Ezra's shuddering breathing evening out against his chest, he couldn't help but think Liam had made the best damn mistake in the universe.

Chapter Eight

I need you tonight, Ezra texted at half past nine in the morning, just as Jesse got out of the morning briefing—which had mostly consisted of them gossiping and eating cake that Iggy had brought in to celebrate Jesse's return to full shifts as of the following morning.

Me: That's what I like to hear ;)

You wish, Romeo, came the acerbic reply. *I need you dressed nice to go out to dinner. Your favourite underwear model just Facebooked me an invite. Apparently he's in town and would love to get together.*

Liam? *Liam* was in town? And wanted to have dinner with Ezra? Because Jesse somehow doubted he was actually part of that invite.

But then, Ezra was obviously a little irritated himself, and that worked wonders for the flare-up of temper that bloomed in the front of Jesse's brain. Ezra wasn't pleased to see him. The prick's agenda wasn't going to work very well if Ezra didn't want him there in the first place, was it? And if *Jesse* was going to be there too, he could keep Ezra distracted from how ridiculously perfect his ex-boyfriend was, and maybe Liam was too polite to accuse him of being—being a bastard to his face.

Then again, he was a lawyer, so Jesse decided not to count on that.

Me: Do we have to? :(

Worth a shot, right?

Ezra <3: Unfortunately, yes. Liam gets worse and more persistent if you ignore him. Anyway I'm back at work next week so he can't pester me anymore :) xx

As am I :D Back tomorrow! Jesse replied, deciding to think of the positive. Ezra said he was pestering. Ezra was annoyed. Ergo, surely, Ezra wasn't open to being convinced that Jesse was what Liam said he was, right? Ezra wasn't going to turn round and decide his ex really was better after all, right?

Ezra <3: My hero ;) Have a good day, babe – love you! Xxx

Ezra had never lied. Jesse pocketed the phone and tried to forget about it.

* * * *

They'd never really gone out to dinner much. Jesse felt uncomfortable in formal gear—he went home to change into dark jeans and a dress shirt, because he couldn't bring himself to wear an actual suit—and Ezra preferred his food to err on the side of simple. And he hated small portions. Jesse had no idea *where* Ezra put the amount of food he ate. Their dates, even early on, had tended to be days out at the weekends, or Jesse's home cooking and a film on Ezra's widescreen TV.

So Jesse felt not only out of his element, but oddly nervous. He stopped at the petrol station to buy more flowers off the rack in the forecourt—a nicely clichéd bunch of dark red roses—and got a taxi the rest of the way to Ezra's, fidgeting in the back seat the whole time. He felt oddly like he was being tested, like this was the first date all over again.

Ezra had obviously just gotten out of the shower when he answered the door, hair damp and wild, dressed in his boxers and nothing else.

"Hello," he said, grinning at the flowers and taking them before leaning in to kiss Jesse—a light kiss, but a lingering one. "I suppose you'd best come in. Can't have the emergency services loitering on my doorstep."

Jesse closed the door behind him and kissed Ezra again, pulling the flowers from his hand and dropping them on the phone table. He felt a little desperate, a little like he had something to prove, and when Ezra wrapped a hand around the back of his head and deepened the kiss, he saw his opportunity.

"We haven't time," Ezra murmured into his mouth when Jesse slid his hands up the backs of his thighs. "We're going for six-thirty."

It was about six already, but—

"Let's be fashionably late," Jesse suggested, laying open-mouthed kisses down the long column of Ezra's neck. Ezra tilted his head and hummed. "Come on," he coaxed, steering them towards the stairs. "He can wait."

Ezra laughed a little, then his quick fingers were at the buttons of Jesse's jeans.

"*Quickly*, then," he murmured, his breath hitching when Jesse bit down on the sinewy juncture of his neck and shoulder, then they were folding gracelessly down onto the stairs, too far gone to bother going up them and to bed.

It was little more than a mutual hand job, but it was what Jesse needed—Ezra's cool hands stroking him in his briefs with expert skill, the tangle of his other hand in Jesse's hair, and the shuddering gasp when Jesse found that jut of tantalising hip and sucked on it until it bruised. The way he dragged Jesse up for a kiss that could have stolen his soul just before the end, and most of all the way, when that end crashed into them like a tsunami of electric bliss, Ezra arched and groaned into Jesse's mouth, long and deep and ridiculously beautiful.

"*God*, I love you," he murmured croakily as Jesse shamelessly wiped off his hands on Ezra's ruined boxers. "Ugh, now I have to shower again."

"Don't bother," Jesse advised, kissing the bruised neck semi-apologetically. "Let him notice."

"Jealous fuck," Ezra grumbled, and kissed Jesse's cheek before rolling himself off the stairs and staggering drunkenly up them. Jesse listened as he lounged, and a little flower of smugness bloomed in his head when the shower conspicuously never came on.

Once he'd gathered himself a little, he went to wash his hands and put the roses in a vase. Flopsy, Ezra's enormous brown cat, was stretched out on the kitchen tiles in the last sunny spot of the evening and opened one eye to glower at Jesse before rolling over, stretching and going back to sleep.

"Yeah, fuck you too," Jesse grumbled at her, and set the roses on the table. The purple daisy-things were still basking proudly on the windowsill. Fuck Liam, too. What kind of abusive boyfriend brought flowers, after all?

He contented himself with poking around in the living room while Ezra got dressed upstairs. The marking was split into two piles either side of the coffee table. Jesse surmised he'd used the coffee table as a chair to do it, because Ezra refused to be disabused of the notion that any and all furniture was to be used however he liked. He was a complete and utter furniture-surfer.

Kitsa emerged from under the sofa to play with Jesse's feet, and he spent a good ten minutes rolling her over and ruffling her belly. She would have been ferocious if she had a temper, but she was more interested in a tickle than actually hunting his hand. Jesse liked Kitsa. Flopsy ignored him or hissed at him, and cosied up to Ezra purring at every chance she got. Manipulative beast. Kitsa was *easy*.

"Leave my kitten alone," Ezra said petulantly from the doorway, and Jesse turned to find him tragically dressed, in dark skinny jeans and some fashionable long-sleeved thing. And a summer scarf.

"Leave that at home," Jesse coaxed, but Ezra held on to it.

"Oh no," he said. "I made the mistake of going out once after you attacked me. One of the brats saw me, and it was all over the school in about ten minutes. I'm not doing that again."

"What was the rumour?" Jesse asked, interested, but Ezra snorted and waved him out the door.

Ezra lived close to the town centre, so they walked. The sun was only just sinking behind the building, casting long shadows across the streets and gold and pink streaks across the sky. There was a light, warm breeze that teased at Ezra's perfectly-styled hair, and his paranoia was justified when they passed a group of kids outside the KFC, and one yelled, "All right, Mr Pryce!" after them. Ezra raised a hand but didn't stop.

"Jamie Burns," he muttered to Jesse. "Spends more time wanking than he does breathing."

"Don't you like any of your kids?"

"Some of them," Ezra admitted. "But not that lot."

"You really are the worst teacher in the world," Jesse said, and Ezra rolled his eyes.

Liam had booked a table at one of the fancier gastropubs. Jesse relaxed on seeing the couples in similar blends of smart and casual clothing, but mentally wrinkled his nose at the specials boards. Why was it necessary to point out that the salmon was organic, Scottish and sustainable? It wasn't very sustainable if it was *dead*, was it?

Then he wrinkled his nose for real when Ezra took him by the wrist and dragged him towards a secluded table underneath a big splat of colour masquerading as a post-modernist painting, where the underwear model was waving.

"I was beginning to think I'd been stood up," Liam said, rising to hug Ezra warmly and a little too long. He shook Jesse's hand, and his grip was weak. "What can I get you to drink? No, really, my round, I insist."

"Couple of pints of Stella, then, I suppose," Ezra yielded quickly enough.

"Stella?" Liam looked faintly surprised, but then nodded and was away. Jesse took the seat next to Ezra and raised an eyebrow.

"He had me drinking wine at uni," Ezra confessed.

"Can't see it," Jesse said.

"It didn't last long afterwards," Ezra agreed, reaching for a menu. "Play nice, babe. I don't want to have to referee a slanging match tonight."

"I'll play nice if he does," Jesse bargained, and Ezra laughed lowly, squeezing his thigh under the table.

"I know you're not happy about this," he said lowly, "and neither am I, really, but if you play nice, I'll reward you later."

"Why are we even *here*?"

"Because he was a nice guy, and I would like to have him for a friend. I promise, if he doesn't get the message tonight, that's it. But you have to behave."

"Do I get to spend the night?"

"If you're *really* nice."

"Deal," Jesse said, and Ezra offered a quick kiss on the cheek before Liam came back. The model's face darkened slightly at the sign of affection. "So, Liam, what do you do again?"

"I'm a family lawyer. The firm specialises in divorces, child custody cases and power of attorney requests, but my area is mainly divorce."

"Figures," Jesse said.

Liam narrowed his eyes. "Why's that?"

Jesse shrugged. "The unhealthy interest in other people's lives."

"Jesse," Ezra said warningly.

"It's fine, Ezzy," Liam waved it off, but his expression didn't change. "You're a firefighter, aren't you, Jesse? That must pay well."

"Shift allowance is pretty good," Jesse returned.

"Good God, you'll be comparing cars next," Ezra muttered. "Cut it out, the pair of you. Liam, what are you even doing here?"

Liam shrugged. "Had the week off work—about time I had a break—and frankly, Ezra, I couldn't stop thinking about running into you in Norwich."

Jesse ground his teeth.

"I thought I'd come and catch up, see how you're doing." Liam's gaze slid to Jesse briefly. "What you're doing," he continued slowly.

Ezra shrugged. "Teaching. Trying to stop my cats from destroying my house. Still running, and I took up yoga as well."

"Yoga?"

"Yeah, he's very bendy," Jesse interjected, and Ezra elbowed him in the side. "What? You are!"

"It's a shame," Liam said, then put down his wine glass and held up both hands. "I'm not, you know, I'm not disparaging your life choices."

Jesse didn't know what 'disparaging' meant but he could take a guess.

"I'm just saying, you know, it doesn't half look like you've—well, *settled*, Ezzy."

"Liam—"

"You were one of the best in your year. You have a *brilliant* mind, not to mention your looks. You have all the potential, and yet—"

"I like teaching, Liam," Ezra said shortly. "I'm bloody good at it, too. One of my kids found the courage to come out at Christmas, and you know why? She told me herself it was because I was so open about it, she felt like it was okay. That's why I teach. If I can help one kid a year, it's worth it."

Liam hummed. "Yes, but—"

"Let's order?" Ezra interrupted almost pleadingly. Jesse touched his hip lightly under the table. "We had this argument in the third year. You didn't get it then, you don't get it now, so let's just order."

The near-argument was waylaid. Liam insisted on buying dinner too, taking one last stab at their salaries before heading for the bar with the menu, and Jesse whistled before he was even out of earshot.

"What a prick," he said casually.

"He's not," Ezra said tiredly. "He's just very, *very* set in his ideas."

"You make him sound old."

"He kind of is," Ezra grumbled, and squeezed Jesse's hand. "*He* wouldn't have accosted me on the stairs. Liam is a gentleman."

"You liked it, don't lie."

Ezra laughed. "I did," he admitted, and a hot wash of arrogant pleasure blossomed in Jesse's stomach.

It didn't last. Liam seemed to take the time at the bar to recover himself, and returned all guns blazing on the charm. He was ridiculously good-looking anyway, but smiling and openly flirting made him *disgustingly* good-looking. He oozed suave sophistication, and he oozed it all over Ezra as he told him stories about his recent trip to Vietnam. Jesse didn't believe for a minute that he'd actually done charitable work out there—he was a *lawyer*, for God's sake, he'd probably never left the Ho Chi Minh Hilton—but Ezra soaked it up, laughing and sympathising in all the right places, and even letting Liam put his hand on his arm for a little while.

Jesse felt...oddly left out. By pure coincidence over the course of their relationship, the odd times Ezra had gone out with his colleagues had been times when Jesse was on shift, and Ezra never really socialised much with his yoga club or running club outside of the actual sessions. He was a bit of a loner. If he went out, it was with Jesse. So it was a strange position, to sit listening to Ezra sharing inside jokes Jesse didn't understand, and it was an unpleasant one, too. They reminisced, and Liam flirted. They caught up on the lives of people Jesse didn't know, and Liam flirted. They discussed politics, where Jesse was plainly out of his depth, and Liam flirted. Just before their meals arrived, he openly called Ezra beautiful, right there in front of Jesse, and the itchy angry feeling was rising back up.

"You're still into your Italian then, Ezzy?" Liam said, and beamed. "Do you know, I can actually cook now?"

"I don't believe it," Ezra said flatly.

"I can!" Liam insisted brightly. "I learned—took cooking classes at the weekends, very therapeutic after you've spent a week with some irate husband shouting at you over his wife's affairs, you know—and my class tutor was Italian herself. Call me next time you come to Norwich or London, and I'll cook you a proper homemade risotto."

Jesse twitched. "Why Norwich *or* London?" he demanded tartly.

Liam chuckled. "Oh, yes, well. I find the commute a bit of a bore. I liked Norwich, you know, went a couple of times on day trips with Ezzy, even if he did refuse to introduce me to his family. And I can't abide living in London, so I thought, why not? I have the money. I rent a flat Mondays to Fridays in Edgware, and I have a mortgage on a house near Norwich town centre for the weekends."

Sweet Jesus. He didn't just earn a bit more—he earned a *lot* more. Jesse felt slightly sick. His salary was less than Ezra's, and teachers were hardly well-paid either. Jesse would never be able to afford just *one* flat in London. But Liam was rich, he'd been to Vietnam and Jesse wasn't stupid—Liam hadn't taken cooking classes run by some Italian by *accident*. He'd taken them for Ezra. If he'd wanted to catch up, he could have called, not just turned up out of the blue.

This wealthy lawyer had an agenda to get Ezra back, and Jesse's dislike blossomed into outright hatred.

All his comfort of the past week was ebbing away. So maybe he wasn't like his father, but it wasn't enough, was it? Liam was still infinitely better than him—money, success, experiences—and Ezra was… Ezra was perfect. Ezra was far too brilliant to ever settle for Jesse. Far too brilliant to settle for anyone who was anything less than brilliant themselves, and even if Liam was a prick, he was a bloody brilliant prick. He had two fucking homes, for God's sake.

"I think I'll pass," Ezra was saying. "Seems like a skill you'd want to reserve for your new guy."

"There is no new guy," Liam said brazenly. Jesse bristled.

"No one at all?" Ezra pushed.

"Nope." Liam swirled the wine in his glass. "Not since you," he said meaningfully, and Jesse pursed his lips, tongue itchy with the need to tell him to put a fucking sock in it.

"Well, get one," Ezra said bluntly. "It's not healthy to mope around and reminisce all the time."

"I don't think you quite realise the effect you have on people, Ezzy," Liam said slowly.

"Doesn't matter," Ezra said briskly. "There's no success in wanting things you can't have."

Except he could have it, and both Liam and Jesse knew it. Liam's hungry look over the wine glass didn't abate. Jesse daringly slid a hand across the wood and wrapped his fingers around Ezra's.

"Yeah, I see how that is," Liam muttered.

"No, you don't," Ezra said sharply. "I've told you before to drop that subject, and you haven't. So, for the last time, Liam, *drop it*. It's not like that. *Jesse's* not like that."

Liam held up his hands. "I didn't mean to offend," he said. "I just want to look out for you, Ezzy. You've always been very—trusting."

"I have good reason to be," Ezra said, but he was calming down.

Jesse was still curling his toes under the table. He wanted this lawyer *gone*, and he wanted him gone *now*.

"All right." Ezra suddenly pulled his hand free and pushed back his chair. "Nature calls. Play nice—*both* of you," he added, throwing Liam a dirty look. Liam smiled back agreeably.

For as long as it took Ezra to get out of earshot. Then he leaned forward over the table and said, "I'm not stupid."

Jesse didn't dignify that with an answer.

"I get it, you know. Ezra's attractive and funny and trusting. That's the problem. He might trust you, but I'm not blind."

Jesse ground his teeth. "He trusts me because I've never done anything to make him not trust me," he snapped.

"He's too blind to see it," Liam said sharply. "You know what he told me the other day? Do you? Stop texting him so much because it makes you jealous. That's nice, isn't it? You ask him to say that?"

"No," Jesse replied, and didn't add the "But I would have done" that he desperately wanted to.

"Uh-huh. Listen." Liam jabbed a finger at him. "I saw the bruises *you* left on his wrists. Ezra *admitted* you did it. And maybe you get off on playing the macho fucking hero—you're in the fire service, it wouldn't surprise me—and maybe you think Ezra's just going to play along and let you bully him and control him, but—"

"Don't you fucking dare," Jesse snarled. "I've *never* hurt him. I *would* never hurt him. I—"

"You bully him," Liam returned, equally heatedly. "You're controlling, you're domineering, you push him around. And when he resists, you—"

"I back off," Jesse snapped, and winced when a look of triumph flashed across Liam's all-too-handsome face. "If Ezra doesn't want something, I fucking respect that. Unlike *you*," he added suddenly, Ezra's laughing account of his graduation day bubbling up in Jesse's memory. "I don't make plans for the both of us like he can't have his own dreams. I listen to his dreams. You didn't."

Liam flushed angrily. "I was young and naive and we didn't communicate enough, but I have accepted those flaws about myself and I am working to—"

"Great, you work on them, but not with *my* boyfriend."

"He's not a possession."

"I'm not the one who wanted a fucking trophy wife!"

A passing waitress from the kitchens glanced uneasily at them, and Jesse struggled with his blood pressure. Who the *hell* did this smug, sanctimonious *prick* think he was? What, was he going to swan in here and rescue Ezra from the fucking dragon?

"This isn't about me," Liam said coldly.

"I think it is," Jesse snapped. "You want him back, and you know the only way it's happening is if you're some bloody hero who gets to save Ezra from an—"

He couldn't say the word.

"From a bad relationship," he amended. "But it's not bad. It's not perfect but it's fucking good and I would *never* hurt him or bully him or any of it because I'm not a fucking scumbag!"

Liam gave him a look.

A look similar to Ezra's—raised eyebrows, pursed mouth, almost pitying expression.

The look that said, "Aren't you?"

Jesse saw red and curled his fists. Liam saw, and pulled another face. The face of a condescending, pretensions *dick*.

"Is that how you solve your problems?" he sneered.

"Shut the *fuck* up."

"What happens when you argue with him, Jesse? Do you just shout until he shuts up, or do you hit him? You certainly leave fingerprints. Do you shake him as well?"

"I've never hit him in my life," Jesse snarled.

"You do surprise me," Liam snarled back. "You must outweigh him by a considerable amount, and it's all muscle, I can see that. Never put it to use?"

"Not with violence," Jesse snapped.

"But you do *use* it, then?"

Of course he used it. Ezra liked being manhandled, he'd said so himself. *Right?* "Never in any way he wouldn't—"

"Of course, violence isn't the only part of an abusive relationship. He said you were jealous, which is typical of the insecure type that instigates these things. Possessive, too, I can see that for myself. Do you check his phone and Facebook account as well? Like to know where he is all the time? Check up on him?"

"No, I fucking—" Jesse began, then the dark part at the back of his brain, the bit that likened him to his father, reminded him *how* he'd found out what Liam was saying about him, that Liam was even in touch with Ezra. On Ezra's *phone*.

"So you do," Liam said flatly. "And when that's not enough? When he gets angry at you for doing it? Then what?"

"Listen, you fucking weasel, if you don't shut your fucking trap, I'll—" Jesse exploded.

"You'll *what*?" Liam sneered.

"Oi!"

They both jumped.

"That's not playing nice," Ezra said, sliding back into his chair just in time to stop Liam getting a smack in the mouth. "I could hear the two of you arguing from the toilets."

Jesse flexed his fingers. Ezra almost casually slid his hand across the wood and slipped it into the space. Jesse gripped back gratefully.

"What were you arguing about?" he asked.

"Nothing," Jesse said, flagging down the waiter for another beer. A sorely needed beer. Because if this underwear-modelling wanker carried on, even Ezra's serene influence might not be enough to stop Jesse rearranging those perfect teeth.

"Yes," Liam said slowly, and smiled at Ezra. "So how do you work around Jesse's…shifts at work?"

"Okay, no," Ezra shook his head. "No, I'm not doing this. You're not here to catch up, you're here to wind Jesse up and make digs at my relationship. Stop it, Liam. I like you, you're a great guy, but then you get like this and you turn into the massive prick that your firm hired. Jesse and I are leaving, and you're going to think about the simple fact that no matter what you say or do, I am *not* getting back together with you, and if you want to actually try and be friends, without taking shots at my boyfriend all the time, I'll listen. But for now, back off."

"Ezzy, I—"

"No," Ezra said sharply, then he was standing. "It would have been nice to see you, Liam, but you've changed," he said, tugging Jesse by the hand. Jesse was more than happy to go and slid his arm around Ezra's waist briefly as they approached the door.

He glanced over his shoulder. Liam was staring at that arm and looking unnervingly grim.

Chapter Nine

The walk home was silent.

Jesse felt—weird. Liam's voice just kept ringing in his head, and his fingertips burned as if he was touching Ezra's phone again, going through his texts, finding those messages again—and the card. He'd ripped up the card Liam had handed over with his phone number, slipped it out of Ezra's jeans and torn it up in that hotel in Norwich—

Except he wasn't. He wasn't *like* that. Was he?

Ezra was giving him funny looks as Jesse chased his own thoughts, and the moment they were home, he dropped his keys on the side table and said, "Jess? What's up?"

"D'you think I'm jealous?" Jesse blurted out.

Ezra raised his eyebrow. "Well, yes."

He flinched. It wasn't what he'd needed to hear. It wasn't what he *wanted* to hear, because where was the line? If he went digging through Ezra's phone and pockets, if he said he didn't like him seeing Liam, then what? And he *didn't* want him to see Liam anymore. He *wanted* to tell him not to, but—but—

"So why are you here?"

Ezra's eyebrows hiked higher. "I'm sorry?"

"Why are you here?" Jesse repeated, folding his arms and hunching his shoulders. "If I'm such a jealous, belligerent, possessive—"

"Hey, hey, I didn't say—"

"You don't need to," Jesse snapped.

Ezra was frowning and shaking his head. "Jess, I'm really not following you here."

"If I am such a jealous prick, why in the *hell* are you—"

"I never said you were a prick about it, I just said you were jealous, and don't raise your voice to me," Ezra said through gritted teeth.

Jesse ran his tongue around the inside of his teeth. He felt jittery, a hot anger burning low in his stomach at the condescending expression on Liam's face, at the way he'd *known*—

"Liam thinks I fucking hit you, you know that?"

"Yes, I do know that," Ezra said coolly. "He texted me a couple of days after we met him in Norwich, and he's been banging on about it ever since. It's driving me nuts. What's that got to do with—?"

"He asked me to my fucking *face* if I shook you to get you to shut up!"

Ezra's mouth tightened. "Jesse."

"And he starts banging on about how it's not just physical, it's—"

"Jesse!" Ezra interrupted loudly. "Why in the hell do you *care* what Liam thinks?!"

"*Because he's right!*" Jesse exploded.

Ezra stared at him. For a moment, the silence rang between them and for a moment, the truth yawned open, then Ezra shook his head and slammed the gap shut again.

"Come on," he said.

He dragged Jesse into the living room by the wrist, pushing him to sit on the sofa. Kitsa lurked for a moment, then darted away under the television with an affronted yowl. Ezra sat on the coffee table, elbows braced on his knees, and frowned up at Jesse from an unusually slouched posture.

"Jess," he prodded in a much gentler tone. "You know as well as I do you've never hit me."

The anger and the—the *hurt* were thrumming in Jesse's veins like a second pulse. This was it. The moment he'd feared, the moment he turned into that bastard who'd killed his mother, the moment that—

"*Jess,*" Ezra pushed again. "You've never hit me. You *know* that."

"I will," Jesse blurted out.

"What?"

"I *will,*" he said. "Liam's *right,* Ez, I *will,* this is just—just the beginning, just how it all starts, isn't it. I went through your pockets to get that card and destroy it, I went through your phone and found his messages, I—I don't want you seeing him, I *don't,* I was planning on telling you not to after tonight, and what kind of a fucking boyfriend does that, what kind of—"

"Someone," Ezra said, pitching his voice very, very deliberately, "who feels threatened."

Jesse clenched his jaw.

"You're afraid, Jess," Ezra said, squinting at him. "But I don't understand *why.* You know this is bullshit. Not liking your boyfriend going to dinner with their ex, you know, whatever. That's normal. I wouldn't like it either."

"You wouldn't ban me from going."

"Neither have you."

"I would have."

"But you haven't."

"That's not fucking important!"

"Yes, it is!" Ezra snapped. "Yes, it bloody well is, Jesse! What's the point in getting caught up in hypothetical—"

"I fucking would have!" Jesse shouted, the anger rising like heat. His chest felt too tight. His heart felt swollen and confined. "I don't like you fucking talking about him, I don't like *him,* I don't want you seeing him again or talking to him on Facebook, or—"

"What the *hell* is so threatening about him?!" Ezra yelled.

"He's fucking perfect!"

"Perfect? He's a fucking bellend!"

"He's better than me!" Jesse bellowed.

Ezra jerked back, startled. Kitsa shot out from under the television and disappeared into the kitchen, and Jesse felt something crack in his chest. His face felt hot.

"What do you mean, he's better than you?" Ezra asked slowly.

Jesse worked his jaw, his chest heaving.

"He is," he said simply.

"Jess. What—?"

"Are you fucking blind?" he snarled, some of the anger finding an outlet in his voice.

"Don't you fucking—" Ezra started, flaring up as Jesse had known he would, then the dam burst.

"He's a fucking lawyer with a fucking second flat, he earns more in a year than I do in five, he's got a university education and he's taken cooking classes from a fucking Italian chef and he can probably fucking talk to cats, too!" Jesse exploded, throwing himself up off the sofa and beginning to pace furiously. "He's a fucking perfect dick, he was probably the best you ever had in bed as well as out of it, so why the fresh fuck are you with me? What, the firefighter thing get to you? Getting your fill of some heroic, powerful piece of rough before you get bored and head back to—"

"*Shut it!*" Ezra roared. It was his teacher's voice, his fire alarm voice, his *this-time-I-mean-it* voice, and Jesse had heard it once and only once before—but this time, unlike last time, he kept going.

"I won't fucking shut it, Ez, it's the fucking *truth*!" he bellowed back, the room ringing in the wake of all the uproar. "He's fucking perfect and I'm a fucking mess and either you're fucking lying to me, or you're fucking stupid!"

"Oh, my God, you seriously have the most fucked-up self-esteem issues I have ever seen!" Ezra shouted.

"Yeah, that helps!"

"Shut your mouth and *listen* to me, for once in your bloody, blind little life!"

"I've tried fucking listening, but you're obviously—"

"You obviously fucking haven't if you haven't got the message by now, you idiot! I bloody love you, even if I really don't fucking like you right now!" Ezra hollered.

"Love's a funny thing to call an exciting fuck!" Jesse roared back, beside himself with hurt fury and uncontrollable, spiralling anger that pinked the walls of the room—and, as the last syllable died away, thumped in his ears over Ezra's suddenly quiet voice.

"Get out."

Jesse stopped pacing.

"Get the fuck out of my house," Ezra snarled.

Jesse unclenched his fists slowly. He had dug bloody crescents into his palms with his own nails.

What the hell had he just *said*?

"I said *get out*!" Ezra screamed, and the anger burst out again.

"What, you going to call Liam and tell him how he was fucking right the minute I'm out the door?" Jesse sneered.

"Get the *fuck* out before I call the fucking police and have you *dragged* out!" Ezra threatened, and when his hand strayed towards the heavy paperweight he kept on the coffee table to pin down his papers and protect them from stray paws, Jesse's brain finally kicked in above the boiling rage, and he stormed his way out. Flopsy yowled from the bottom of the stairs as he stamped past.

"Oh, *fuck off*!" he roared at her, and slammed the front door behind him hard enough that the doorbell bounced off the wall and shattered on the step.

* * * *

By the time he got home, Jesse felt lousy.

For the first half of the walk, he'd still been spitting mad. He'd cut through the park, and had punched two trees just for being trees and kicked what had possibly been a stray cat when it shot across his path in the dark. Because fuck Liam, and fuck Ezra and fuck Jesse himself, too. And he'd reached the other side of the town centre, and his wrist had started throbbing from being asked to duel with a tree so soon after healing from its fracture, and with every pulsating twinge, his anger slowly bled away.

And left him feeling sick.

He knew he had a temper. He always had. That was why he feared becoming his father so much, because he carried that same hotheaded tendency to just—to just explode when things went wrong. It was why he'd never tried to join the police. The first time anyone spat at him, he'd blow up and smack them one, and that would be it. He wasn't like Ezra. Ezra could take the verbal lashing all day at the school and just roll his eyes. Ezra could stare at someone while they called him all sorts of names, then ask if they were done and walk away. Even when it did get to him, he didn't show it.

Shit, Ezra.

In the haze of anger, Jesse had barely heard himself, but the more he calmed down, the more of it came back. And the sicker he felt. The swearing, the calling him stupid, the aggressive stamping up and down, the terrified cats and the *look* on Ezra's face—oh God, the *expression*—

Maybe he'd never hit him, but verbal abuse? Had he ever crossed the fucking line. How in the hell would Ezra ever give him a chance after that? How could *Jesse* give himself that chance?

"How could you?" he asked himself in a hoarse croak, throat sore from the shouting, as he turned into his own street, and the blocks of flats jutted up either side of him like looming, scowling faces. "You stupid fucking *arsehole.*"

It wasn't nearly enough. He was worse than an arsehole. He had just proven everything. He wasn't good enough. He'd never been good enough, and after that, after calling Ezra all those things and just—just—*being* like that, he'd be lucky if—

He'd be more than lucky if Ezra let him ever come back. Oh shit, they'd probably just—

"Oh God, it's over," Jesse whispered, and sank down onto the steps outside his building, head in his hands. There was a burning in his face again, but it wasn't anger. It wasn't even annoyance. "Fucking Jesus fucking Christ—"

It was over. It was over. He'd just destroyed the best relationship he'd ever had, the only real relationship he'd ever had, and destroyed it so thoroughly that there was no rebuilding it. There was no coming back from this. There was no way Ezra would take him back—because he wasn't stupid, he was absolutely brilliant and totally ruthless and nobody's fool, not even Liam's, never mind Jesse's, and—

"It's over," Jesse croaked, and the hot ache in his throat erupted. His voice cracked, and a tear launched itself towards the concrete.

His phone buzzed in his pocket, but he didn't dare to look.

* * * *

The alarm clock went off, but Jesse had barely slept. He felt thick-headed and fuzzy, sore and aching. He didn't want to go to work, but he was on the six-to-two shift, and Alan didn't look kindly on people shirking because their personal lives had just imploded through every fault of their own.

But one look at his phone said it was too early to try to call Ezra. Not because it was five in the morning, but because of the text messages. The first, sent not ten minutes after he'd left, simply told him to stay away. The second was a string of inventive swearwords. The third—the third made his hand shake.

Ezra <3: On second thoughts, don't come near the fucking house at all. I'm about this close to fucking boxing your stuff up and sending it second-class via Burkina Faso, so don't let me catch fucking sight of you until I've calmed down, you son of a bitch.

Jesse swallowed, and scrolled through a few more.

Ezra <3: You're a fucking idiot. Liam's a bellend, but you're a bloody fuckwit.

Ezra <3: How the fuck am I meant to help you when you don't fucking talk to me??? Tell me about your father, great, thanks, but don't think maybe you ought to mention THE HUGE EGO PROBLEM YOU HAVE!

Ezra <3: You've terrified my cats, frankly you've terrified me, and holy shit this is your idea of talking it out?!

Ezra <3: You broke my DOORBELL!

Jesse half-laughed, half-sobbed at the last one, pausing on it and fighting to get his raging emotions under control. He didn't want to go on. He had fifteen texts and three missed calls, and though he could almost hear Ezra slowly calming down, he *knew*—he just *knew*—that there was a break-up text in there somewhere. How could Ezra not dump him after that?

Ezra <3: This is seriously the dumbest fucking fight I've ever had.

Jesse forced himself out of bed, abandoned the phone and headed for the shower.

He hadn't meant to explode. He hadn't meant to do anything. He'd meant to just go home, see Ezra to the door, make his excuses because of this early shift, and come back to the flat. He'd never meant to start the row. He'd never meant to say any of the things he'd said, and it was all because of Liam.

Well, no.

It wasn't.

It was all because of Jesse.

Because he'd never stopped waiting for the other shoe to drop. Never stopped waiting for Ezra to get tired, or bored, or realise that dating an ignorant ex-shelf-stacker-in-a-cheap-supermarket wasn't going to be long term for a brilliant chemistry graduate. Never stopped waiting for Ezra to wake up and smell the coffee. And Liam had smelled that coffee, had fucking *drunk* the damn coffee, and—

Jesse leaned his head against the cold tiles.

He *hadn't meant it.*

He'd known, somewhere in his head, it would never last because he just wasn't good enough for Ezra—and he was never going to be, really, not for *Ezra*—but he had hoped, all the same. He'd hoped. Hoped maybe he could become good enough, if he learned enough about Ezra and learned how to keep him happy all the time. Hoped maybe Ezra would choose to overlook the crappy bits about Jesse, because Jesse wasn't totally useless, and he'd hoped maybe Ezra would decide he liked the good bits enough—

There was no enough. Now there never would be.

He dressed in a numb haze. He deleted the rest of Ezra's texts, too scared to read them, and headed out into the five-thirty world with no care for the clear sky, that washed-out pale shade of blue that said it was early morning even after the sun had risen. It was a warm morning, but Jesse didn't care. A pleasant breeze ghosted through his hair and plucked his collar, but he didn't notice. His thoughts were on Ezra, and his mind strayed away to the little house around the corner as he passed by the cul-de-sac on the main road, twisting despite himself to glance at the closed curtains and silent car, just visible near the end. Flopsy's dark shape was upright and majestic on the gatepost.

Jesse's heart lurched at the thought of never going back, or going back only to have a box of his spare things shoved into his arms and be dismissed with a cold look and an icy word.

He felt sick all over again.

"You look like shit," Alan said the moment Jesse walked in, at three minutes to six.

"Up all night," Jesse said.

"Doesn't look like it was for the right reasons." Pete whistled, and ducked away when Jesse glowered at him. "Sorry, mate, just sayin'."

"Well, don't," Jesse snapped, tossing his bag into his locker and hauling out his kit.

"You can sit and stew in the back, then," Alan grumbled. "They want us cruising. Reckon we're due."

"We are," Pete said flatly. "Not been a good blaze since Dawkins and Henley got themselves smashed up."

"I'd *like* to keep it that way," Alan said, but it was a stupid dream.

Still, Jesse liked cruising. It kept his mind on the banter around him. It was his first proper shift since the accident, and Mac hadn't come back yet, still waiting for his skin grafts to heal fully, so Jesse got the lot, both barrels in the face, and he wanted it. Badly. It would take his mind off the mess he'd just made of his personal life, of what he'd said and done in the living room of that little house around the corner, and maybe in the break, he could dare to hope.

His hope was shaken when Ezra texted at eight o'clock, though.

Ezra <3: Come over at four-thirty. We need to talk.

No kiss. No endearment. No request to stay safe. Cold, clinical, detached.

We need to talk.

"Dawkins, box the phone," Alan grunted.

Jesse stuffed it in the box where they kept all phones in the truck, and swallowed.

"I fucked up last night," he confessed.

"Don't wanna hear about you fucking last night, thanks," Ryan cut in immediately, and a general jeer went up.

"Fucked *up*, you tosser, open your ears," Jesse grumbled, smacking him around the back of the head.

"Same shit," Pete protested.

"It's not," Jesse said, and swallowed. "I think I'm single again."

"Oh shit." Pete grimaced. "Sorry, mate. You were keen on that one, weren't you?"

"If you only think, you know, maybe it's not," Ryan offered awkwardly.

"You know," Pete said. "If the missus is mad at me, I go all out—flowers, jewellery, cards, the lot. Offer to cook. Everything. That'll sort you out!"

"Yeah, 'cept for the bit where his missus is a bloke," Ryan interrupted, and Alan shook his head.

"I run a team of fuckin' gossipy harpies and *girls*," he said severely. "What God did I piss off, eh?"

"Well," Pete started, then the radio cut in, chattering like a monkey on speed.

A moment later, the sirens were on and Alan was turning a thirteen-tonne vehicle in the time and space usually required by a three-tonne vehicle, and the banter was abandoned as they scrambled to don their gear. Car crash. Possible fatalities. Police en route, ambulance only just launched from the A&E across town, four vehicles involved. A cruncher, as Pete would call it, when he wasn't being serious and shrugging on his jacket.

"Usual pairings!" Alan snapped as they barrelled along the road, ploughing through traffic barely parting fast enough for them, and Jesse forced his life aside, the adrenaline flooding his system and soothing his nerves.

That was, until he jumped down from the truck as it screeched to a halt behind the grisly scene of crumpled cars stinking of burnt rubber and spilled oil, and stopped dead, his brain stalling at the sight in front of him.

A car had crossed the central reservation and across a lane of traffic. It was a crushed, mangled heap, its bonnet buried in the front of a blue car, and both passenger-side doors were crushed from the impact of a Jeep into its side. A fourth car had rear-ended the Jeep, and a woman inside it was screaming. Jesse could see blood, the shimmer of heat off exposed engines, the coughing grumble of one car still attempting to turn its engine over, and the hiss of rapidly cooling petrol. Glass and metal were strewn across the road and passers-by gawped and took pictures but made no attempt to help. A police car had screamed up on the opposite side and two coppers were just jumping out, but Jesse couldn't move. It was his job, technically, to liaise with them, but he couldn't move.

Because in the middle of the smash sat the crumpled remains of a very familiar Peugeot 207.

Chapter Ten

His heart stopped—then it jumped, the adrenaline spiking in his system like cool water flooding his veins.

"Pete, with me!" he roared, and was moving without feeling it, sprinting the thirty metres across the skid-streaked road towards the crumpled mess that was the remnants of Ezra's car.

It had been hit dead-on, the bonnet less than two feet in length, the driver's door crumpled and battered in its now-crooked space. The windscreen was cracked and webbed, but intact. The white flash of the airbag obscured the steering wheel and was streaked red with blood.

"Casualty!" Jesse dimly heard Pete bellow over his shoulder, then Tony was shuffling into place to pop the stuck door.

"Shit, Dawkins, is that—?"

"Get me that fucking ambulance," Jesse replied harshly, and the door burst open with a bang.

The car barely shuddered with the violent motion, still snaked and bound to the other wreck, where Ryan and Alan were popping the other door, and very noticeably not calling for medical assistance. But Ezra was alive, Jesse realised in the same second, slumped over the airbag in a boneless heap, but for his face.

His face was twisted in agony, eyes screwed shut and sweat standing out on his forehead in huge cold beads.

"Sir—" Tony began, new to the crew and ignorant of most of their personal lives.

"Ez," Jesse interrupted, and Pete was dismissing Tony to check the second vehicle with Ryan and the boss. "Ez, sweetheart, it's me."

Ezra took a shuddering gasp, a hand shakily wavering up from the steering wheel. There was something off, horribly off, about the way he sat, and yet Jesse's brain refused to compute it. The driver's recess was crushed into a third of its usual space, Ezra's legs entirely hidden by—

Oh, Jesus. Oh, holy sweet Jesus.

The steering column had collapsed onto his thighs, and the crumple zone had not been enough to stop half the car's guts from being forced backwards like a sandcastle before the tide. His legs would be crushed.

"Okay." Jesse caught the hand and squeezed it tightly. "Ezra, listen to me. The ambulance is coming. Your engine is off, the car has stopped moving and the road's closed. There's no further risk from the car, you hear me?"

Ezra squeezed his hand until the bones creaked, and didn't say a word. His eyes were still closed. His breathing was coming in rapid, jerky pants.

"Pete," Jesse whispered.

"On it," Pete said, and slipped away to tell the boss and flag down the first arriving ambulance. In the car that had smashed into Ezra's, Jesse could see Ryan unfurling a foil blanket and draping it over the destroyed driver's side.

Dead.

"Ez," Jesse lowered his voice. "Look at me, baby."

Ezra was gasping. Jesse dared to rest a hand as gently as possible on his bloodied hair and rubbed a thick lock of the irrepressible blond between his thumb and finger.

"I'm right here, baby," he whispered, glad Pete had retreated to a safe distance. They couldn't proceed until the ambulance arrived anyway. He would need cutting out, but with his legs smashed under the weight of the engine block, he might bleed to death within minutes of being freed if they didn't have paramedics on standby. There was nothing to do until those distant sirens were on top of them. "Look at me, sweetheart. I'm right here."

Ezra's eyes opened to thin slits, but he wasn't really looking. He sucked in a deep breath, hissed, coughed and began to gasp again.

"J'ss…Jess, *pl'se,*" he whimpered, and Jesse squeezed his hand tightly.

"Just breathe, sweetheart," he urged, pitching his voice low and gentle, like they taught in first aid courses. He knew shock when he saw it. "Nice and slow. Once the ambulance gets here, we'll get you out of the car. And I *promise,* I will not go anywhere until you're on that stretcher and safe. All right?"

Ezra just squeezed his hand again. The sirens were close, and Jesse could hear the attending police shouting it in their direction. A shadow fell over his shoulder, and he glanced up into Alan's grizzled face.

"How we doing?" he grumbled.

Ezra didn't react to his voice in the slightest.

"Shock and unknown leg injuries," Jesse said shortly, trying to find the phraseology that wouldn't panic Ezra more than he already was. "Steering column," he settled for eventually, and Alan nodded.

"You stay here," he said gruffly, and Jesse was struck with the urge to kiss him. Which had never happened before and was a little disturbing.

"You hear that?" he murmured as Alan moved away. "Boss' orders, I have to stay here and hold your hand all the way through this. And I will get you through this, Ez, I promise."

"I can't do it, Jess, pl'se, God, get me out, pl'se—"

He was slurring, his voice rapid and panicky, and Jesse cupped his wrist to feel for a pulse. It hammered under his fingers, thready and erratic.

"Ssh," he soothed again, squeezing his hand again when Ezra whimpered. "I know you're in pain, baby, and I know this is like your worst fucking nightmare and I can't wake you up this time, but I'm here."

"M'sorry."

"What?"

"F'Liam," Ezra whispered, eyes screwed shut again. "I'm sorry, m'sorry, so sorry, Jess, didn't think how it'd look to you—"

"No, Ezra, ssh, stop it. I'm sorry too. And you're right, we need to talk, and I was going to come over tonight, I swear, sweetheart, but right now, we don't think about fighting, all right?" Jesse urged desperately. "I'll get you through this. I know I've been awful lately, but you do trust me, don't you?"

Ezra squeezed his hand tightly, eyes half-open and gazing at him as though peering through a heavy fog. "Mhmm," he murmured, then blinked rapidly.

"Stay with me, sweetheart," Jesse coaxed softly, cupping the exposed cheek.

"M'scared, Jess."

"I'm not going to let anything happen," Jesse promised.

"What have we here, then?"

A cheery paramedic with red hair in a jaunty ponytail and a round, motherly sort of face appeared at Jesse's shoulder, snapping her gloves on and taking in the scene with a professional flick of the eyes.

"Looks like you've got yourself in a bit of a mess, eh, lovey?" she asked cheerfully, elbowing Jesse aside. Tony had popped the door right off, though, and Jesse was able to crouch by the twisted front wheel and still hold Ezra's hand, stroking up to his elbow when Ezra whimpered at the movement.

"I'm right here," he repeated gently, and looked to the paramedic. "Name's Ezra Pryce, twenty-five. Steering column's collapsed on his legs, can't tell if the engine block is involved as well."

"Adjustable column?"

"Yep."

"And you two know each other or not?" she asked, wrapping a blood pressure cuff around the outstretched arm.

"B'yfriend," Ezra suddenly croaked, clutching Jesse's fingers tightly. "Pl'se—need'm, pl'se—"

His voice had dropped back into a near-impenetrable slur, and from his new vantage point, Jesse could see the edge of a vicious cut on Ezra's forehead, sticking his face to the airbag with half-dried blood.

"It's all right, lovey, long as he doesn't get in my way then he's quite all right to sit here with us," the paramedic said cheerfully. Her jaunty attitude was clearly part of the job. "My name's Ellie, and the hulk over here is Rob. I need to take your blood pressure and oxygen levels, get a nice little recording of what your heart's up to in there, and work out the best way to help you out, lovey, because you've obviously hurt your legs and I'll bet your back's smarting a fair bit, too."

It hit Jesse then, when she said that, why Ezra's position had looked so off. The driving seat had retained most of its original position, the steering column rammed into the seat where Ezra's knees would have been, and yet he was sagging forward as though the bend in his spine to let him rest his head on the airbag was in his lower back, not his upper back. An unnatural bend, even for a yoga enthusiast.

A cold fear prickled in Jesse's stomach.

"Can you tell me what happened, Ezra?" Ellie asked loudly, stroking back some of his bloodied hair and pulling down each eyelid one at a time to shine a penlight into his eyes. One pupil contracted sharply. The other didn't.

"Don't—I don't—"

His breathing began to pick up again, but Ellie was not for the flustering.

"That's all right, lovey, perfectly normal, don't worry," she soothed, and the death grip on Jesse's fingers eased fractionally. "What's your boyfriend's name?"

"J'ss."

"Speak up for me a bit, lovey."

"Jesse."

"What's his last name?"

"D'wkins."

She glanced aside at Jesse and he nodded.

"Do you know why he's here?"

"Fire service," Ezra mumbled, and tugged his hand in towards himself, refusing to let go of Jesse's palm. "Jess? M'legs hurt, Jess."

"I'm not surprised, lovey," Ellie said briskly. "Try and slow down your breathing for me, eh? I don't want you hyperventilating in there."

Instead of calming, it sped up again, and Ezra closed his eyes again, screwing his face up and turning slightly into the airbag and the padded steering wheel under his face.

"He's claustrophobic," Jesse said tightly, and leaned over her to touch Ezra's hair and whisper in his ear again. "Ez, it's all right, babe. I know it hurts, but I need you to keep calm for a little bit longer, all right? The sooner Ellie can tell me what's wrong with your legs, the sooner Pete and I can bust you out of here, okay?"

"While you're up there," Ellie interrupted briskly, handing a fabric neck brace to him, "fasten that around his neck. He'll have whiplash at the very least. Then I'll need you out so Rob and I can brace his back."

"No!"

It was the clearest thing Ezra had said yet, and Jesse's fingertips bloomed blue as the grip turned from hard to vice-like.

"Okay, Ez, ssh," Jesse urged. "Ellie," he said over his shoulder. "Yell for Tony, would you?"

She had a set of lungs on her. Moments later, Tony was hovering anxiously, shifting on his feet.

"Tony, pop the passenger door off for me," Jesse said. "And get started on getting that bloody Nissan off the front of this car." They would have to unprise the column, the driver's seat and the engine block to get Ezra out, and Jesse had a fair idea that it would be twice as hard and twice as painful for Ezra if they didn't get the two vehicles untangled first.

"Boss already has us on it," Tony said, and mouthed, "*Two dead,*" before disappearing around the other side of the car. The wrenching sound of the door being prised open was deafening from the inside of the Peugeot, and Ezra let out a choked sob, face creasing even further.

"Just one moment," Jesse soothed, then the passenger door was wrenched off, and Tony gave him a thumbs-up in the gap before returning to the work on the ruined Nissan. Untangling a multi-car wreck felt like it took seconds, usually. Now, it felt like hours.

The next twenty minutes were nothing short of painful. The paramedics worked feverishly to get Ezra braced and ready to be moved the moment it was possible. His rising awareness, and therefore rising panic, kept Jesse anchored on the torn mess of the passenger seat, squeezing his upper body into the small recess to hold Ezra's other hand and murmur reassurances under Ellie's questions of what hurt, what he could feel and whether he'd ever injured his back before. Ezra's panic ebbed and surged in waves. His strangled gasps turned into screams twice, and broken pleas a half-dozen times, begging Jesse not to go, begging Ellie to help him, even begging the God he didn't believe in to save him, and Jesse had never seen anything so horrific in his whole damn life.

Then the car started to groan.

Ezra seized up with a gasp. Jesse forced himself farther across the space and pushed a hand across that fine blond hair, clumped with rusty splotches of now-dried blood. It hurt to see Ezra so panicky, and Jesse had never appreciated before how terrifying this must be for the driver. He squeezed Ezra's hand tightly, mindless of the scratches along his arm, and exchanged anxious looks with Ellie as the front of the car screamed, the Nissan finally being pulled back enough to allow them to spread the Peugeot back out.

"Can't breathe, J'ss, I can't breathe," Ezra whispered frantically, and Jesse hushed him and kissed his knuckles.

"Yes, you can, baby," he soothed. "You know what that noise is? That's the guys getting ready to force this car back open. You following me, sweetheart? Just a few more minutes and they'll open this one up and Ellie and Rob will take you off to hospital."

The look Ezra gave him—wide-eyed, panicky and half-mad with sheer fear—was the worst expression that Jesse had ever seen.

"I don't want to die, Jess," he whispered, and Jesse's heart seized for a brief, dizzying moment.

Then he leaned close and said fiercely, "You are *not* going to die. I'm not going to let you, Ellie and Rob aren't going to let you and the hospital isn't going to let you. We will get you out of here, and you will recover from this, you being the bloody-minded bastard that you are, and I will be there *every. Step. Of the way*. You hear me?"

The panic shifted in his eyes. When Alan called for Jesse to get out of the car and help them, Ezra squeezed his hand one last time.

"I love you," he croaked, sounding terribly pathetic in the mangled confines of his ruined car, and Jesse swallowed against the lump in his throat.

"Tell me again when I come back," he said, and let go.

Untangling a car hit by a lorry was intensive work but untangling two cars that were fairly light in the first place was relatively easy. Once they began, it was over in a matter of minutes, the crumpled recess groaning as it was split open again, and Tony reaching in to lift the ruined steering column free of Ezra's legs. Jesse had pushed him to do it, not trusting himself not to shake or throw up when the footwell came into view. The moment Ezra's legs were out, the column was dropped back, and Jesse forced himself to hang back with his colleagues as Ezra was lifted clear by the two paramedics, a couple of burly policemen and a nurse who had been walking to work and had stopped to assist them.

Alan clapped a hand on his shoulder. "I can't let you go right now."

"I know," Jesse said shortly. Partner or no partner, he had a job to do here.

"Vehicle removal are en route," Alan said shortly. "Another half-hour and we'll be clear. Then I'll run us back to the station so you can get out of your kit and go."

"I—sir?"

"You heard me," Alan said flatly. "You're no good to me if your head's elsewhere. We finish up here, then you go. I'll put you in for compassionate leave for the rest of the week."

Jesse looked towards the ambulance as the doors slammed. Rob lifted an arm in a wave, then it was sliding away down the hot tarmac, sirens bouncing off the surrounding buildings.

Jesse's heart hurt as though it was trying to follow.

"Thank you, sir," he choked, and Alan tactfully pretended not to notice him dashing away a tear.

* * * *

It was an hour and a half before Jesse managed to get to the hospital, and by the time he did, there was only a nurse with an apologetic face and a compensatory cup of tea waiting for him. Ezra had been taken straight into surgery and wasn't bound to come out again for several hours.

"Can you tell me anything?" he begged her, unashamed of it. "Anything about how he was, about—about what they were saying?"

About the outcome.

"I'm sorry, sir."

And she did look genuinely sorry.

"I can't tell you anything. I don't *know* anything, but—"

She squeezed his elbow and pressed him to sit in a hideously orange plastic chair.

"I can say your partner's in the best of hands. Dr Anwar is on duty today, and she is a phenomenal surgeon."

Surgeon. Surgery. Somehow it felt jarring, because of *course* Ezra was having surgery, everything from his hips down would be an absolute mess, but—but Ezra was having *surgery.* It was frightening, and Jesse clutched the cup of tea desperately, the adrenaline that got him through the day ebbing and bleeding away. It wasn't even eleven. Ezra had texted him at eight. Not three hours ago, he had been trying to think of what to say, how to get past the ugly shouting match and what he'd blurted out, how to persuade Ezra not to leave him.

Now maybe Ezra would leave him anyway.

He had never waited this side of the door. He'd been brought in himself at least twice a year since he'd started working with the fire service, for everything from last month's fractured wrist to excessive smoke inhalation and first-degree burns. Ezra had been on this side of the door twice for Jesse. Maybe he'd sat right here, wringing his hands and tapping his right foot in that antsy way he had. Both times had been in the middle of the night, though. Both times, Ezra had been tired and grumpy and beautiful in that ruffled way.

Jesse dropped his head into his hands and stared blindly at the tiles.

He knew nothing about medicine. He knew nothing about car accidents apart from how to cut people out of them. He never knew whether the victims lived or died unless it made the papers or they were already dead when they arrived to help. He had no idea what—what was going to happen. What *was* happening, somewhere in this hospital.

There were things to do. When Jesse came to hospital, things were simple. Make sure someone called Ezra and wait for him to show up. But Ezra had family. Ezra had a mother and a sister—though maybe he could skip the sister—and he was supposed to go to work in the morning, and—

And none of it would stick. Jesse felt shaky and sick, and he wanted someone to tell him what to do. There was always someone to tell him what to do. Ezra. Alan. A doctor. There was always something to be done, and someone to tell him to do it, and—

Now there wasn't.

He abandoned the cup of tea and staggered towards the lifts. The nurse made no attempt to stop him, though she watched him go. He followed the signs without any real idea of why, and the little unassuming door opened into a near-empty room, lit in gentle red and soothing blue, cushioned seats in a row facing a great window that overlooked a memorial garden. A middle-aged man with a green jumper looked up from lighting candles on a tray, the little flames glimmering suspiciously in the evening light, and he looked both welcoming and solemn.

The hospital chaplaincy.

"Would you like to speak or be alone?" the man asked.

"I don't know," Jesse said honestly, and sank into the nearest seat. The door cut out the hospital behind him. There was a carpet in this room, and the smell of antiseptic was fainter. He had always pictured chaplaincies to be more like churches—pictures of Jesus and crucifixes like Mrs Pryce's—but the absence of them was calming. He supposed it wasn't just Christians who lost people in hospitals.

The man offered him the burning stick.

"Would you like to light one?" he offered.

"He's not—" Jesse started, and shook his head. "He's in surgery," he said, and the man nodded as if he understood.

"A family member?"

"My partner."

There was no real reaction. The man blew out the burning stick and laid it down in the tray with the candles. After a moment, he came to sit in the chair opposite, folding his hands between his knees.

"I take it that whatever has happened has come as some surprise?"

"Car accident," Jesse said hoarsely. "I don't know how he is."

"No news is good news, as they say," the man said.

Jesse tried for a smile and failed.

"We argued," he said. "We were supposed to meet up after work and talk about it, and—I've been an idiot."

The man said nothing.

"I've been so caught up in thinking I'm not enough for him, that I'm not good enough—and maybe I'm not—but I've been forgetting what I can do, what I am doing for him, and now—now I—"

"What is his name?"

"Ezra."

The man raised his eyebrows. "Rather Biblical."

Jesse laughed wetly, and a few tears escaped. A moment later, a handkerchief was being pressed into his hand, the tiny letters 'RR' stitched into the corner.

"His family are Catholic," he said, and gestured vaguely at the room. "I figured, you know, I could…pray or something. It couldn't hurt."

"Unfortunately, I think God ceased to work like that around the time He had a son," the man said. "Fatherhood changes people, and I suspect the Almighty wasn't any different."

Jesse laughed again, the humour soothing a little of the raw, impotent pain in his chest, and he looked up at the window. It was arched, framed in dark wood like a chapel window, but with no stained glass or forgotten saints.

"I was with him," he blurted out. "I held his hand while they—while they cut him out of the car, and I—I couldn't stop the pain, but I could be there. Is that enough? If he—if—"

"Being there is the greatest thing any one person can do for another," the man said softly, and sat back a little. "I was a porter here, before I retired. I can't tell you the number of times I left my trolley and sat by someone's bed to hold their hand. I almost never spoke to them. I never knew them. I very much doubt any of them had ever noticed me before. But I would sit and hold their hand, because if there is one thing we can do for each other, it is be there."

Jesse choked and his vision blurred. He dropped his head, and the burn of his eyes carried down his face in wet streaks. Quite suddenly, the man was grasping his hand.

"I have been thanked by people who barely have the strength left to breathe, who have been unconscious for days," he said gently, his voice a deep and soothing timbre in the quiet room. "I believe the dead have not left us until they are quite, quite dead. If you have been there, then it will have been enough. If you could offer even a little comfort to him, then he will grasp that and understand it, no matter what comes next."

Jesse squeezed the rough hand in his and pressed the handkerchief blindly and ineffectually to his face.

"You love him?"

"He's everything," Jesse croaked.

"Then it will have been more than enough," he said. "If we can all go out of this world saying that someone loved us, and someone was there for us, then we can all go content and in peace. It sounds as if your Ezra has had both."

Jesse shook his head. "I've been an idiot."

"You're human," the man said, and when Jesse looked up, he was smiling softly. "I was married for eighteen years before my wife passed away. Every single one of those we fought, we argued, we bickered and we reconciled. I nearly walked out once. She threatened to divorce me twice. And I would change nothing. I loved her, with all that I knew how, and I was there for her in every way that I could be. When the end comes, it comes. I very much doubt my last words to Janice were of love. I probably asked her to get milk at the supermarket on her way home. By the time I learned of what happened, she was gone. But she died a woman loved, and I had been there every time that I could. So, yes, it hurt. But she rests in peace, and I wouldn't change that."

It was some time before Jesse could find his voice again, the possibility of life without Ezra yawning like a chasm in front of him, like an abyss from which there was no exit, and when he could breathe again, the man was still there, hands folded in front of him again, serene.

"What happened?" he asked eventually.

"To Janice?" the man hummed. "An aneurysm. Swift and quite thorough."

Jesse took a deep breath through his nose and twisted the handkerchief in his hands. "I—I wanted to pray," he said, "but I don't know how. I don't even know if I'm praying to anyone."

"Voicing our fears makes them less frightening," the man said. "Some call that talking to God."

He rose and waved to Jesse to keep the handkerchief.

"Talk," he said. "I'll keep myself busy for a while. And keep hope, if not faith, because hope can be much more powerful, I find."

He shut the door quietly behind him. The sun was finally beginning to sink towards the horizon in the arched window, and Jesse folded his hands around the wet handkerchief and stared out into the dusk.

"Please," he said.

That was all.

Chapter Eleven

"Mr Dawkins?"

Jesse started. It had been hours since he'd arrived at the hospital, hours since he'd half-prayed, half-begged a window in the chaplaincy and hours since anyone had seemed to remember that he existed. The teacup nurse had long since gone home and the early-morning children had long since given way to the middle-of-the-day accidents and mishaps.

He half-rose to meet the doctor who came marching towards him. She was a tiny woman, barely five feet in height, with dark hair piled up under a plastic cap and large, keen brown eyes.

"Dr Marwa Anwar," she introduced herself, shaking his hand firmly. "I've been told that Mr Pryce is your partner?"

"Yes. Is he—?"

"Come with me." She turned on her heel and marched away again, and Jesse sluggishly followed. Doctors were unreadable. Nurses had things written all over their faces, but doctors were inscrutable, and he wanted to just shake her and wring the answers out of her.

"How is he?" he tried hoarsely as she led him into a lift, and her face relaxed minutely.

"He will live, Mr Dawkins," she said gently, and Jesse sagged against the side of the lift. Her tiny hands were immediately on his sides, bracing him with a surprisingly strong grip.

"He's—he's going to—"

"He will live," she repeated firmly. "I cannot discuss much of his condition at this point, but, barring complications, he won't die."

"And how likely are complications?"

"They're not," Dr Anwar said shortly as the lift coughed them out. "I am a *very* good surgeon, Mr Dawkins."

She led him down a short corridor and paused before a glass window.

"I can't let you in until he has been fully assessed by the consultancy team, but I thought you would appreciate at least a look," she said, though Jesse already wasn't hearing her.

In the short ward were four beds, all facing the window, and a nurse was fitting a drip into the back of Ezra's hand. He had obviously only just been settled, by the activity, but he was unconscious, face ashen against the sheets, hair still matted and dark with his own blood. The ugly gash on his forehead had been stitched, and the blankets were badly misshapen, one shoulder visibly strapped up—but he was alive. A jumping line across a dark monitor tracked his heartbeat. He was safe and alive, and Jesse sagged against the glass, pressing one hand to it as though he could get through.

"When—when can I see him?" he breathed.

"Come back tomorrow in visiting hours, and the consultant will have more answers," she said. "He will need full assessment then, but I imagine, unless he deteriorates during the night, you should be permitted to sit with him for a few minutes."

"I need—"

"Mr Dawkins, you need to go home," Dr Anwar said firmly. "Mr Pryce is in safe hands, I can assure you. His injuries were not in themselves life-threatening. He may have lost a limb—may still, if infection sets in—but he would not have died. He will still be here in the morning, and I would be greatly surprised if he woke any time before tomorrow, even if we were to reduce his drug dosages."

Jesse tore his gaze away from Ezra's still, slack face. Dr Anwar stared right back at him, face open and patient.

"You're sure?" he croaked.

"I am certain, Mr Dawkins. You need to go home and rest."

Slowly, he nodded. Ezra was safe. He wasn't going to lose him. Maybe things were going to be difficult for a while, but he wouldn't be—

"Go," Dr Anwar insisted gently, and steered him away from the window.

Jesse let her.

* * * *

Jesse didn't go home.

He called for a taxi from the A&E entrance, and in the ten minutes it took for the battered private car to creep into the drop-off point, he changed his mind and asked the driver to go to the fire station instead.

The station was quiet, but Jesse turned his back on it and walked to Ezra's house, the crisp air clearing the fog and the shock from his mind and body. Ezra would be all right in the end. He wasn't going to die. Every step up from that was only an improvement, and whatever the long-term impact of this, Jesse was going to be there. He was always going to be there, because he had been such an *idiot* lately, and absolutely none of it was important.

The only important thing was Ezra, and whatever it took, Ezra would get better.

A couple of months previously, Ezra had given Jesse a key for the back door in case he wanted to come over but Ezra hadn't got back from the school yet. Jesse almost never used it, mainly because it involved wrestling with the sticky latch on the side gate, but tonight he popped it open and slid around into the back garden. Kitsa joined him at the back door, slipping out of the bushes to wind around his feet and meow plaintively, obviously upset at his departure the night before.

It was—peaceful. Distracting and peaceful, to have to feed the cats before anything else, to line up his boots on the kitchen mat, and see the post waiting in the hall. To see Flopsy asleep on the sofa. To see the plate and cup in the sink from breakfast, and the teaspoon that said Ezra had been having a yoghurt bender again.

And it felt wrong, too. Jesse sat heavily on the sofa and stared at the empty living room. It felt *wrong*. It wasn't that he was here without Ezra—he'd stayed behind some mornings, lounging about and playing with Kitsa, when he'd stayed the night and Ezra had

had to go off to work first thing in the morning. But it wasn't the same as this. This time, Ezra wasn't going to come back at four with an armful of books and muttering about dumb kids, dumber colleagues and the latest change to the curriculum. This time, Jesse would go to bed alone *and* wake up alone. This time, Jesse wasn't feeding the cats because they were pestering him—he was feeding them because Ezra wouldn't be, for *weeks*.

He hadn't expected to ever be allowed back in this house again. Now he was here under nearly the worst circumstances possible, and it *hurt*.

Jesus. No matter what happened, it would be weeks before he got out of hospital. Months, even. Jesse might be uneducated, but he wasn't a complete moron. Ezra *had* to have broken both legs, which meant a wheelchair, which meant there was no way he'd be able to come home. This little house just wasn't built for wheelchairs. Which meant, even if they were easy breaks, simple breaks, it would take six weeks or more, and the way the car had been—

Jesse swallowed hard against the lump in his throat.

He busied himself. Jesse knew himself—stay busy, stay okay. So he puttered about the little house, half-pretending Ezra would be home soon, putting water in the flower vases, weeding out the junk mail from the pile on the mat and putting a load of laundry through the washing machine. Flopsy ignored him. Kitsa followed him around, purring and rubbing her head against his hands whenever he stooped to pet her. Ezra did his chores in the evening, not before work, so there was plenty to do. Jesse even made the bed, changing the sheets out of the need to do something and not wallow, washed the scant dishes and wiped down all the kitchen surfaces, just to not *think* for a few minutes.

Eventually, he collected himself back together. Eventually, he sat down with Ezra's phone book and the cordless handset, Kitsa immediately jumping into his lap. He had to dial twice, he was so on edge, and when the phone finally connected, it rang and rang for what seemed like hours.

Until it didn't anymore.

"Ceri Pryce speaking."

Jesse took a deep breath through his nose. "Mrs Pryce, it's Jesse Dawkins," he said. "Ezra's partner."

There was a pause. Then, "What happened?"

Jesse almost smiled. Ezra was sharp. He supposed it fitted that his parents were equally suspicious.

"There was—" he struggled. "He was in a car accident earlier today."

She drew in her breath sharply.

"He's in the hospital, but he's all right," Jesse added hastily. "Well, you know, he's not *all right*, but—he will be. He's not—it's not fatal."

"I see."

"He had a long time in surgery, though, so—I figured you ought to know," Jesse finished lamely.

"I—yes. Yes, thank you," she said, and Jesse grimaced at the hoarse tone to her voice. "What—no, never mind, I'll—I'll come down as soon as I can. He is—you're sure—"

"The surgeon told me herself he'd live," Jesse said. "And I was—I was there, Mrs Pryce. My team were called to the accident."

She let out a shuddering breath. "He was—"

"He talked to me, he was, you know, coherent and everything. And the doctor said he'd be fine."

"Right. Right, yes, I—I'll—I'll come down as soon as I can. I'll need—I'll need to find someone to look after Mum, and—I'll try and get there by tomorrow. Thank you," she added suddenly. "For calling. So soon."

It was a brief, awkward and horrible conversation. Jesse had never had to make a call like that. He'd *had* one, when Mum had killed herself, but he'd never made one. She hadn't had any family, no real friends to speak of. The funeral had been attended by him, the vicar and a couple of neighbours who'd lived next door to Mum's old house. He'd never had to make that kind of a call, and especially not to his boyfriend's—ex-boyfriend's?—disapproving, Bible-thumping mother.

Kitsa meowed and headbutted his hand.

He stretched out on the sofa, petting the kitten and staring absently across the tiny living room. Ezra had said he was his boyfriend. That was what he'd told Ellie. And the way he'd clung to Jesse's hand, he couldn't—he couldn't hate him, right? For last night? Maybe the talk had been to talk it out and clear the air, not break up with him. Maybe that had been Ezra's intention all along.

Whatever his intentions, Jesse wasn't going anywhere now. He felt oddly resettled, like the black temper had been shaken out of him. Ezra had needed him. He'd reached for him and *needed* him, really needed him in that car, and there was nobody else who could have done what Jesse did. Nobody else could have helped Ezra through that. He'd needed *Jesse*, and no one else.

It hurt to realise what Ezra had been telling him all along—hurt to realise it like *this*.

So Jesse sat and stroked the cat and stared across the room, at a picture Ezra had framed on his bookshelf. A picture of them, crushed in close in a shot taken at

Christmas by one of Jesse's gym buddies on a night out. Ezra had come out to join them after his yoga class, his fluffy hair half-hidden by a black beanie, his smile wide and beautiful. They both looked beautiful, Jesse thought, because they looked happy. Ridiculously happy, with cheesy grins like everything was perfect. And it *was* perfect, no matter what, never mind about Ezra's stupid ex-boyfriend and his stupid sister and his current boyfriend's stupid self-esteem issues.

Ezra smiled like that because of him, and Jesse couldn't believe he'd missed it all this time.

* * * *

The hospital was quiet at eleven o'clock the next morning.

Jesse had woken up still stretched out on Ezra's sofa, Kitsa sleeping curled up on his stomach and Flopsy a warm, heavy weight across his ankles. He had slept deep and hard for most of the day, exhausted by the crash and the waiting game in the hospital, and he had only woken when the sun had poked him rudely in the eyes the following morning. He had taken half an hour to shower and change into the spare clothes he kept in Ezra's bedroom before heading right back out, and the antiseptic smell of the hospital was somehow oddly soothing. Ezra was here. Ezra was *safe* here, even if he was still—still hurt.

It took two nurses, three phone calls from said nurses and retracing his steps twice to find Ezra. He had been moved in the night and undergone a second surgery at eight o'clock that morning, but the nurse refused to tell him why, obviously clocking that Jesse wasn't technically family. But eventually he found his way to a ward for post-surgical care and managed to persuade another nurse with bobbed blonde hair to let him in to sit by the bed for a little while.

"I swear the minute you tell me to go, I'm out," he pleaded, and she eventually relented with strict orders not to touch *anything* and to call her if Ezra so much as twitched.

Then he was there, and the raw ache in Jesse's throat started up all over again.

He looked very much the same. Very much small and fragile in the hospital bed, hair scraped back instead of floating around in its usual mess. An oxygen tube ran under his nose, and his neck was still in a brace. His shoulder was strapped up, in a high sling that Jesse's experienced eye recognised from hundreds of practice drills gone wrong—a dislocation. At this closer vantage, the awkward shape of the blankets was due to the open casts on both legs, and two tubes disappeared under those blankets towards his ribs.

But he breathed. He breathed, slow and gentle, and a heart monitor tapped out a calm, steady rhythm by the bed. Slowly, Jesse slid his fingers under Ezra's, too nervous to properly hold his hand, and leaned close to whisper in his ear.

"I'm here," he breathed, and sat back to watch his face.

His very scratched and bruised face. Five blue stitches stretched garishly across his forehead, and his eyes were both spectacularly black, the left one probably swollen shut. He was a complete mess. But he was still breathing.

"I love you," Jesse whispered, and bit his lip. "And I'm sorry. I've been fucking stupid, and I'm sorry and

I'll tell you again when you wake up. Promise. Okay, baby?"

Ezra, of course, didn't respond, but Jesse was okay with that.

"If you wake up and smile at me, just for a second, I promise to—" Jesse thought about it. "To never complain about your cats again. Or to promise you shoulder massages whenever you want them, because take it from me, baby, you're going to get cramps and soreness like nothing else while that shoulder heals."

"Mr Dawkins?"

He jumped. The doctor that had materialised at the foot of the bed simply raised an eyebrow.

"You are the patient's partner?" he asked coolly.

"Yeah," Jesse said, slipping his hand back out from under Ezra's. "How is he? What—what did you have to do?"

The doctor eyed his clipboard. "Are you in a civil partnership, married or cohabiting?" he asked.

"I—what's that got to do with anything?"

"Mr Dawkins, I cannot simply—"

"Ezra!"

And Mrs Pryce was hurrying across the ward, her hair askew, clothes rumpled, skirting around the surprised doctor without seeming to notice either of them. She bent over the bed to stroke her son's face gingerly, worry twisted into her haggard face, before whirling on the doctor and shrieking, "What *happened*?!"

"May I ask who—"

"I'm his *mother*!" Mrs Pryce snapped. "I received a phone call yesterday afternoon from Jesse here saying my son was in the hospital! Don't just *stand* there, tell me what's going on!"

The doctor drew the curtain around.

"I need your permission for Mr Dawkins to stay," he said flatly. "As the patient's family, you—"

Jesse's heart lurched. Mrs Pryce paused, biting her lip.

"No," she said finally. "No, of course he can stay. Jesse will be—will be looking after Ezra, you see. I live in Norwich."

"Very well," the doctor said. "I suggest you both take a seat."

Mrs Pryce sank into the visitor's chair. Jesse leaned against the bedrail, trailing a hand down to stroke lightly over Ezra's elbow.

"The patient was brought in with severe trauma after what we were told was a head-on car collision. His right leg is fractured in five places, two compound, and three toes were crushed. That leg is the major concern at the moment. His left leg suffered a compound fracture to the shin, but that was relatively simple to set. Both ankles are broken. Both legs have been set and are in open casts until the skin heals. He's suffered multiple contusions, none particularly serious, and required stitches in his forehead. His right hip and right shoulder were both dislocated and were restored by Dr Anwar prior to the surgery. Four ribs suffered hairline fractures, and three more suffered bruising on the bone. There was moderate internal bleeding from his liver which Dr Anwar corrected, and we will be monitoring closely over the next few days. He also suffered whiplash," he added, almost unnecessarily.

Jesse squeezed the elbow under his fingers and let out a long breath.

"Oh, Jesus," he muttered.

Mrs Pryce, on the other hand, looked quite composed again. "And the prognosis?"

"For the moment, we need to ensure the right leg does not develop any infection or complications. If it does, we may need to consider amputation. Until the bones heal, we cannot be certain of the ongoing mobility of that leg in any case. The left leg should heal without much problem, as should the ankles. The crushed toes will have to be monitored for gangrene. The whiplash, the shoulder, the ribs and the hip will heal easily enough, although the patient is likely to be in physiotherapy for several months. The liver should recover—he was previously in a good state of health and Dr Anwar reported that, trauma aside, the liver had been functioning well."

"And if it doesn't?" Mrs Pryce pushed.

"I imagine it will," the doctor countered. "The liver is a resilient organ. In a healthy young man, it should recover."

"When will he wake up?" Jesse blurted out.

The doctor raised an eyebrow. "Entirely? Not for several days, Mr Dawkins. He will be in and out of it a little, but pain management at this stage more or less involves keeping the patient under."

Jesse glanced down at Ezra's still face and bit his lip. Mrs Pryce was immediately battering the doctor with fresh questions. She might have been quiet and tired in Norwich, but Jesse finally saw the evidence of her caring and he left her to it. The doctor was irrelevant.

He slid his fingers back under Ezra's and pretended that Ezra squeezed back. On the one hand, it was good that he was sleeping. Jesse didn't want him to be in pain, and he'd recover faster if he slept. But on the other hand, Jesse wanted to talk to him, for Ezra to hear how sorry he was about the whole bloody argument and how'd he take it all back in a heartbeat if he could and how he realised now just how fucking stupid he'd been.

The doctor and Mrs Pryce slipped out, but she returned alone momentarily with a chair, settling on the other side of the bed and taking Ezra's other hand. She looked tearful but composed again. Jesse bitterly wondered where Grace was. The charitable part of him could pretend she was looking after her doddery grandmother. The less charitable part insisted she wouldn't have come if he'd called saying Ezra had an hour to live.

It was, surprisingly, Mrs Pryce who broke the quiet, when she murmured, "I feel the strangest sense of déjà vu."

Jesse winced. "It must be—hard for you," he offered hesitantly, and a wan smile crossed her face. Sitting with all her focus on her son, she didn't look like the anxious, dismissive woman from the house outside Norwich. She looked like a mother.

"Ezra and Grace were upset, but physically quite fine," she said softly. "They had both collected worse injuries as young children. All three of mine had a thing for trees, you see," she added, and a little laugh escaped, quiet and wary, into the room.

"They fell out a lot?"

"All the time," she said. "Ezra especially. He hit puberty very early, you see, and suffered terrible growth spurts. He'd grown to his full height by the time he was fifteen. Very awkward as a boy."

Jesse struggled to imagine a tall but baby-faced Ezra.

"But he and Josh could have been twins," she murmured, and smoothed back Ezra's hair in an obsessive little motion. "They looked so alike it was uncanny. He looks—"

Jesse bit his lip.

"I sat with Josh," she murmured. "My husband was dead, my youngest were traumatised, and I sat and held my son's hand as he passed away. He never knew I was there."

"Mrs Pryce, Ezra's not—"

"Oh, I know he isn't," Mrs Pryce said. "But it still feels…"

She trailed off. Jesse squeezed Ezra's hand and didn't know what to say.

"I know I was a bad mother afterwards," she said suddenly, and Jesse winced.

"You weren't—"

"I was. I let Grace take out all her anger on Ezra, and I let Ezra hide himself away until he was a stranger to us, and I let my own grief consume me. My children were hurting too, but I couldn't comfort them, and suddenly they're adults and don't tell me a thing. You know, I didn't know that Ezra had a new—a new—"

"Partner," Jesse supplied gently.

"Partner," she echoed, and smoothed that wild blond hair back again. "I didn't know about you until he called and said you both would be visiting. He doesn't tell me things."

"Because he gets upset you disapprove," Jesse blurted out, and Mrs Pryce gave him a startled look. "I'm sorry, but you can't expect him to tell you all about his relationships if you give him the whole 'gay men are an abomination' thing."

"Please don't compare me to my daughter," she said tightly.

"You're not that different," Jesse pushed.

"I do not believe my son is going to hell!" she snapped.

"Do you think I am?"

She paused, and Jesse shook his head.

"You might not be as loud as Grace, but you're the same," he said. "You think there's something wrong with him and he's defying God, and whatever, fine, you might be right. But he's happy. Doesn't that count for something? We're both consenting adults, we're not out to convert anyone or ruin other people's lives. It's nothing to do with anybody else. It's just me and him, that's it. And if there is a god, then he and Ezra can hash it all out when Ezra actually dies, but for now, can't you just let him live his life?"

It was the most he'd ever said to her—or anyone, really—regarding his sexuality. Jesse didn't see much religious homophobia. He saw the casual, two-poufs-walk-into-a-bar style homophobia that was less abrasive, less grating. All his mates at work teased him about having a missus that looked awful in a skirt, and he didn't mind. It was just a laugh. And Jesse was big enough and nasty-looking enough that he'd never really had to put up with the darker, uglier side of it from pubs and clubs the world over.

Ezra's experience of it, on the other hand—that was worse. That wasn't funny at all.

"I'm not asking you to go on gay pride marches and shit," Jesse said, staring at Ezra's thin, white face as though in a trance. "I'm just saying, you can't complain he shuts you out if every time he tries to talk to you, you tell him he's doing something wrong."

"It *is* wrong," she said quietly, but she lacked the fervour that Grace had when she said it.

"Mrs Pryce, with all due respect, I come from an abusive household. My parents were straight, but my dad cheated on my mum, he hit her, he called her all sorts of awful things, he drank, he smoked, he did drugs, he fathered at least one bastard and eventually he ran off with someone else. Then my mother killed herself," Jesse said flatly, and ignored her startled flinch and gasp. "By comparison, I don't see how any god with any brain could call me and Ezra wrong, and my parents right."

"I—" Mrs Pryce croaked, then she subsided and looked back to her son, her hand trembling a little as she stroked back his hair.

They didn't speak again for the rest of the afternoon.

* * * *

Jesse had been in the fire service long enough, and done enough on-call shifts, to react instantly to something changing, and so Ezra's fingers had barely begun to contract around his before Jesse was sitting up, scrubbing the sleep from his eyes with one hand and leaning towards the bed.

"Ezra?" he murmured.

It was just after six. Ezra's mother had left at five to go back to her hotel and Jesse had dozed in the chair since. He had refused to go before visiting hours ended at eight, because the doctor had said Ezra would be in and out of it and Jesse didn't want him to wake up alone and confused and hurt. Not after that.

And now his tired patience was being rewarded, as dark eyes hazy with drugs and exhaustion finally cracked open.

"Hey," he murmured, leaning his elbow on the edge of the mattress and stroking his other hand lightly against Ezra's cheek. "You with me, sweetheart?"

Ezra closed his eyes again with a heavy sigh but turned his face into Jesse's fingers regardless. "J'ss…" he breathed.

Jesse kissed his forehead and smiled widely. His mouth felt uncontrollable in how wide it stretched, but fuck decorum. Fuck it if he looked like an idiot.

"How are you feeling?" he whispered.

But Ezra was only drifting. He squeezed Jesse's hand weakly and was gone again, the painkillers pulling him back under from one heartbeat to the next. Jesse pressed the button for the nurse and sat stroking his hand until the curtain was pulled back and the cup-of-tea sister from the first day clicked her way into the cubicle.

"He woke up a minute ago," Jesse said, keeping his voice low as if he'd disturb Ezra again.

"Did he say anything?" she asked, plucking the chart off the end of the bed and scribbling a note.

"He said my name, but he went under again pretty fast."

"Perfectly normal," she said briskly. "He'll sleep like the dead. Best thing for him. Did he seem to be in pain?"

"I don't think so," Jesse said, rubbing a thumb rhythmically across the back of Ezra's hand. "He really should be out of it that fast?"

"You've obviously never broken your thigh, dear," she said, patting his arm as she bustled around him to check the drip. "This can come down for the night and we'll see if he can't be woken enough to take fluids by mouth in the morning," she murmured half to herself.

"Yes," she said to Jesse again, "it's extraordinarily painful to break the thigh. He'll be feeling it when they take down the morphine, that's for sure."

Jesse nodded, already beginning to tune her out. Ezra's face was relaxed, and his fingers limp in Jesse's—but it was just sleep now, not unconsciousness. Nothing worse than sleep. When the nurse slipped out again, Jesse bent over the bed to kiss Ezra's temple, feeling the slow, calm whisper of a pulse in the thin skin there, and breathed lightly into his hair for a moment.

"I'm here," he whispered, and Ezra's fingers twitched.

Chapter Twelve

For the next four days, Jesse fell into a routine.

He returned to early-morning shifts, rising at five and working through until two or three in the afternoon, at which point he showered and changed at Ezra's, fed the cats and headed to the hospital. Sometimes Mrs Pryce was there and they made awkward small talk or sat in silence. Sometimes she wasn't, and Jesse could sit and hold Ezra's hand and talk to him instead, even if Ezra couldn't hear him and certainly couldn't talk back.

Visiting was for family only until Ezra woke up properly, but Jesse had apparently passed muster as the partner. The side table was crowded with cards and plastic flowers sent from the school, the biggest from his tutor group, who dedicated it to 'Mister Ez!' in a slightly inappropriately cheerful fashion. But Jesse liked it all the same.

"That's how important you are, babe," he murmured after going through them on the second day, and Ezra's fingers fluttered lightly in his.

Ezra was in and out of it, much as the snotty doctor had predicted. His right leg swelled up like a constricted balloon on the second day, and had to be drained, but he slept through it, wholly unaware of the entire palaver. When the evening nurses finally unstrapped his shoulder on the fourth day at the consultant's approval, Ezra didn't so much as frown. If he woke up at all, he mostly blinked and went straight back to sleep. His fingers would twitch a lot, and his face sometimes screwed up like he was in pain or having nightmares, but he never really woke. Jesse was left to talk to himself, doze in the visitor's chair and practice his apologies for when Ezra *did* come round.

It was a lonely sort of existence, but it was his, for the moment.

On the fifth day, Jesse arrived very late. The shift had badly overrun thanks to a blaze that had gutted an abandoned farm building just north of the town, and he arrived flustered and still smelling slightly of woodsmoke, only to be pulled aside by Nurse Cup-of-Tea.

"He's a bit agitated," she explained when Jesse glanced questioningly towards the bay entrance. "He's starting to come out of it more, but he seems to be quite wound up and we're not sure why."

"Is he in pain, or—?"

"He's managing the pain very well." The nurse shook her head. "I can't explain it, dear, he's just very antsy. See if you can calm him down a little, perhaps? If he does get more upset, we'll have to have him sedated and you won't be able to stay, I'm afraid."

Her warning was chilling, but when Jesse slipped through the curtains into the cubicle, Ezra was asleep again. The heart monitor had been removed, but the oxygen tube was still there. The swelling in his face was reduced, even if his eyes were still ringed in dark, furious purple.

"Hey, baby," Jesse whispered, pulling up the chair and tucking his fingers gently under Ezra's. "Nurse says you've been edgy?"

He got a very gentle flex of the fingers and squeezed them lightly. They flexed again, stronger.

"Ezra?"

He was offered a breathy sigh, then Ezra's fingers spasmed in Jesse's hand and those foggy eyes were sliding open, pupils huge from the drugs, focus drifting absently over the ceiling.

Then he seized up, and Jesse moved.

"Hey, hey, relax," he urged, half-rising to lean over the bed and force his way into Ezra's line of sight. "You're in the hospital, baby," he said, and Ezra stared wide-eyed up at him. "Ez? Can you hear me, sweetheart? You know where you are?"

Ezra caught his sleeve with clumsy fingers. "*J'ss*," he breathed, then his eyes were flicking around the cubicle, his hand beginning to tremble on Jesse's arm. "Jess, can't move. Can't move m'legs, Jess, *please*—"

For a brief moment, Jess could smell petrol.

"No, sweetheart, ssh," he coaxed, stroking a hand through his fine hair. "Listen to me. You're in *hospital*, babe. You've broken your legs, that's why you can't move. You're safe, sweetheart, I promise."

Ezra clutched, still shaking, still wide-eyed with drug-induced panic. He couldn't focus, Jesse realised. He couldn't focus enough to realise that he wasn't trapped. All he understood was the fear.

"Here, come here," Jesse urged softly, sitting slowly back down and pushing himself as close to the bed as possible, laying an arm heavily over Ezra's chest. That sometimes worked for nightmares or panic attacks—maybe it would work even here, despite the drugs. He pressed his head onto the thin pillow beside Ezra's, until Ezra finally turned his face and tucked his nose into Jesse's cheek, screwing his eyes shut and letting out a choked, breathy sort of sob. Jesse squeezed his shoulder, and felt the tremors beginning to die out again.

"Jess—"

"That's it, sweetheart," he murmured soothingly. Ezra's fingers were tangled in his shirt at the elbow, and he felt them curl into the fabric at the endearment. "I've got you. You're okay."

It took another forty minutes for Ezra to doze off again, coming to in little fits and starts of momentary panic, but eventually he slept again, safe under Jesse's arm, face tucked towards him.

Jesse held on, kissed his hair occasionally and ignored the nurse when she looked in and smiled.

* * * *

The next day, the curtains were open and the bed was gone. Jesse hovered in the doorway uncertainly, glancing about as if Ezra had been moved one cubicle down, and Nurse Cup-of-Tea appeared at his elbow.

"He's down in X-ray," she said cheerfully. "They'll be putting a full cast on his left leg today. The skin's healed quite nicely."

Jesse fidgeted. "What about the other leg?" he blurted out.

"They're still not sure." She shrugged. "Cup of tea?"

When the orderlies came back, Jesse was perched on the visitor's chair with a cup of unbelievably strong tea, and Ezra was actually awake, half-reclined instead of flat on his back, and he smiled drowsily in Jesse's direction, a hand coming out vaguely towards him.

"Hey," he mumbled, catching Jesse's fingers as the orderlies parked the bed back in place and Nurse Cup-of-Tea fluttered about, checking his drip.

"Do you think you can manage a drink, dear?" she chirped.

Ezra curled his fingers around Jesse's and hummed. "Maybe," he said.

She waited, but nothing further was coming. Jesse suggested orange juice, and she disappeared. "You feeling better?"

"Mm," Ezra sighed. "M'ribs hurt. And m'leg."

He was more alert, though, and Jesse bit his lip. "You remember what happened?" he murmured.

"'Member you," Ezra mumbled. "Where'd you go?"

"Hm?"

"Y'sterday. Or…earlier. Can't 'member—"

"I went to your house," Jesse said, propping one elbow on the mattress to stroke his fingers soothingly over Ezra's forehead. His eyes were still drifting lightly. "Fed your cats, watered your spider plants. Ate your leftovers."

Ezra half-smiled, turning his face into Jesse's touch. "Good," he murmured.

"How much do you remember?" Jesse prompted again, half-hoping he remembered nothing, and half-hoping he remembered everything. Hoping he at least remembered that Jesse had been there.

Ezra frowned. "You."

Jesse's heart swelled. "Me?"

"I—" He blinked slowly. "My leg hurt. Felt trapped, an'…you. I j's—you were there."

Jesse swallowed against the sudden lump in his throat.

"Made it okay," Ezra mumbled, and his thumb twitched jerkily over Jesse's knuckles, like he was trying to rub them but lacked the fine motor skills. "I wasn't—I could do it, 'f you were there."

Jesse took a shaky breath and the feeling clawed its way out. "Can I…just speak for a bit?" he whispered.

A spark of something—worry, curiosity, wariness—lit behind the fog, and Ezra curled his fingers into weak hooks digging into the joints of Jesse's hand.

"You're everything to me," Jesse blurted out. "You mean the entire world. You're funny and you're kind and even when you think I'm being stupid or a freak, you still roll your eyes and smile at me, and you just—you love me, I know you love me, but I never knew why. And I've been waiting, you know, for the other shoe to drop. I've been waiting for you to wake up and realise I'm just this big, lumbering, stupid bloody idiot who breaks things all the time and says the wrong thing to your mum and picks a fight with your ex. I'm just this bum, muddling his way through, and you love me, and I've been waiting for you to stop loving me."

Ezra was frowning, and shifting like he was trying to sit up properly and argue. Jesse dropped a hand to his shoulder, pushing lightly to keep him still.

"I always felt like I wasn't enough. Your family don't think I'm enough, and your ex-boyfriend is, like, infinitely superior to me, I mean, he's well-off and well-educated and everything, and I felt so out of my depth. Like you were going to wake up at any minute. Then you were in your car and you were panicking and you were hurt and you nearly broke my knuckles, you held on so hard, and—and that was it. You just needed me, you needed *me,* and I realised I've been stupid and acting like an idiot over Liam and I'm sorry."

"J'ss—"

"No, wait." Jesse squeezed his hand as tightly as he dared until Ezra stilled. "I've never been enough, Ez. I wasn't enough for my dad to stay, and I wasn't enough for my mum to be happy once he'd left, and I wasn't enough for anyone to ever actually date until you came along—and you were so perfect, how could I possibly have been enough for you?"

Ezra shook his head, a shine over the fog. Jesse winced. He hadn't meant to cause tears.

"Always," Ezra mumbled, and scowled, fighting to speak past the drugs. "Always enough for me. More'n enough," he managed finally, and Jesse leaned close to kiss one gritty cheek and smile tremulously at him.

"I think I finally get that," he murmured, and Ezra held up one weak, wavering hand to touch his ear. "You love me," he said simply, "and you're not the kind of guy to love someone who isn't worth it."

Ezra smiled sleepily. "Nope," he agreed, and Jesse grinned, bumping their noses together. "J'ss?"

"Mm?"

"Love you."

Jesse smiled, because it was true. It had always been true, he'd just been too thick to really hear it.

"Love you too," he murmured, and Ezra's smile was brilliant despite the haze. "You know I do. And I'm so sorry."

"F'r what?"

"For the things I said," Jesse murmured. "For the whole bloody argument."

Ezra sighed, tugging weakly on Jesse's shirt collar. Jesse cupped the curved fingers and squeezed them.

"N't now," Ezra mumbled. "Can't focus properly. We n'd—need to talk 'bout't."

"I know, but I *am* sorry," Jesse insisted gently, and bit his lip again. He didn't want to ask, but—but— "Ez? Do you remember telling the paramedic I was your boyfriend?"

"Vaguely. S'a bit fuzzy."

"Is that still true?" Jesse mumbled, and went red when Ezra frowned at him. "I just—the argument was so—I was sure you were going to dump me, when you told me to come over. I thought—I thought we were over."

Ezra huffed, grimaced, pressed a hand to his ribs and exhaled slowly into Jesse's shoulder when he pressed closer to try to soothe him.

"N'idiot," he mumbled.

"What?"

"You. Y'r a nidiot," he mumbled, and clutched at Jesse's collar again. "Not dumping you. N'd to talk, but not dumping you. Not f'that."

Something loosened in Jesse's chest, and he smiled into Ezra's hair and kissed his scalp again, feeling suddenly freed. Feeling like the colour had come back into his world. Ezra wasn't going to fight him on this. He was going to be there, all the way through this recovery, and Ezra was going to let him.

Nurse Cup-of-Tea returned with a tall glass of orange juice, and Jesse was shunted to the side while she sat Ezra up and persuaded him into drinking half of it, chattering on all the while about when he could start on foods and that if he woke up a bit more the doctor would come to talk to him tomorrow, and on and on and on—

Jesse held Ezra's hand, stroking his cool knuckles, and let his shattered nerves heal.

* * * *

The next day was Jesse's rest day, and he came in the moment visiting hours began, with a box of Ezra's books and his fully-charged iPod. He also brought his toiletries, because the more Ezra woke up, the more ratty he was going to get about being bed-bound and smelling of hospital.

Ezra waking up properly had meant his visitors' restrictions had been lifted, and it showed. A steady stream of visitors came and went for most of the afternoon. Several colleagues with yet more cards and presents from the kids, and a letter from Ezra's substitute, threatening him with emasculation if he didn't get in a damn wheelchair and return to work by the end of the week, preferably sooner. Jesse had never met Ezra's kids *or* Darren Collingwood, but by the tone of the note, he didn't need to. A woman from the floor below who'd been in one of the other cars came up to see him, and a policeman came to get Ezra's statement. The policeman had been a surprisingly entertaining visitor, because he insisted he'd met Jesse at last year's local gay pride and nearly had to arrest him for being too drunk, and Jesse went purple and tried in vain to remember him—or any of that day, really. Ezra simply lay and laughed quietly at the pair of them.

"I knew you used to get up to no good before I came along," he murmured hoarsely once the policeman had taken his full statement and gone. "God," he groaned, and Jesse edged his chair closer to hear him properly. "My insurance is going to suck."

"For the car? I doubt it," Jesse said. "They'll pay out. It went down on our records as a drunk driver."

"Mm."

Ezra was pale. Jesse stroked his fingers over the sheets.

"Pain?" he murmured.

"Mm," Ezra repeated, and grimaced. "My leg. Bloody aches."

"Well, you did mangle it," Jesse offered. "The nurse said the doctor's going to come up today and talk to you about it."

Ezra went white.

"Hey, hey, come on," Jesse coaxed as the clatter of the nurses bringing lunch began to sound in the main corridor. "It'll be fine. Whatever happens, it'll be fine."

"What if they cut it off?" Ezra croaked.

"What?"

"I heard them," Ezra said hoarsely. "I heard them, when they drained the fluid off my knee the other day. The doctor was saying the surgeon should have cut to the chase and sawn it off, and—"

"Hey, no." Jesse slid an arm gingerly around Ezra's shoulders, careful to avoid his battered ribs. "I talked to the surgeon, the day the—the day you came in. She was all optimism. She said, you know, it'll take ages and everything and maybe it won't be the same, but she said you won't lose it."

Ezra's lip wobbled dangerously, then he twisted into Jesse's arm with a grimace of pain, but clutching hard, determined to have the damn hug. Jesse clutched back, smoothing his hair in lieu of properly squeezing him like he wanted to, and grimaced when Ezra's shoulders hitched alarmingly.

"It'll be okay," he promised. "Whatever happens, I *promise* it'll be okay."

"If they cut it off—"

"Ez, *I* would have cut it off if it would have saved your life," Jesse said urgently, and Ezra's fingers dug into his back. "You're alive, sweetheart. And you're going to stay that way, and you know, that's all I'm asking for. Two people *died* in that crash. *You* could have died. If you'd—if you'd gone into deeper shock, or you'd panicked too much, you would have had heart failure, or bled to death, or just plain died of shock. You would have died. And now you're not going to, and they can cut off both legs, but to me, you're alive and that's enough."

Ezra sniffed wetly. The nurse approaching with a tray gave Jesse a look, and he shook his head.

"We're fine," he mouthed.

She gave him a sympathetic nod, set the tray on the side table and snuck away again.

"Come on, sweetheart," Jesse murmured into that fine fair hair. "Even if you do lose it, you're alive. And I'm here, aren't I? No matter what, I'm here."

Ezra heaved a deep, shaking breath and whispered, "Couldn't do this without you, Jess."

Jesse swallowed against the lump in his throat and breathed out through his nose.

"S'why I'm here," he managed, and untangled them. "Come on. Lunch. The cup of tea lady said if you manage all three meals today you can come off the drip, and I'm sick of trying to hug you around that line."

Ezra offered a wet smile, eyes still shimmering like liquid, but settled awkwardly back and let Jesse set the tray across his lap. He picked at the food rather than really stuck in, but it slowly disappeared, and when the same nurse passed on another round, she gave Jesse an approving look.

"The doctor will be up in half an hour or so," she said when she came to remove the empty tray, and Ezra grimaced.

"It'll be fine," Jesse said. "You know what I thought when I first saw you in the car?"

"What?"

"I thought you'd broken your back," Jesse said. "I was imagining, you know, wheelchairs and a new house and all sorts. So, from my point of view—"

"I get it," Ezra mumbled, squeezing Jesse's hand. "Thanks," he added after a moment, and sighed. "Just—for being here."

"Always," Jesse promised.

Twenty minutes later, a doctor appeared, one Jesse hadn't yet seen—tall, red-haired, and, although he must have been forty-five if he was a day, very good-looking in a confident, refined sort of way.

"Mr Pryce," he greeted brightly. "And, ah—" He checked his notes. "Can I assume you're Mr Dawkins?"

"Jesse."

"Your mother a wild west fan, then?"

Jesse snorted. "They told her I was going to be a girl."

"Oh dear." The doctor smiled. "Well…" He flipped over a couple of sheets of paper. "I'm Dr Yates. I'll be handling your treatment from now on, Mr Pryce, and arranging things with other departments. What news would you like first? The excellent, the good, or the bad?"

Ezra's grip tightened alarmingly on Jesse's hand and the colour drained out of his face. Jesse wrapped both hands around Ezra's fingers and squeezed them back as much as he could before saying, "Start with the best and work our way down, maybe?"

Ezra simply nodded.

"Well," Dr Yates said cheerfully, "your liver function is back up to normal, looks like you've got no permanent damage there, and Dr Anwar and I are both of the firm opinion that you're not in line for any more surgery for the moment."

"So –"

"You're not going to lose your leg," he clarified kindly.

Ezra sagged back against the pillows bonelessly. Jesse lost control of his smile and leaned over to hug him and hide it in his shoulder. Ezra was trembling faintly, but for once, neither of them cared.

"Oh, thank God," Ezra breathed suddenly, and sniffled. A tear escaped. Jesse brushed it away and kissed his cheek. "Jesus, thank you."

"Thank the surgical team," the doctor said. "If not for Dr Anwar, I have no doubt you would have lost it, and on the table, too. But she's an excellent surgeon. She's written in her report a recommendation that you don't have the metal rods taken out, however, and she can't vouch for the functionality of your knee. The ligament damage was somewhat extreme."

"I'll take what I can get," Ezra croaked, and wrapped both arms around Jesse's shoulders, hiding his face. Jesse had the distinct idea that the tears had won.

"What's the rest of it?" Jesse asked.

"That's the good news," Dr Yates said. "The infection window has passed with no sign of it. The physiotherapy team sat down with myself and the surgical team yesterday afternoon and discussed the scans and the surgical images. Now they are convinced you should regain full use of your hip, with time, and you will be able to walk again, after a fashion."

Ezra twisted his face out of Jesse's shoulder, but didn't disentangle himself. "After a fashion?" he managed wetly.

The doctor shrugged. "That's the bad news, I'm afraid. Two hours of your surgery were spent attempting to repair the damage to your knee, and neither team can say for certain that they succeeded in giving you that functionality. The bones will heal, as should the muscular tears, but there is severe ligament and tendon damage, and if those cannot be repaired or strengthened with the physiotherapy, then your knee won't function properly."

"By not function—"

"You won't be able to control it," he translated. "It won't stop or start when you want it to. You would have to walk with a crutch, but you would be capable of movement. You aren't going to be confined to a wheelchair forever."

Ezra took a shaky breath, shook his head and buried his face back in Jesse's shoulder. "That's hardly bad news," he mumbled.

"You've obviously never had physiotherapy," the doctor said dryly, and smiled again. "The head of the physiotherapy team and I will drop by tomorrow afternoon to discuss your treatment and long-term care. You will be confined to a wheelchair until your legs heal, I believe that goes without saying, and it's unlikely you will be released until one of them—the left—is out of plaster and you can get yourself about on crutches. But we can't make any promises about how well your right leg will work after all of this."

"It's better than cut off," Ezra whispered, so low that Jesse had to repeat it for the doctor—and agreed with it. Crippled was better than gone. A dodgy knee was better than a missing leg.

"It is indeed," Dr Yates said, flicking through his notes. "The bones in both legs are healing nicely so far. The break in your right ankle is rather worse than originally thought, but that should still heal perfectly well. You're a lucky man. A less fit patient would almost certainly have lost functionality of the right leg by now."

Ezra coughed out a laugh. "Knew the yoga was good for something," he mumbled, and Jesse combed his fingers through his hair. "Can you—when can I start using the wheelchair?"

"We'll get the plaster put on your right leg in a couple of days," Dr Yates said, "and we'll try transferring you into the chair for a few hours each day and letting you get about the hospital a bit. If you cope very well, we might let you out for a couple of hours to go to lunch somewhere with your partner, let you have a change of scenery. But you do *not* move yourself in and out of the chair. Your right leg is still very delicate and jarring it even slightly could undo all the work Dr Anwar put into saving it."

Ezra nodded. Jesse stroked a hand down his arm and ignored the doctor in favour of the light coming back on in Ezra's eyes. He was going to recover, and he knew it. That steely determination was beginning to stir up again.

When the doctor disappeared again to find another patient on his list, Jesse leaned across the bed to kiss Ezra's cheek.

"I love you," he said, and it felt, for the first time, completely natural to say.

Chapter Thirteen

Ezra came home in late July.

The lads at the station had wanted to throw a party. The summer term had just ended, and Jesse heard rumours of the teachers wanting to do something similar, but he managed to waylay both attempts until the weekend, guessing that going home would be painful, exhausting and embarrassing.

And he was right.

Ezra was released on the last Monday in July, a simmering hot day that made the roads sticky and the air stickier. Jesse had taken two days off work to help him get home and get settled and had roped Pete into helping with the physical 'getting Ezra into the house' stage. Ezra had barely waited until he was set up on the pulled-out sofa-bed before dismissing Pete, obviously half-furious, half-upset at being seen in a less than ideal state.

"He's seen worse, you know," Jesse told him once Pete had gone, but he was brushed off too.

Ezra was more or less better, apart from the right leg. His dislocated shoulder cramped occasionally, and the cruel gash across his forehead had scarred, but in Jesse's opinion it only made that long face more beautiful. His left leg had healed and the cast had come off last week. The right one was still in plaster and still ached for ninety-nine percent of the time. He was constantly tired, because he hadn't been able to move much for almost two months, and irritable from a mixture of sexual frustration and that love of tactile contact that had made Jesse deem him 'a whore for hugs' within the first month of their relationship.

Jesse had unfolded the sofa last night into its double-bed contraption that looked rickety but was surprisingly solid. Ezra would be living downstairs for the time being. The downstairs bathroom had a shower, whereas the upstairs one only had a bath, and Jesse hadn't liked the idea of Ezra having to go up and down stairs to eat if he was out or at work.

By the time he came back from showing Pete out, Ezra was asleep, a cat at each hip, and breathing deeply. Jesse stroked back his hair and wandered off to do some chores, mostly getting the bathroom ready for when Ezra woke up and demanded the inevitable shower, and beginning to make a lot of freeze-able meals for when he had to go back to work. Ezra couldn't cook at the best of times, never mind with one leg in a floor-to-arse cast, and Jesse had no intention of letting him try.

It took an hour and a half for the noise to start.

Jesse hated that noise. The half-choke, half-cry that was filled with such complete *fear* that his gut twisted into a hard knot and he was out of the kitchen and into the living room before it could repeat itself. He'd left both doors open for just this reason. Flopsy was sitting on the carpet, eyeing the bed dubiously, and Jesse stepped right over her as another strangled plea rose from the sofa-bed, an incoherent word in the middle of it.

"Ezra!" he called loudly, bending over the bed and tapping his cheek sharply. "Ezra, sweetheart, it's all right. Wake up now, come on, baby."

Ezra struggled. The shift of his hip turned the whimper into a scream, and Jesse slapped his cheek again, light enough to avoid a mark but hard enough to break through the first layer of the dream and force Ezra's eyes open, lost and roving. He was white as the sheets and sweating, eyes huge and terrified in the afternoon light.

"Please, please, Jess, I can't do this, *please*—"

"Ssh." Jesse cupped his face in both hands, pushing down until their foreheads touched. "Ssh, baby, you're not in the car. You're home, you're safe, you're with me. It's all right, sweetheart. Come on, wake up for me. Just wake up, baby, that's it."

Ezra blinked, clutching painfully at his biceps, then the awareness flooded in and he relaxed back into the pillows, breathing harshly. "Jess?"

"It's okay, sweetheart," Jesse smoothed back his hair. "You're safe, I promise. There's plenty of room. You're not trapped."

He had been expecting this. Coming off the painkillers a few weeks ago had lessened the frequency of the nightmares, but hadn't stopped them, and Jesse reckoned they wouldn't stop until the cast was taken off and Ezra could move his leg freely again. He'd had nightmares long before the accident, about being trapped or the crash that killed his father and brother.

Now—now, it would take a lot longer for the bad dreams to fade away.

"Hey, hey," Jesse soothed as Ezra locked his arms around his neck and began to cry, still shaking in his hands. "Ssh, baby, you're okay. You'll be even better once I can get you some painkillers, but you're okay. It's fine. You're *fine*, I promise you. Ssh, sweetheart, calm down." He slid his hands gingerly around Ezra's back, trying to avoid moving his hips. By the tension, Ezra was in pain. By the grip, he didn't care.

When the panicked crying eased, Jesse dared to sit up a little, Ezra's hands sliding back to his bruised biceps and his breathing rattling around tears and pain.

"I'm going to get you some painkillers, all right?"

"No," Ezra croaked.

"Ez—"

"*No.*" The edge of panic was still here. "Stay here, Jess, please. *Please.*"

"Okay. Ssh, sweetheart, okay," Jesse sat on the edge of the mattress, tangling one hand in Ezra's hair and stroking gently, his other holding Ezra's left hand in his lap and rubbing his thumb across healed knuckles. The tears had abated, but the tightness in his face hadn't, and Jesse bent to kiss away one of the telltale lines.

"I want you here," Ezra croaked.

"I was just cooking."

"No, I mean—I don't want to sleep on my own."

Jesse's heart flinched. "Babe, I can't exactly cuddle you right now. I'd hurt you."

"*No,*" Ezra insisted, and wiped the last of the tears away with the heel of one hand. "I mean—don't go home. Tonight. Stay here with me."

"You want me to stay here while you recover?"

"Mm," Ezra squeezed his elbows. Jesse bent to kiss his temple.

"Okay," he said simply. "I was kind of hoping you'd let me anyway. I don't feel great about having to leave you here on your own while I'm at work as it is."

Ezra sighed, closing his eyes and tugging lightly. Jesse settled on the bed beside him, sliding an arm under his thin shoulders and feeling the tension leech away as he rubbed his palms and fingers rhythmically over the tight muscles in Ezra's back.

"Go back to sleep," he coaxed. "You're safe with me, you know that."

"Don't think I can sleep though," Ezra mumbled. "When's Mum coming?"

Mrs Pryce had returned to Norwich after Dr Yates had pronounced Ezra's leg to be manageable. She had, after all, a demented mother-in-law and a job. Grace had never materialised at all, and Jesse was thankful for it. The last thing either of them needed was that sour-faced bitch hanging around. But when Ezra's discharge date had been set, his mother had decided she'd come down and see him again, and Ezra had been so pleased when she'd called, Jesse hadn't the heart to feel irritated about having their first real private time since the argument and the crash interrupted.

"About two, I think," he said, scratching at the hair at the nape of Ezra's neck and watching the lines in his face smooth out a little. "You've got time to sleep more if you want."

"No," Ezra said, though his voice was erring on the side of tired. "I'll just dream again."

"You've never had a nightmare when I've been hugging you," Jesse pointed out.

"I have woken up panicky, though," Ezra mumbled.

Jesse didn't bother pointing out he hadn't had one of those starting-awake fits since their early days together, and simply rubbed his thumb in circles over Ezra's upper arm. He'd doze off by himself in a few minutes.

"Jess?" Ezra murmured, tucking his head against the top of Jesse's shoulder. "You're a git sometimes, but I love you."

"I'm a git?" Jesse pouted. "What'd I do to deserve that?"

Ezra huffed, laughed and didn't reply.

* * * *

The knock on the door came at quarter past two, waking Jesse from a doze. The sunlight was streaming through the windows onto the bed and baking them both in warmth, and the combination of the lazy heat and the weight of Ezra on his arm had lulled Jesse into a stupor in front of the chattering TV while Ezra napped.

The knock disturbed him, though, and Flopsy unglued an eye from her position curled around Ezra's feet. Ezra stirred, blinking dazedly, and Jesse squeezed his shoulder before getting up and going to answer it. Thankfully, he was prepared for the sight of Mrs Pryce on the doorstep, looking almost pretty in a pale green blouse, though he was surprised to see the bent form of Nana and less than pleased with the presence of Grace's long golden hair.

"Living room," he said shortly, pointing them through to the right door, and eyed Grace with the same curled lip she offered him. "Where have you been?"

"*Someone* had to look after Nana," Grace said shortly.

Jesse privately doubted that was anything more than a feeble excuse and preceded her back into the living room. Nana had taken up the armchair with an imperious manner and was already knitting, although Jesse was certain she'd not brought any into the house with her, and Mrs Pryce was perched on the arm of the sofa helping Ezra sit up against the pillows and asking questions in a low, motherly tone. Jesse distracted himself by fetching tea, listening in the kitchen to the low cadence of Ezra's voice, deep amongst his female relatives, and Nana's bright chirps of nonsense. By the time he returned with a tray, she was calling Ezra lazy for lying about in the middle of the afternoon, and even Grace was allowing a small smile to crease her icy features. Jesse settled back onto the bed, sliding his arm around Ezra's waist, basking in the warm smile Ezra offered him, and felt—

Comfortable.

He was suddenly struck by how comfortable he was, despite the glance Mrs Pryce gave to his hand on Ezra's waist, and despite Grace's mere existence. He felt at ease, like their disapproval was irrelevant, like it simply didn't matter.

Like what Ezra had said all along was true.

He didn't really listen to the conversation, too preoccupied with his quiet epiphany. Too relaxed. He didn't need their approval, all of a sudden, and it was liberating, to not care if he was making a bad impression by lounging on the sofa-bed beside Ezra, not to worry about displaying any affection in front of these people.

Spurred on by the thought, he leaned over to kiss Ezra's forehead lightly, and earned himself a slightly surprised look.

"Are you married?"

"What's that, Nana?"

"Are you married?" she repeated sharply, beady little eyes on Jesse's hand at Ezra's waist.

"Um, well, no," Ezra said.

She harrumphed noisily and said, "Well, you better not be having sex, young man."

"Mum!" Mrs Pryce exclaimed.

"You mustn't let any man put his penis in you before you have a ring on your finger!" Nana exclaimed hotly, and Ezra choked on his cup of tea. Jesse hastily removed it before it could spill everywhere, and took the opportunity to *try* to fathom what his boyfriend's extremely elderly grandmother had just said. Jesus *Christ*!

"Mum, really, that's hardly appro—" Mrs Pryce attempted.

"I did it!" Nana cried. "And look where it got me! Men are only after one thing, Ezra, so you get a ring on your finger before you let that great oaf of yours do anything!"

"*Mum!*" Mrs Pryce said furiously, going an interesting shade of purple. Jesse couldn't stop it and started sniggering helplessly. Ezra just dragged the sheet up over his head and hid from the world.

"Don't you 'mum' me, young lady!" Nana protested. "Don't think I don't know what you and Zach were up to behind my back! And I'll bet you didn't even use any condoms either! Foolish boy that he is—I raised a waster of a son, and you've made a waster of my grandson too. Ezra! Ezra, come out of there and answer me!"

"No," Ezra said firmly, and clutched the sheets with a vice-like grip when Jesse attempted half-heartedly to pull them down. "I'm never coming out again."

"Mum, you can't just say things like that!" Mrs Pryce looked horribly embarrassed, and Jesse felt somewhat sorry for her.

"It's, um, it's all right," he tried, and Nana turned up her pointy nose at him.

"Don't speak unless you're spoken to, young man," she said, and squinted at him. "Who are you, anyway? Are you Michael's youngest? You're a bit old, aren't you?"

"Oh, Mum, for goodness' sake—"

"Oh my God, she either thinks I'm a girl, or has converted to the rainbow," Ezra mumbled into the sheets. "*Jess*. I'm on fire."

"You wish," Jesse said.

"Where's Zach?" Nana asked, apparently sick of the subject. "And where have Josh and Ezra gotten to? They'd better not be fighting again."

"They're not fighting, Mum," Mrs Pryce said awkwardly. "Drink your tea and, um, check your knitting. I think you've dropped a couple."

It was a good distraction technique. Nana's attention was tidily diverted from her embarrassed grandson—or temporary granddaughter, because God only knew what was going on in her head—and daughter-in-law. Ezra unburied himself, scowling at his grandmother in a manner that suggested he knew all too well what her clouded mind was like, and yet couldn't get over the kind of things it came out with every now and then. Jesse smoothed his ruffled hair and rolled his eyes when Ezra turned the scowl on him.

"She's *your* grandmother," he murmured.

"And if she were in her right mind, she wouldn't even sit here and watch the pair of you," Grace sneered suddenly.

"Grace, stop it," Mrs Pryce said wearily.

Grace huffed and stood up. "I'm going for a fag," she said, dragging out the last word deliberately, and stalked out of the living room towards the front door. Jesse watched her go, frowning at her slender back until she sashayed out of sight, and Ezra flicked his arm.

"Leave it," he murmured.

Jesse was tired of leaving it, though.

"I'll be right back," he murmured, shifting free and following her, half-curious and half-angry in an idle fashion. He didn't have a brother—or a sister, for that matter—but he liked to think he'd never treat them like Grace treated Ezra, and he was sick of it. What had Ezra *done* to deserve it?

He followed the smell of fag smoke. Jesse hated smokers, smoking and generally anything that involved flicking hot ash over flammable materials. He'd seen too many people killed in house fires started by not stubbing out fag ends properly, or by flicking the ash onto things it shouldn't touch. So the smell was distinctive, and he followed it like a bloodhound.

She was sitting on the fence by the gate. From the back, she looked very much like Ezra's sister. The same long limbs, the same way of folding herself gracefully down onto the boards, the same shimmering colour to her hair in the summer light. She half-turned her head when Jesse closed the front door behind him, and a sneer crossed the otherwise pretty mouth.

"What do you want?"

"Why are you here?" Jesse asked flatly.

Grace shrugged. "Mum insisted."

"Look, I get it. You don't like me. You don't like Ezra. Whatever, that's your problem. But do the Christian thing and lay off. He's been badly injured, he could have died, and—"

"Good."

Jesse's brain rebooted. "*What*?"

"I said good," she repeated coldly, and patted the fence next to her. Jesse didn't take the invite. "I know you think the sun shines out of Ezra's arse, but it doesn't. He's a selfish little shit and he always has been."

"*Lay off*," Jesse snapped.

"I'll tell you a secret, Jesse," Grace said, stubbing out the cigarette and rummaging in her pockets. "I'm a Christian, but I don't worship God."

Jesse frowned at the back of her head. She twirled a fresh cigarette between her fingers and lit up again.

"For my tenth birthday, God gave me a birthday present," she said. "In His infinite wisdom, He killed my father and my brother. He murdered my father, who was a good man who worked hard to provide for us, and Joshua, who was everything I could have ever asked for in a big brother. Who did He spare? The *faggot*."

She spat out the word with such venom it stunned Jesse, and where he had snapped and snarled earlier, he stood dumb now.

"The pathetic middle child, who sinned just by breathing, who kissed other boys and thought his perversions were normal—he was spared. But the eldest, the bright one, the best of us all? God took him away. What kind of a God does that? What kind of a God murders His good and loyal followers and spares the pervert?"

She turned her head again, not quite looking at him. Her eyes glittered in the sunset.

"I believe in God, Jesse, but I also believe God doesn't deserve our worship. God is a child playing with us. God is cruel, God is vindictive and God destroyed our family to spare the sinner."

"You can't blame Ezra for *living*, Grace," Jesse said numbly.

"I think you'll find I can," she said coldly. "I knew. I knew when we were children that he was gay. He kept quiet all those years, but we both knew it. Joshua knew it before he died. We tried to help him, we tried to set him straight, but Ezra has always refused to think about others. It broke Mum's heart when he came out, said he was dating that law student. She cried for hours."

Jesse felt sick. Ezra had been right. Grace was the nutjob. Mrs Pryce, with her 'homosexual' word usage and her pursed lips, was sweet and welcoming next to this vitriol. At least Mrs Pryce still loved her son, even if she thought he was damned.

"It's an insult to Joshua's memory, to Dad's memory, that Ezra is all that's left of the Pryce name," she said coolly. "I'm not about to let Ezra spit on their memories by, what, pretending that his life choices are okay? No."

A cold feeling was creeping up Jesse's spine as the pieces suddenly fell into place. Let him? How could Grace *not* let him, how could –

It clicked.

"Liam," he said.

Grace snorted. "Liam followed Ezra around like a puppy," she drawled. "He adored him, the sick fuck. I knew he'd never let go, so when Mum said Ezra was visiting at Easter and bringing a guest, I knew it would be the new boyfriend," and she shrugged.

Jesse stepped back, into the door. She'd called Liam.

"What did you tell him?"

She shrugged again, dragging on the cigarette until it glowed a brilliant amber. "That I was worried. My poor brother seemed to have this dangerous boyfriend from Brighton. I'd seen bruises. The usual. Got the idiot going all right. You see"—she turned her head to look over her shoulder at Jesse—"Liam's never *met* me."

So Liam wouldn't have known that Grace was the most vindictive, spiteful little cat south of Mansfield. Hell, south of the bloody Outer Hebrides. He would have mistaken her for a genuinely concerned little sister, and—

She'd tried to play them off against each other, tried to exploit Jesse's insecurities and Liam's continued feelings. She'd tried to ruin her brother's relationship, because—because he was *gay*, and had *dared* to survive the car crash that had killed their father and brother?

"You're the sick one," Jesse said, his voice shaking. "You're a sick, vindictive little bitch who's acting out like a fucking child because you lost your daddy. I get it, Grace, it's hard to lose a father. I was eight when I lost mine. But you can't blame your brother for surviving. That's the sick part. You're a sick, lonely, pathetic woman and you will never find someone who loves you. You will never understand love, and that's why you hate him, because Ezra moved on with his life and you didn't. You get off on wrecking other people's lives, and guess what? You failed."

She drew on her cigarette, long and hard, and said nothing.

"You fucking failed," Jesse said, shaking his head. "You're just—Jesus fucking Christ."

He turned on his heel, unable to look at her any longer. The conversation in the living room ground to a halt when he marched back in, and Ezra frowned up at him.

"What's the matter?" he asked as Jesse sat on the edge of the bed with more force than was strictly necessary, and Jesse licked his lips.

"Grace told Liam I'm abusing you," he blurted out.

"What?" Mrs Pryce said.

"*What*?" Ezra echoed angrily.

"Grace told Liam. Grace told Liam so he'd come in and try splitting us up," Jesse said, and shook his head. "I know I probably shouldn't say this about anyone in your family, but—your sister is a massive fucking cunt."

Mrs Pryce reeled back in her chair. Ezra's expression went from angry to downright furious.

Nana said, "Language, dear," and carried on knitting.

"I—" Ezra began, then shook his head. "Jess, get my phone."

"Ez—"

"Get my phone."

Jesse got it. Ezra immediately scrolled through his contacts and put in a call. Mrs Pryce scurried outside, presumably to talk to her daughter. Nana knitted away, oblivious to the hubbub.

"Liam," Ezra said sharply. "Yeah, fine. Question for you. Did Grace ever talk to you about me? Or Jesse, for that matter?"

Jesse settled on the mattress, resting a hand lightly on Ezra's biceps, rubbing against the tense muscle. He felt oddly…calm about the whole thing. At Easter, he would have blown a gasket, yet now…he felt calm.

Hated the little bitch, that was for sure, but…he was calm.

He half-listened to Ezra's conversation with Liam, and half-watched Nana, in case she decided to do something random and nutty, and jumped when Mrs Pryce stole back into the room, pink-eyed and smudged-looking, and began to gather their things.

"Ezra, dear," she said when Ezra hung up. "I think it's best we go."

"Yeah, I think so," Ezra agreed icily. "And tell that fucking *cow* that if she—"

"Hey, hey, relax," Jesse urged, rubbing at his arms and pressing him back into the pillows again. "Relax," he insisted, and Ezra huffed.

"Mum, just—just go," he said, waving her off. "I'll—I'll call you next week or something, just—"

She hovered a moment, then set about coaxing her mother-in-law up out of the armchair she'd adopted as her own in the short visit. Jesse ignored her, turning his focus on Ezra.

"Relax," he urged, eyeing the tight lines in Ezra's face. "Don't let her get to you."

Ezra huffed angrily but squeezed Jesse's hand tightly. "I'm more pissed at Liam than her," he grumbled.

"Why?"

"I *told* him she's a horrible witch, but he obviously never bloody—"

"All right," Jesse interrupted. "But there's nothing we can do about it now. I mean, *we're* okay, right? She didn't get to us."

"She did for a while," Ezra said pointedly.

Jesse worried at his lip. "That was—worries I already had surfacing."

Mrs Pryce led Nana out. Ezra watched Jesse's face in silence until the front door closed, then wound his fingers through Jesse's and tugged.

"Yes," he said. "And we need to talk about that. *Now.*"

Oh, *shit.*

Chapter Fourteen

Jesse made attempts at postponing the talk. He brewed fresh tea, fed the cats when they pestered and went to check the front door was properly locked. But when he returned to the living room, ever hopeful, Ezra hadn't settled down and dozed off again. He was sitting up, petting Flopsy at one hip like a Bond villain, and waiting.

"Come on, Jesse," he coaxed, and patted the sofa-bed.

Jesse perched gingerly on the edge, pulling at a loose thread in the sheets, and sighed. "I'm sorry," he said.

"For what?"

"For the fight," he said, and felt a coil of sour guilt stir in his stomach. "I didn't mean—"

"I think you did," Ezra said quietly.

"Not all of it." Jesse shook his head and reached out for a hand, curling his fingers around it loosely. "I didn't mean any of the things I called you, I swear. I—"

"I'm not worried about that," Ezra said. "I'm worried about the bits where you've not been listening to me for months, the bits where you've let your jealousy get to you and the bits where you apparently think you're not worth loving, Jess."

"I don't—"

"Well, what else is saying you're not enough for me supposed to mean?" Ezra prodded gently.

Jess bit his lip. "I—"

"Jess." Ezra leaned forward with a pained hiss. Jesse shuffled a little closer. "You need to talk to me."

"I told you about my dad."

"You didn't tell me about this," Ezra insisted gently. "Come on, Jesse. Why would you not be enough for me?"

Jesse took a deep breath. "Okay—look, I—I was stupid. I get that now. After—after this," he gestured at the cast, bulky under the sheets. "After the crash, I realised just how stupid I was being, but—"

"But what about before the crash?"

"Just look at it from my point of view," Jesse said, shifting until he was sitting loosely cross-legged, holding Ezra's hand in his lap and rubbing the joints in a habitual sort of tic. "So last October I see this gorgeous guy in a club, and it's just like every other gorgeous guy I've ever seen in a club. He'll dance with me, he'll have a drink with me and he'll even kiss me. Only this one gives me his number, and when I call, he actually agrees to go out with me."

"You can't tell me that's entirely new, Jess," Ezra said softly.

"Not yet," Jesse said bitterly. "So I take this guy on a date, and he's not just gorgeous, he's brilliant and funny and he doesn't think I'm cheap or a moron for not liking fancy restaurants because I don't know which fork to use."

Ezra laughed a little. Jesse smiled and squeezed his hand.

"See?" he said.

"Mm. But—"

"And the date is amazing and he lets me walk him to his car and when I call about doing it again, he says yes. And this is new, Ez, you're like one of maybe four guys who ever went on a second date with me. And by the fifth date, you're the *only* guy who hung around that much. All I ever had before you was sex. Guys want me, you know, they want to be able to say they got off with a firefighter, but that's all they want. They don't want to date one. Some of them don't want to date at all. They're just into the club scene and random shagging and I was looking for something more and it was—it was bloody depressing, Ez."

"Jess, that doesn't mean—"

"But it *did*," Jesse insisted, squeezing that captured hand tightly. "It did mean that, Ez. It meant nobody was interested in me, not really, then suddenly life dropped this amazing, beautiful guy into my lap who was everything I'd ever wanted, and—I couldn't believe it."

"Oh, Jess."

"It's always been like that, Ezra," Jesse confessed, feeling hot and shaky and sick with the outpouring, and yet grounded, with Ezra's fingers rubbing little circles into his hand and the firm answering grip if he squeezed. "I've never, ever had a boyfriend before you. I'm twenty-five—well, was twenty-four—and I'd never had a boyfriend and it's not like I came out in my twenties, you know? I knew I was gay since—since forever, really, I've always known, but I've *never* had a boyfriend. I've never even had someone interested in me that *I* didn't want to date. It's never happened."

"Jesse, sweetheart, all that means is you didn't meet the right guys for ages," Ezra urged gently. "If I'd made a habit of gay bars, we would have met a couple of years ago. And some people *will* look at your job and think it's too heavy, you know? That's really heavy when you don't know how much you like this guy yet, that he might have to rush off in the middle of a commitment to go to work and he'll come home at all sorts of stupid hours and maybe someday he won't come home at all."

"Yeah, but, Ez, nobody ever gave me the chance," Jesse said. "Not until you."

"Oh, sweetheart. That—"

"So, think of it from my point of view," Jesse reiterated. "I suddenly have this boyfriend. This gorgeous boyfriend who doesn't think my job is a liability, and thinks my taste in music is actually half-decent—"

"*Only* half."

"And I have no idea what I'm doing," Jesse said. "I make mistakes and I forget things and I bring flowers just in case I did something stupid I need to apologise for, and sometimes I make this guy so mad I think he's going to dump me, and—"

"Oh, Jess, *no*—"

"And"—Jesse swallowed—"and he introduces me to his ex. This ex who could have modelled underwear and cologne at the same time. And earns a six-figure salary. And took a cooking class run by an actual Italian chef, just to impress this guy that *I'm* dating, and I felt—I felt so bloody inferior, Ezra. I felt like you never needed me and I was just you settling for what you could find in Brighton. I felt like you were dating a fucking waster and any minute now you'd realise what you gave up at the end of your degree and—"

"Come here," Ezra whispered, tugging on the hand. Jesse went, settling on the pillows beside him and winding his arms around Ezra's waist and shoulders, hugging him close. "This is what I mean, Jess. You don't listen to me. You—"

"Wait," Jesse murmured. "Let me finish."

"Okay..."

"Then a drunk driver smashed into the front of your car and I realised just how fucking stupid I've been," Jesse said lowly. "You were—Jesus, Ez, you were in so much pain and so panicky, and you needed me. You wouldn't let go of me. You begged me not to go, and when I had to go around the car to let the paramedics brace you, you were crying and—I just—nobody else could have helped you but me."

Ezra petted his hair and hummed softly.

"You needed me," Jesse repeated, "and I think that's what I was missing all along. You're always so independent and caustic and—and *you*, and I love you for it, because you know, I never wanted some clingy, needy boyfriend because how the hell would that work with my job anyway, but—"

Ezra kissed his forehead and tugged until Jesse shifted enough to let him kiss his cheek. "Of course I need you, you bloody idiot," he murmured.

"But I didn't get that," Jesse said, dropping his arm until both were round Ezra's waist. He stroked a strip of exposed skin with his thumb. "I felt like an accessory next to Liam. I was just waiting for you to get tired of me. It didn't—it didn't sink in how much you needed me, too."

"Do you need me?"

Jesse shifted to stare at Ezra. "Of *course* I need you."

"Why?"

"Because—because I do, Ez," Jesse struggled. "I mean…I get to come here after work and hug you when I have a bad day and you just—you make it better even if you're ignoring me and doing your marking or whatever, and you text me when I'm at work, and—I love you, that's why."

"And that's what I mean, sweetheart," Ezra said. "You've not been listening to me. I've told you I love you, and when you think about it, you *know* I love you, but the minute I suggested visiting Mum, it was like you forgot. Like you stopped hearing me."

"I was scared," Jesse admitted, and tucked his cheek against the top of Ezra's shoulder. "I was scared you were going to realise I wasn't enough."

"You weren't listening," Ezra said. "There are literally thousands of gay guys in this country who earn more than you, and have jobs better suited to actually dating than you, and actually know how to wash their clothes without mixing the darks and lights and turning everything grey, but I don't love those guys, Jess. If we're saying you get points for every good quality, then all the good stuff only ever adds up to a hundred, but me being in love with you gives you, like, a thousand."

Jesse squeezed him tightly and curled closer. Ezra scratched his hair lightly and murmured a low endearment.

"I get it now," Jesse murmured, and kissed Ezra's shoulder through his T-shirt. "I do get it, Ez. The way you needed me in the car, and in the hospital when you were still so ill—"

"But you need to get it all the time, Jess, not just when I physically need you," Ezra coaxed.

"I'm so—"

"Don't apologise to me. Just *listen* to me." Ezra pushed. "You have a real self-esteem problem. And I get where it's coming from, I'd probably be just as screwed up with your family history, but you've *got* to sort it out. If you don't, we're just going to repeat this again and again somewhere down the line. It'll be some attractive colleague, or Grace scheming again, or even Liam, because God knows the man's like a terrier with a rat when he thinks he's onto a winning bet and I doubt he's going to back off just because I put a flea in his ear about listening to Grace. You have *got* to sort this out."

"How?"

Ezra sighed. "I want you to see someone."

"What?"

"A counsellor," Ezra clarified. "You can organise it free through work. Just give it a go."

Jesse cringed at the idea of telling a stranger all his secrets and letting them psycho-whatever him. "I don't want to be psychomanaged," he said.

"Psychoanalysed."

"That."

"I'm not burying this," Ezra said. "You *need* to drop that way of thinking, sweetheart, or every time we fight, you'll think I've stopped loving you, or I'm going to dump you, or you're not worthy of me, or whatever."

"I've learned—"

"You *think* you've learned, but I'm going to recover and the shock of this whole thing will wear off and you'll fall right back into your old habits and we'll start all over again."

Jesse sighed heavily against Ezra's collarbone.

"I do love you, Jess, but we need to fix this," Ezra coaxed. "Just give it a try, all right? And while you're at it, talk to the counsellor about this fear you're going to turn out like your father."

"Ez," Jesse said warningly.

"Listen, I get it that you want to be careful," Ezra said. "You do have a temper. You get wound up and explode, often over very silly things, but you're not a violent man."

"I don't have to be *violent*," Jesse said. "I just—I'm threatening, Ez. I—"

"Really?" Ezra said mildly. "Hm. I've never felt threatened by you."

Jesse rubbed his thumbs over Ezra's flushed-warm skin and said, "Good," in a very small voice.

"Jess?" Ezra shifted a little to peer at his face. "I mean it. I mean, come on, that was an ugly row and I've no intention of having it again, but you never so much as came near me, never mind—"

"You tense up if I pin you down in bed," Jesse said in a whisper.

"Now you're being thick," Ezra said sharply. "You know that's nothing to do with you."

"Ez—"

"It's not," Ezra said, scratching at his hair gently. "I was the same with Liam. *Worse* with Liam. And come on, Liam's about as threatening as a newborn kitten."

Jesse snorted with laughter and buried his face in Ezra's neck to laugh helplessly at the mental image. Ezra sniggered and smiled into his hair, the little kiss he dropped there wide and amused.

"And you know it's when you surprise me, or I'm too tired to process why I'm stuck," Ezra murmured gently. "We both know I don't get edgy when I know what's coming. Literally," he added, and Jesse squeezed warningly. "Jesse, I trust you. With my life, also literally. If it was anyone else, I would outright panic at being pinned down by—how much do you weigh now? Fifteen stone?"

"Sixteen," Jesse said.

"And most of it muscle," Ezra said agreeably. "Drop sixteen stone on top of me, and I will be less than happy, but sixteen stone of *you*, Jess—you see what I'm saying?"

"Mm-hmm."

"Just give the counsellor a try," he coaxed gently. "If it'll even help a little in sorting out your fears—"

Jesse kissed his neck. "Okay," he conceded. "I'll do it for you."

Ezra pinched his shoulder. "I'd prefer if you did it for yourself, but I'll take that, I suppose."

"If I don't like it or—"

"How about we agree on a minimum time?" Ezra suggested. "Let's say you arrange for twelve weeks' worth? And if it's not working or you really hate it, then you can pack it in and we'll think of something else."

"Ten weeks. Tops."

"All right."

Jesse shifted to sit back on his heels, facing Ezra again, and took both hands in his. "I'm sorry," he said.

"Jess, I know, let's—"

"No," he interrupted. "I need to say this. I was way out of line that night. Of course you can have dinner with whoever you like, and I realise now how stupid I've been thinking you're just going to up and go back to Liam in a heartbeat, and I am so sorry for the things I said to you, and nothing I said about you was true. Nothing."

"I'm more worried about the things you said about yourself," Ezra said lowly.

"And I'll go to this counsellor for a while and I'll try and work things out, but right now, I have to apologise for what I said to you," Jesse insisted. "I was like a little kid throwing a massive tantrum, and I'm so sorry. And when your leg gets broken out of its tomb, I'll take you out for the best dinner of your entire life."

"Mm." Ezra eyed the window. "I suppose I could do with some new flowers to brighten the place up."

Jesse grinned and kissed him, short and sharp and hopeful.

"Done," he said. "New flowers tomorrow."

"Red ones," Ezra demanded imperiously.

"Red ones," Jesse agreed.

"And right now, you could make it up to me a bit more."

"How?"

"Put a film on and hug me?"

Jesse braced his hands either side of Ezra's hips to kiss him soundly, his nerves soothed when Ezra cupped his face, and smiled when Ezra broke it to press their foreheads together and murmur something Jesse couldn't quite hear.

"Love you," Jesse said.

"Love you too," Ezra whispered, and Jesse knew it was true.

* * * *

Jesse woke sharply when something landed on the end of the sofa-bed.

Ezra had dozed off halfway through the film, had had another nightmare that Jesse cut off in the middle and had clung and cried in startled terror for a good few minutes before managing to collect himself and tearfully demand help to shower. The second nightmare had been worse than the first, and he'd seemed…unsteady, maybe, emotionally speaking, while Jesse helped him cover the cast and wash. He'd insisted on hobbling into the kitchen on his crutches to help with dinner, even though Jesse banished him to the table to play with the kitten and refused to let him help.

Said kitten was now sitting on Jesse's toes and eyeing him through the gloom.

Jesse had left a lamp on, hoping the light would soothe Ezra's overactive mind a little bit, and Kitsa's eyes glittered an eerie green. Tiny claws plucked the sheets, and she stalked up Jesse's body to butt her head against his chin and purr.

"Hello," he whispered, tickling her side, and glanced at the DVD player. Half past one. Bloody cats.

Ezra was quiet. He'd not insisted again that Jesse stay, but after the second nightmare, Jesse hadn't felt comfortable leaving, so he'd crept into the other side of the sofa-bed at half ten and curled an arm over Ezra's chest, still wary of the ribs that had long since healed. He'd moved since, and they weren't touching at all now.

Yet through the gloom, Jesse could see the frown on Ezra's sleeping face.

"Out the way, moggy," he mumbled, lifting the kitten off his chest and dropping her on the floor. She meowed pathetically. "Nope, sorry."

He turned on his side to mould himself up against Ezra's left. His left leg was stretched out as if it was still in the cast, Ezra's brain having apparently not caught up with the news that it was actually a leg again and not an unwieldy club attached to his knee. Jesse brushed his toes against the ankle and slid an arm over Ezra's waist.

"M'here, sweetheart," he murmured, kissing his shoulder and squeezing very lightly, hoping to not wake him. Ezra murmured, shifted his shoulders and the frown smoothed away slowly. "That's better."

The next few weeks were going to be unpleasant, Jesse knew. He'd have to arrange counselling around work and looking after Ezra around his shifts and Ezra was going to be by turns grumpy as fuck—he was an awful patient, Jesse had learned—and upset and tearful as the nightmares worked their way out of his system. He'd started physiotherapy for his leg last week, and it had left him exhausted, frustrated and emotionally wrung out.

He was going to need Jesse.

He was always going to need Jesse, really, and Jesse stroked his thumb across Ezra's lower ribs and watched his face relaxing and listened to a soft murmur that was possibly his name. Even when this was all over, he'd be able to hold on to that. Ezra had needed him, in the car and afterwards, and there was nobody else who could have done it. Nobody else who could have got him through it.

Nobody else who *had* Ezra, wholly and completely, and Jesse dared to press forward to kiss his ear. Nobody else who would have been enough.

Jesse was enough.

Jesse was more than enough.

Epilogue

September arrived as a baking thing, hot and airy and floating two inches off the ground. The road shimmered in the sunlight and an arid, smoky sort of breeze teased Jesse's hair and felt thick in his lungs. It looked like autumn, with the dried-out leaves dying in the gutters and clouds skidding waywardly across the deep blue abyss of a sky, but never settling. By the heat, summer wasn't quite ready to let go just yet.

Work had been busy, spontaneous fires and water rescues all over the place, as stray cigarettes lit up the dried-out countryside and people who ought to have known better swam in risky places to get away from the soaring temperatures. But work had also been regular, everything peaking in the middle of the day and tailing away in the evening.

Thus, Jesse walked home at eight-thirty, damp from the station shower and rapidly drying in the still-fierce heat. The sky was paler now, but still a long way from twilight, and his boots sucked greedily at the tarmac of the road, as if they too were thirsty.

"Hello, girl," he said, when he reached Ezra's gate and Kitsa leapt up onto the fence to rub her head against his elbow and meow plaintively. "If you want inside, use your cat-flap. Stupid cat," he crooned, rubbing her ears and fishing out his keys. He'd had one cut for the front door, sick of the side gate. "No?" he asked, when she stayed on the fence and didn't follow him to the door. "Fine, then, fuck you."

The house was even warmer than the street. Jesse shed his boots and yelled a greeting, judging the echo expertly and following the change in sound. The back door was open, and a head of wild blond hair was visible over the back of the deckchair.

"Hey, gorgeous," he said, bending over the chair to offer a kiss. Ezra smiled into it, his face pleasantly hot from his basking, the notebook he'd been flicking through dropping to the heavy textbook in his lap. "Still determined on going back next week?"

"Absolutely," Ezra said. "And those brats are going to regret ever thinking a substitute means they don't have to learn."

Frankly, Jesse didn't give a shit about the kids. The last fortnight had been devastatingly hot, and it had done Ezra a world of good. The waxy pallor to his features had faded under a crop of freckles, and he'd stolen some of Jesse's dumbbells to idly lift while he lounged in the sun. He didn't look ill anymore. He didn't look *frail* anymore, despite the crutch and the cast, and the tiredness that still plagued him. Mostly due to the extra energy he needed to walk anywhere and the gruelling physiotherapy sessions five days a week.

"Well, put your stuff away," he said, teasing the flyaway hair. "It's dinner time. Want to hobble round the chippie with me?"

"But the *suuuuun,*" Ezra whined, tilting his head right back until he was almost looking at Jesse upside-down. Jesse took the hint, and kissed his forehead, nose, chin and finally mouth. "Mm. Well, all right then."

"Up to it?"

"Watch me, flame-boy."

The most painful part was watching Ezra get up. Once he was up, he was relatively steady, if still easily tired and occasionally in a degree of pain. But getting up was an exhausting, laborious process—and to top it off, Jesse had been banned by the physiotherapist from helping.

'He has to manage on his own,' Tracy had said sternly. *'Now he can do it, you're not needed.'*

Ezra's right leg was still a ruin entombed in a cast, and the left weak and wobbly. The ankle was stiff and prone to cramps. The knee was next to useless and the subject of most of the physiotherapy sessions. Tracy still wasn't sure whether Ezra would ever regain proper use of it, and nobody knew anything at all about the outcome for the right leg once the plaster could be broken open. But Jesse didn't much care. He was still operating under thankfulness that Ezra was alive and hadn't got shot of him after that fight.

"All right," Ezra said, once he'd struggled out of the chair. "Let's do this."

"Sure?" Jesse said, locking the back door behind them as Ezra hobbled into the house.

"Stop fussing," Ezra said, but there was no bite to it, and Jesse leaned in to kiss him as they reached the front door. "Mm. All right, keep fussing, whatever."

"Knew you'd see it my way," Jesse said.

The walk round to the takeaway usually took five minutes. It was just the other side of the main road and a cut through an alley that ran between the houses. With Ezra's limp, it took closer to fifteen, and the faint traces of sweat were darkening his hair at his temples by the time Jesse pushed the door open and held it for him.

"Doing okay?" Jesse asked when Ezra lowered himself with difficulty into one of the plastic chairs.

"Mm."

"Ez—"

"I'm fine," Ezra said, and grimaced. "Could do with a couple of painkillers when we get back, though."

"Tracy go hard on you? Usual, please, Mo," Jesse asked as the takeaway owner's teenage son stuck his head out of the kitchen.

"She's a bitch," Ezra said grumpily, and growled when Jesse ruffled his hair. "Are you seeing Amanda on Monday?"

Amanda was Jesse's counsellor. He had been reluctant, but if seeing a counsellor was the price to pay to keep Ezra, he'd go every week until the day he died. And she wasn't that bad. Nosy, but he supposed that was in the job description. And far too keen on exploring his acceptance of being gay, even though Jesse had pretty much bypassed the entire gay crisis and had enthusiastically explored every facet of his sexuality during his teenage years.

"Ten o'clock," he grumbled, and Ezra laughed, reaching up to squeeze his hand.

"She's doing you good," he said.

"Yeah?"

"Mm," Ezra toyed with his fingertips, and smiled. "You don't look at me like I'm a mirage anymore."

"A what?"

"A vision."

"But you are."

"An *imaginary* vision, Jesse. Like I'm going to pop and disappear," Ezra rolled his eyes. "God, you're thick."

The remark didn't sting. It didn't even so much as twinge. Perhaps Amanda really was helping. Jesse smiled and bent to kiss him quickly while Mo was preoccupied, and had stepped back by the time the spotty youth reappeared with their order.

Jesse swung the bag by the handle and offered his elbow as they returned to the street. Ezra tucked his fingers into the crook, lightly brushing the hairs on Jesse's inner arm, and made some caustic remark about being an old lady with her walking stick. Jesse simply watched the play of dying sunlight in his hair and considered the beauty of him. And yet, he didn't feel lucky anymore. Not so specifically. Oh, he felt lucky about how his life had turned out, but not—not so specifically about having *Ezra*.

He needed Ezra—but Ezra needed him too, to offer an elbow and laugh at his remarks and love him, and Jesse did all of it and more.

"I don't want to go back to the flat tonight," Jesse said as they crossed the main road, the bottom of Ezra's crutch making a wet *schluck* every time he prised it off the sticky road surfacing. "Can I stay over?"

"You've stayed over every night for two weeks."

"Yeah, but it's nicer at your house."

"Why?"

"You're here. And when you're grumpy, I can cuddle Kitsa. There's nobody to hug at my flat."

It wasn't even home anymore. Ezra's house was home. The flat was just a flat.

"I should bloody well hope not," Ezra grumbled, wincing as they paused at the gate for Jesse to unlatch it. Kitsa was still sitting on the fence and eyed the bag hopefully.

"Hold that," Jesse said, passing the bag while he unlocked the front door. Ezra made a questioning noise, and Jesse stooped to slide both arms around Ezra's hips and lift him bodily into the air.

"Fucking hell, Jess!" Ezra yelped, dropping the crutch with a loud clatter and clinging to Jesse's shoulders, caught off guard. "What the hell are you playing at?!"

"Weightlifting." Jesse grinned up at him, and Ezra raised his eyebrows imperiously.

"You saying I'm fat?"

"Nooooo," Jesse said, carrying him into the living room. Ezra huffed. "Fine. I can't keep my hands off you, and it seemed like a good idea at the time."

"You can't be serious."

"I am," Jesse said and let Ezra slide down his body until his mouth was within kissing range. Ezra arched his back, keeping his face just a little too high, until Jesse persuaded him down with plucking kisses to his neck and jaw. Then Ezra finally gave in, dropping the chippie bag on the sofa and wrapping both arms around Jesse's neck and shoulders. Jesse kept a firm hold even as Ezra determinedly attempted to destroy his remaining brain cells. Or suck them out via his mouth. Whichever.

"Missed you today," Ezra murmured into his mouth. Jesse smiled and squeezed his hands until Ezra's breath hiccupped. "Bastard."

"Love you too, sweetheart," Jesse scoffed, and shifted his hold into a bridal carry before lowering Ezra gingerly to the sofa. Ezra winced and settled himself, rubbing at his shin and grumbling. Jesse fetched the painkillers, poured the fish and chips onto plates and came back with the peace offering held aloft like a treasure.

"Marry me," Ezra said, and knocked both pills back like an addict.

"Maybe when you won't need a properly accessorised crutch to go with your tux," Jesse quipped, and Ezra poked him in the ribs. "You never said I could stay the night."

"What do I get if you do?"

"Cuddles."

Ezra pointedly eyed the hand Jesse had dropped onto his knee. "I have cats to cuddle," he said flatly when Jesse simply blinked at him.

"Um, better cuddles?"

"Debatable. You don't purr."

"Oh, please."

"You *don't.*"

"Fine." Jesse walked the hand a little higher. "A massage to get all the kinks out."

"All of them?"

"All of them."

"Even the ones that turn up during the massage?"

"Especially those ones."

"Fine," Ezra said, tucking himself into Jesse's shoulder and blinking wide, innocent dark eyes up at Jesse. He pouted deliberately and Jesse kissed it away. "Deal, I suppose."

"You suppose?"

"Depends how good this massage is."

Jesse laughed, transferred his hand from Ezra's thigh to his waist, hugging him tightly. Both cats had come investigating in the hope of scamming—Flopsy some fish and Kitsa a chip, because Kitsa was the most ludicrous excuse for a cat Jesse had ever seen. It was comfortable and easy, sitting together on Ezra's sofa and throwing chips for Kitsa. The dying sun streaked shadows across the little room, and Ezra's hair made the slow slide from white-hot liquid iron to a gentle, burnished gold. Jesse wanted to be startled by how simply happy he felt, and yet he wasn't. It was the happiness that had been waiting while he'd tried to get over himself.

It was a happiness that couldn't be contained, and the moment that Ezra leaned forward to put his empty plate on the coffee table, Jesse caught at him, leaning over him to press a kiss into the opposite side of his neck, and work his way steadily down until he found, at the corner of Ezra's T-shirt, the scar from the crash that had killed his father. He kissed it reverently, then abandoned it in favour of mouthing at Ezra's throat until the strong pulse in the jugular began to pick up and Ezra's fingers were combing through his hair in time to breathy sighs.

"Skipping the massage, are we?" he murmured softly, and Jesse tugged on his earlobe with his teeth.

"Come upstairs," he breathed.

Ezra simply slid his arms around Jesse's shoulders in invitation, and Jesse wriggled off the sofa and hefted Ezra back into his arms with minimal effort. He had lost weight in the hospital that he hadn't yet regained, but the fire was still burning beneath his skin. Jesse thumbed the jut of hip as he carried his prize towards the stairs, and Ezra's tongue lapped at his ear in a flickering, evil tease.

Dropping him to the bed, Jesse snapped open his shorts and peeled them off effortlessly, sliding his hands down one exposed leg and bending to kiss the scars as they passed under the crumpled fabric. Two on the thigh, four or five around the knee, countless tiny puckers and hollows in the skin of the shin, and a savage white slash above the knee, testimony to where Ezra's car keys had gone in the midst of the chaos. Once the shorts were gone, Jesse dropped his own and kissed his way back up, sucking wet bruises into skin until he returned to Ezra's chest and pushed up his T-shirt to find his two favourite spots on that lean chest.

"Oh, shove off," Ezra whispered breathlessly, and pushed him off long enough to shed the shirt, drawing Jesse back down with a kiss that was more pornographic than sweet, and made Jesse's hands briefly forget what they were doing. "Too far away."

Jesse obediently shucked his own shirt before settling bodily over Ezra and paying homage to his chest. Ezra's leg was shifting restlessly, the foot sliding up Jesse's thigh and down again in sporadic bursts, but Jesse ignored it. And when Ezra tried to tug him up for another kiss, Jesse pinned his wrists to the mattress under his own hands and carried on. He might leave bruises, but Ezra's breathless squirm and vague blasphemy said he didn't mind too much.

"Jess—"

"What do you want?" Jesse coaxed, sucking on the jutting hip and letting go of those wrists to slide his hands down to the waistband of Ezra's boxers.

"Everything," Ezra murmured, tangling his fingers in Jesse's hair, but not pulling. Yet. "Come *on*, Jess."

Jess mouthed briefly at the front of Ezra's underwear before sliding it off. Ezra kicked it free, grimacing at the sharp motion, but when Jesse paused in sudden concern, made a strange hissing noise and dragged him up by the hair for another kiss.

"Ez, if you're—"

"Jess," Ezra breathed wetly into his mouth. "I have been more than patient. I am happy to let you fucking wait on me hand and foot and carry me round on a pillow tomorrow, but for God's sake, right now, I want you. You asked what I want, and I want you to fuck me. So bloody well *do* it."

Jesse laughed, reaching for the bedside table, and fumbled blindly in the drawer while Ezra held his head trapped and bit down on his earlobe until his blood didn't know where to go or what to do. "I fucking love you, you know," he said breathlessly, finally shedding his own underwear and rolling his hips up into Ezra's until the litany of quiet swearing and passive-aggressive threats was broken by a shuddery breath.

"Prove it," Ezra breathed, and Jesse pushed at his hip.

"Turn over," he whispered.

He offered the promised massage, one hand kneading at Ezra's thigh in deep, rhythmic circles, the other working him open, slick with lubricant and shaky with the urge to just go for it already. Ezra had a long, lithe back with a valley for a spine, and Jesse occupied that valley with his tongue, mapping August-induced freckles and nipping at the rolling shapes of his shoulder blades as Ezra squirmed and swore at him, inhaled in bursts and exhaled in shivers. When he reached back and seized the hand at his thigh, Jesse knew he'd gone far enough, and he pressed in and forward until they were chest to back and he could feel Ezra's shallow, rapid breaths pushing against his ribs.

"Okay?" he asked, tangling their fingers together.

"Oh my God, move," Ezra gasped, eyes closed and hair askew on the pillow. "*Move*, Jess!"

Jesse moved, and those first sparks of an electrical storm overrode any concern he felt, any hesitation, any caution. He groaned into the nape of Ezra's neck and picked up a rhythm, losing himself in the tight grip and the salt on Ezra's damp skin, the weight of him in Jesse's hand when he wormed it between Ezra's hips and the mattress and wrapped his fingers around him firmly, the searing heat and the muted groans of pleasure and want. Pure, unadulterated, unseemly want.

It had been too long, and Jesse's emotions were too close to the surface, for it to last long. All too soon, the tsunami hit the shore and, for a brief moment, Jesse felt nothing but white-hot, mindless pleasure, crashing out of him like a storm, and leaving everything in a perfect, peaceful glow once he came back to himself.

"I love you," he whispered into one exposed ear, stroking clumsy fingers through the damp hair surrounding it, and pulled free gingerly, kissing Ezra's shoulder at the groan it elicited. "I'll be right back, baby."

When he returned with a flannel, Ezra barely let him clean them up before tossing the cloth aside and trapping Jesse's arm around him, dragging him down into the crumpled sheets and obstinately ignoring the wet spot.

"Just stay here," he mumbled, and burrowed back into Jesse's body when Jesse reached down to massage the too-tight thigh again. "Leave it."

Jesse ignored him, kissing his shoulder and feeling completely at peace with his world right at that moment. What could be more perfect than this? Than lying tangled up with Ezra, pleasantly exhausted and too warm, fingers twisted together at Ezra's chest and the muscle of his thigh slowly giving way under Jesse's questing palm.

"Jess?"

"Yeah?"

Ezra squeezed his fingers tightly.

Jesse squeezed back. "I know," he murmured, and kissed his neck.

* * * *

Jesse woke when the sun bled through the weak cotton masquerading as curtains. It poked idly around his head for a while before slithering across the cheap sheets and burning Ezra's fair hair into a brilliant straw-yellow, leaving Jesse blinking sleepily at the fluffy nest and carding his fingers through the clumps above a hidden ear, teasing the knots out as gently as possible. He could feel Ezra's heat in the idle pulse behind his ear, feel the murmur of blood beneath the thin skin at his temple, and feel his breathing pushing lazily at Jesse's arm where he had it locked around strong ribs.

The sheets were tangled around their legs in a messy cluster, and were probably why Ezra hadn't woken up complaining of feeling trapped yet from Jesse's smothering hug. There were bruises in the shapes of Jesse's fingers blooming darkly against the narrow bones of Ezra's hips. A black and purple imprint of Jesse's dental work was stark against his collarbone, drowning out the tiny freckles that had been the result of sitting in the garden for nearly a month. His mouth still looked blood-full and swollen, and Jesse couldn't quite tell if his own brain was just tired and pleased, or whether some of the afterglow had carried over through the night.

Jesse tightened his arm and kissed a bare shoulder, pulling Ezra into him more fully, and absorbing the shift and the murmur. When the murmur turned into a groan, he kissed the bruised neck, then Ezra was twisting in his grip, his yoga meaning that his chest met Jesse's before his hips even began to turn, and he was moulding himself into Jesse's front, a slender arm curling around his waist, his nose pressing into Jesse's jugular in a way that let Jesse feel his voice rather than simply hear it.

"It's too bright."

His hair, soft and wavy from the lack of mousse or spray, brushed against Jesse's chin. Jesse dragged a hand up to play with it, bending his head to kiss the hot scalp beneath when Ezra let out a contented hum. "If you were a cat, you'd be purring right now."

"Mm. Damn right."

Jesse stroked the palm of his hand down Ezra's arm. He'd left fingerprints there, too, just above the wrist. It was tough pinning down a yoga fanatic. But not all that much of a hardship. He untangled them enough to lean down and kiss the bruises, half in apology and half in a smug sense of 'mine', and Ezra's hand was in his hair and he was being reeled back in for another kiss. It was stale, tainted by the night, but he didn't care, and sank into it with a warm, idle sort of affection that had to be drugging Ezra too, by the way he simply let Jesse pour himself all over him and didn't so much as twitch.

"I love you," Ezra whispered into his mouth, and Jesse untangled the sheets without breaking the lazy, open kisses, peeling them away until nothing separated them at all and he could coast his hands over miles of freckled, flawless skin. "God, Jess, I love you. I love you, I love you—"

The night before had been quick and sudden, the want hitting Jesse like a tonne of bricks and leaving him mindless in the face of it. This was slow, languid and relaxed, lost in a multitude of kisses and stroking touches that were at once fleeting and lingering. Jesse didn't so much burn with need as swell with want. He *wanted*, so intensely that it was *everything*, and yet so idly that it was like the incoming tide, inevitable and natural, expected like sunrise in the east. He buried his face in Ezra's neck when he felt the roll and whispering, shuttered gasp that told all, and the rush of heat between them, and he mouthed his own love when he came with scattered thoughts and the brief white-out of *nothing* that brought the tide crashing down.

"You're everything," he whispered to Ezra's jaw, brushing his mouth up his sweat-damp skin and wild hair to kiss his temple. "Everything," he repeated, even as he pulled them slowly apart, wanting to stay but needing to go.

Ezra reached and caught his hair, dragging him back into a soul-destroying kiss. "Later," he commanded, tugging the sheets up. "Let's take the morning."

"Shower."

"Later," Ezra whispered, and his word was Jesse's quiet command.

This was enough. This had always, always been enough.

Want to see more from this author? Here's a taster for you to enjoy!

Best Behaviour

Matthew J. Metzger

Excerpt

By the time Jim swallowed his pride, he was standing on the pavement with three bin bags and an overgrown spider plant.

"Can you come over?" he asked. "I need your help." Then he hung up.

Sarah rang back, of course, but Jim didn't answer. He just sat down on one of the bags, put the plant down next to his boot and leaned back against the railings.

Fuck.

That was the only thing that came to mind. *Fuck.* How the fuck had he ended up—well, no, he knew exactly how he'd ended up like this. Stupidity and pride and a whole host of other things that weren't all that flattering. And yet, even as he combed through them all in his head, he'd not change any of them. So, what did that make him?

At least it wasn't raining.

Stretching out his legs in front of him, Jim examined his tatty boots and absently wondered if he ought to try building sites. But even they needed certificates and shit these days. Only thing Jim knew how to do was put boxes on shelves and say, "Would you like fries with that?"

And even the places that sold fries didn't want him.

It wasn't that he hadn't tried. They'd known for months that the warehouse was going to fold eventually, and he'd been looking for other work. But everywhere asked for qualifications. And the places that didn't took one look at his history—specifically that weird little gap after that night with the car—and told him to get packing.

Well, he was packed now.

Whole life in three bin bags. And a plant. Great success he'd made of himself there. Wouldn't Mum be proud?

He snorted. No doubt Sarah would pass the message along.

He wanted nothing less than to have to ring Sarah, but he was out of options. If he ended up in a cardboard box on the streets—or, worse, a Sally Army hostel—then he *would* end up back in prison. Knew it just as much as he knew the sky was blue. And even his pride wasn't so huge as to want to go crawling back in there.

Still—

He'd had a plan, when he got out. Sort himself out. Get a job, find a flat, settle down with the right eight or ten people he'd like to shag for the rest of eternity. Sounded easy, when there were several hundred odd days to think about it in a cell. Only the right person hadn't been right after all. And the job hadn't lasted. And the flat needed the job.

Chewing on a corner of his thumb, Jim sighed. At least the bailiffs wouldn't be on first name terms with him anymore.

A silver Merc came creeping around the end of the road. It looked absurdly out of place in Jim's road full of burned-out Clios and old Skodas with black alloy wheels. It shimmered like a police car as it inched toward him and stopped right across the entrance to the flats as if it owned the lot of them. Driver probably could have *bought* the lot of them.

Jim lifted a hand and waved.

The driver's door opened. A ridiculously tall heel landed on the potholed tarmac and a slim woman unfolded herself from the car. She frowned down at him like a scolding parent or a disappointed probation officer and Jim could have laughed. She looked more like either of those than what she was.

"Hey, sis."

"What happened?" Sarah asked.

She didn't greet him. She certainly didn't hug him. Strip back all the pretence and they would have looked very alike—both tall, both with honey-coloured hair, both with the glass-cutting jawline. But Sarah's hair was in a perfect bun, her suit pristine, her nails gleaming. She hadn't even been working today, but that was how a mum of three *could* look when she hired a nanny. Then there was Jim—hunched over, hands in pockets, hair on end, unshaven, still wearing his hi-vis vest and dirty jeans as if he had a job.

Like peas in a mile-long pod.

"Lost my job," he said.

"Again?"

"We all did," he said defensively. "They've closed the warehouse."

Her frown eased a fraction.

"Then came home and the landlord was here. Said if I couldn't cough up five hundred by Friday he'd evict me. So I told him about the job, and" —Jim gestured to his spider plant—"here I am."

There was a long, long silence.

So long, in fact, that ice ages came and went. Evolution spawned four hundred new species. Mars underwent a century of its own. The big bang began to revert into the big crunch.

Then Sarah said, "Why did you owe your landlord five hundred pounds?"

"And the rest."

"What?"

"I owed him a grand and a half."

Her jaw dropped. "You *what?*"

Jim shrugged.

"Why weren't you paying your rent!"

"With what?" Jim asked. "They cut the gas off last week. I owe water like…four hundred and something. Even the bank's started threatening with bailiffs. I'm out of options. Why d'you think I rang you?"

Her jaw was still agape, but she spluttered.

"Four hun—the bank—*bailiffs*?"

"Yeah."

He felt about an inch tall and his stomach was clenching up. He was too hot. His leg started to jiggle.

"Why didn't you ask me for help?"

"I did. Am."

"Sooner than being—you've been evicted!"

The hot feeling boiled over. "Right. Yeah. Because asking worked so well last time."

"That was different."

"It really wasn't," he replied tightly. "That was *worse* than this."

She pursed her lips, eyeing his spider plant. It looked sorry for itself on the grubby flagstones. But to hell with her and her demands. She hadn't helped when he'd asked the first time. Why would he ask again?

"I tried everything," he said. "But today was the last straw. So here I am."

"Here you are," she echoed weakly, then shook herself. "Right. Well. Our spare room it is."

He grimaced but said nothing. The truth was, Jim didn't want Sarah's help or Sarah's spare room. He'd tried everyone else while the landlord had been flinging his things in the bin. Old work colleagues who didn't want to know. An ex-boyfriend who'd asked, "Who?" as though Jim had vanished out of existence when they'd split up. He'd even tried Justin, much as he didn't want to be around that smug fucker with his new fiancé.

But, in the end, nobody had been able—or wanted—to help.

So here he was, squinting up at Sarah in the dying light.

"Come on," she said. "Let's get that lot in the boot."

She didn't touch the bags. She just opened the boot and held the plant on her hip like a baby as he moved them. The smackheads over the road were staring and he flipped them off as he banged the lid down.

"Jim! This is a new car!"

"Sorry," he muttered.

"Let me just call Anthony…"

Jim rolled his eyes, unable to help himself. "I'm sure this'll go down really well."

She raised an eyebrow. "Don't you go bringing him into this."

"Why not?" he asked. "You brought him into it last time."

"It wasn't like that."

"Really, because it sure felt like that."

"Well, it wasn't."

Jim rolled his eyes but gave up. He wished he could end arguments like that. He wished his interpretation of events was the definitive one. What it must be like, to have that kind of power? But then he'd never had that power with Sarah. He doubted anyone ever did.

He let himself into the passenger seat as she talked on her phone and sulked in the front like a little kid. His skin itched. His stomach was a lump of lead. He desperately didn't want to be doing this—but it was just temporary, he told himself. Just until he could find another job. A better job. Longer hours and higher pay.

It was a short chat. She waved her hands a lot. And eventually she hung up and got into the driver's seat, mouth tight as though they'd argued.

"Told you he wouldn't like it."

"Enough, please."

Jim shut his mouth and stared at the flats as Sarah turned the car around, and they slowly vanished in the wing mirror.

"I didn't realise things had gotten this bad. You should have talked to me."

Jim grunted.

"You should have talked to Mum."

"Oh, right, yeah—"

"She's just worried about you."

"She screens her calls. She won't answer. Hasn't since I came out."

"I'm sure she—"

"Don't tell me what Mum means," Jim said tightly. "You weren't there. You didn't hear her. I know exactly what she means."

An uneasy silence fell between them. Sarah clenched and relaxed her fingers around the steering wheel in an anxious rhythm, and Jim's leg was jiggling again.

"How good did you think it was?" he asked quietly. "I'm eight grand in debt and I worked minimum wage. What did you think was happening?"

"I don't want to talk about that," she snapped.

It was all she'd ever said since that original no. She didn't want to talk about it. She never wanted to talk about it. If Jim brought it up, she changed the subject. Left up to Sarah, they'd *never* talk about it.

"I would have helped if you'd told me," she said after a while and Jim snorted.

"Since when do you *help?*" he demanded.

She pursed her lips. "Since always. You were just too stubborn to see it."

His jaw ached and he realised that he was grinding his teeth again. Slowly, he relaxed his jaw. He couldn't afford to piss her off now. He'd have to be on his best behaviour, at least until he found another job.

But it was a mutinous silence. Because the rub was that Sarah had been right. Anthony had refused to help because he was a judgemental prick, but Sarah had done this pragmatic refusal that had hurt worse, somehow. Religious bigotry, Jim could kind of roll with that. Anthony was dumb as his dog collar anyway—what did Jim expect?

But Sarah? Sarah's practicality had *hurt.*

And, worse still, it had been *right.*

So he seethed quietly as they left the city behind. The traffic was busy, commuters rushing home from their better jobs to their better homes with their partners and kids, not their sisters and crap in-laws. He stared out at the sea of other people as they inched away to the south and wondered if he'd ever get on track. Sarah had only four years on him, but she had it all figured out. Jim...Jim felt as if he'd been careering from one disaster to another ever since he was a kid.

And bleeding away into the wide avenues, long driveways and conservatories of Dore and Totley didn't help. Sarah fitted in out here. Her Merc, her suit, her manicure drumming ceaselessly on the leather. Jim felt like he had in prison and sank lower and lower in his seat as they left even the outskirts behind and dipped into the countryside proper.

The house lay just shy of the Derbyshire border—Jim could just about see the sign—and the electric gates were a foreboding barrier against the likes of him. The place screamed money. Gated drive. Detached twin garage. A summerhouse visible round the side. Since Jim had last been—when Agnes was born, over a year ago now—they'd had an honest-to-God fountain installed in front of the steps that led up to the front door.

It was more like a mansion than someplace people actually *lived.*

"It's been a while," he said uselessly as Sarah tucked the Merc into the garage next to a gleaming BMW on the latest plates.

"Yes."

"How's everyone?"

"Oh, they're fine."

Another long pause. Jim lifted his bin bags. Sarah took the plant. Then he was looking up at the house and he wanted to scream.

"Come on," she said. "I'll show you which room you can have. And you'll join us for dinner, won't you?"

"Not really that hung—"

"Of course you will," she interrupted as she opened the door. A bell chimed. "Zoe! Zoe, are you in?"

Jim was listening.

He stood in the hall and stared at the spiral stairs sweeping away to the first floor like something out of a wedding brochure. At the marble floor. At the chandelier. At the two-storey windows dominating the back of the hall and showing the gardens falling away to the south of the house. At the money oozing off the walls—and at the white dog collar, sitting proudly on a hook by a collection of tidy coats and above a rack of expensive shoes.

Forget Zoe. Anthony was home.

And this was going to be hell on earth.

PRIDE
PUBLISHING

About the Author

Matthew J. Metzger is an asexual, transgender British author juggling books, an office job and a love of travel with the human need for sleep once in a while. He writes both adult and young adult books focusing on LGBT+ characters and their relationships, particularly those from the less salubrious areas in which he was dragged up over the years.

On the very rare occasions that Matt isn't writing, he can usually be found at the gym, halfway up a mountain or collecting new tattoos. (And yes, he does have book ink...)

Matthew loves to hear from readers. You can find his contact information, website details and author profile page at https://www.pride-publishing.com

www.ingramcontent.com/pod-product-compliance
Lightning Source LLC
Chambersburg PA
CBHW030128180626
46812CB00002B/602

9781839438387